THE MISADVENTURES OF ELLERY QUEEN

THE MISADVENTURES OF ELLERY QUEEN

EDITED BY
JOSH PACHTER
& DALE C. ANDREWS

SPECIAL INTRODUCTIONS BY
RICHARD DANNAY & RAND LEE

WILDSIDE PRESS

THE MISADVENTURES OF ELLERY QUEEN

Published by Wildside Press LLC.
wildsidepress.com | bcmystery.com

CONTENTS

ELEMENTARY QUESTIONS

Your editors are of, ahem, a certain age. We discovered Ellery Queen at a time when his adventures graced the shelves of bookstores and libraries coast to coast, a time when, as kids, we could pedal our bikes to the neighborhood drug store and buy the most recent EQ novel or the latest issue of *Ellery Queen's Mystery Magazine*. We grew up with Ellery as one of our closest and dearest companions.

But there will be some readers of this anthology for whom such was not the case. So before we turn to the stories, which are mostly pastiche and parody, it might help if we addressed three questions: Who is Ellery Queen? What is a pastiche? And what is a parody?

Who is Ellery Queen? At first glance, the answer to that question seems simple enough. From 1929 to 1971, first cousins Frederic Dannay and Manfred B. Lee published over thirty novels and seven collections of short stories using the name "Ellery Queen" as their joint pseudonym. Most—but not all—of these works featured as their main character a professional mystery writer and amateur sleuth who was also named "Ellery Queen."

For almost fifty years in the middle of the 20th century, Ellery Queen was everywhere—in novels, short stories, movies, radio and television programs, even comic books. During that Queenian heyday, noted critic Anthony Boucher put it this way: "Ellery Queen *is* the American detective story."

There were many things about Ellery that captivated his fans.

For starters, it was intriguing that author and character shared a common name, and unique that Ellery the character practiced the same profession as Ellery the author. Throughout the EQ novels and stories, Ellery the character *solved* the mystery at hand while *writing* mysteries of his own.

The tales themselves were the epitome of "fair play" Golden Age puzzles. Ellery the author gave us all the necessary clues, then invariably pulled the rug out from under us with a perfectly logical solution that was right there in plain sight yet never suspected.

But on a closer look, the answer to the question "Who is Ellery Queen?" becomes more complicated.

As we have noted, "Ellery Queen" was a pseudonym—originally reserved for fiction collaboratively written by Dannay and Lee; Dannay did the lion's share of plotting and Lee the lion's share of writing. In the late 1930s, though, when the Ellery Queen character began appearing on the radio and a new script was needed every week, some of the writing was farmed out to others, with Lee supervising and Dannay only minimally involved. Then, in the '40s, several authors were brought in to write a series of "Ellery Queen, Jr." books for younger readers. In the '60s, during a stretch when Lee suffered from a severe case of writer's block, several novels—while plotted in detailed outlines drafted by Dannay—were written by other authors (including such well known names as Theodore Sturgeon and Avram Davidson), with Lee providing a final polish. And in the '60s and '70s, some thirty paperback originals—purporting to have been written by Ellery Queen but not featuring the Ellery Queen character—were ghosted by numerous other writers working under licensing agreements, with only very limited involvement of Dannay and Lee.

What is a pastiche? Let's let Ellery Queen—the author, not the detective—answer that one. In the introduction to *The Misadventures of Sherlock Holmes*, Ellery Queen wrote that "a pastiche is a serious and sincere imitation in the exact manner of the original author." When you read the Ellery Queen pastiches in the first section of this anthology, you will find Ellery himself rendered to the best of the various authors' abilities. Pastiches poke little or no fun at their source material, since—again according to Queen—"as a general rule, writers of pastiches retain the sacred and inviolate form" of the original.

What is a parody? Now this is an entirely different matter. Parodies stray from the path, and do so with tongue decidedly in cheek. Once again in Ellery's words, "writers of parodies, which are humorous or satirical take-offs, have no…reverent scruples. They usually strive for the weirdest possible distortions" and "highly ingenious travesties." So, for example, when you encounter in Arthur Porges' "The English Village Mystery" a detective named "Celery Green," you will know that you're in the presence of a parodist at work.

Just as the question of authorship can be difficult in the context of Ellery Queen, so, too, is the precise categorization of some of the stories that lie in wait for you here. In the third, "potpourri" section of the collection, you will encounter detectives who think like Ellery (such as James Holding's King Danforth and Martin Leroy), who are named in homage to Ellery (such as Josh Pachter's E.Q. Griffen), and even a fictional Frederic Dannay working his way through a mystery in the manner of Ellery (in Joseph Goodrich's "The Ten-Cent Murder"). Such stories defy categorization; they are neither pastiche nor parody. You could call them homages or tributes—but whatever you call them, they too are here for your enjoyment.

So, now that our three initial questions have been addressed, let's turn our attention to the genesis of this volume of E.Q. "misadventures." What we have attempted to do in this anthology is to close a circle that opened almost 130 years ago:

> • In 1892, Arthur Conan Doyle published a collection of short stories titled *The Adventures of Sherlock Holmes.*
> • In 1934, the first collection of Ellery Queen stories appeared, titled *The Adventures of Ellery Queen.*
> • In 1944, Ellery Queen edited *The Misadventures of Sherlock Holmes.*

It wasn't long after *The Misadventures of Sherlock Holmes* was published (and then withdrawn) that pastiches and parodies of Ellery Queen began to appear. In 1947, the first EQ pastiche was published, in France: Thomas Narcejac's *"Le mystère des ballons rouge."* More pastiches and parodies followed over the years, and Fred Dannay delighted in publishing many of them in the pages of *Ellery Queen's Mystery Magazine*, a practice that has continued after Dannay's death under the editorships of Eleanor Sullivan and now Janet Hutchings.

Which brings us to—us: Josh Pachter and Dale Andrews. We both made our first appearances in print in *EQMM*, each with a story featuring a main character named Ellery Queen. Dale's story, "The Book Case" (written in collaboration with Belgian EQ scholar Kurt Sercu), is a true pastiche, a new mystery confronting an elderly Ellery. Josh's "E.Q. Griffen Earns His Name" has as its protagonist a teenaged boy named after the great detective by a mystery-loving father and an indulgent mother.

In the early 1970s, not long after the death of Manny Lee, Josh suggested to Fred Dannay that perhaps it was time for a collection of EQ pastiches, parodies, and other homages to be titled *The Misadventures of Ellery Queen.* Dannay liked the idea, but for reasons lost in the mists of time it never happened. Josh moved overseas in '79, Dannay died in '82, and the idea was forgotten.

Until 2012, when a Japanese publisher released a Japanese-language anthology that was in fact titled *The Misadventures of Ellery Queen* and included translations of both "The Book Case" and Josh's second E.Q. Griffen story, "E.Q. Griffen's Second Case."

Josh and Dale were living only twenty miles apart—Dale in Washington, DC, and Josh in Northern Virginia—but, although we knew of each other's work, we had never met. EQ biographer Francis M. Nevins brought us together in 2015, and we almost immediately began discussing the possibility of compiling this anthology.

With the approval and encouragement of the Frederic Dannay Literary Property Trust and the Manfred B. Lee Family Literary Property Trust, we set to work. Some of the authors whose stories you are about to read—Larry Block, Jon Breen, Joe Goodrich, Mike Nevins, Arthur Vidro—are still living, and they were without exception delighted to agree to the inclusion of their work. In some cases, we were able to track down the heirs of authors no longer with us—Ed Hoch's and Bill Brittain's widows, Thomas Narcejac's daughters, Arthur Porges' nephew—who were equally pleased to grant us the necessary reprint permission. Four other stories—those by Dennis M. Dubin, Patricia McGerr, Norma Schier, and J.N. Williamson—appear by permission of their original publisher, *Ellery Queen's Mystery Magazine.*

One finishing stroke—a last question that should also be addressed:

Why have we, and why have other authors, felt driven to compose these further adventures of Ellery Queen?

This time, we are confident that the answer is a simple one: we haven't been able to stand the thought that all of Ellery's adventures have already been chronicled. So we have each offered up our own takes on the EQ saga.

This volume collects what Frederic Dannay, in his introduction to *The Misadventures of Sherlock Holmes*, described as "the next best thing to new stories." He understood what motivates parodists and pastichers and homagers. "Misadventures" are written "with sincere reverence, despite the occasional laughter and fun-pokings," he observed. Such stories are, in every case, "a psychological form of adoration."

What sparked the authors of these stories to write them? Speaking for ourselves, "adoration" pretty much sums it up. As editors, we hope you will enjoy reading the collection as much as we have enjoyed compiling it. If you like the stories, we hope they will send you back to the original adventures of Ellery Queen…and that you'll check out *Ellery Queen's Mystery Magazine*, in which all but two of these stories originally appeared.

Josh Pachter and Dale C. Andrews
Herndon (VA) and Washington (DC)
January 2018

SORELY MISSED ADVENTURES

Before I comment on the book you now hold in your hands, I'd like first to say something about a book published more than seventy years ago with a similar title and concept but a very dissimilar destiny.

I own the first edition copy in jacket of *The Misadventures of Sherlock Holmes* (Little, Brown, 1944) that my father, Frederic Dannay, inscribed to Ellery Queen fan and book collector John Newton: *To John—This is a first edition of the only Ellery Queen book ever "suppressed." It was also a "labor of love." With best wishes, "Ellery Queen"*

The story of the "suppression" has been often told (not always accurately). In a sentence, the Conan Doyle estate, which detested this (or any) collection of parodies and pastiches of Sherlock Holmes, used a minor permission snafu for Doyle material included in the landmark Ellery Queen anthology *101 Years' Entertainment* as leverage to halt all further distribution of *Misadventures*. So ended forever the circulation of what crime-fiction expert Otto Penzler has called "the greatest of all Sherlockian anthologies."

My principal encounter with parodies and pastiches has been as a copyright and publishing lawyer for fifty years. The legal question, in determining whether these literary forms may be published without the copyright owner's permission, usually turns on whether they are considered "fair use," a complete defense to copyright infringement. Fair use issues, always vexing, have been called by the New York federal appeals court the "most troublesome" in all of copyright law.

To simplify (perhaps oversimplify), parody usually succeeds as fair use because it's seen as comment on or criticism of the original, and these are important fair use purposes. Pastiche, on the other hand, rarely if ever succeeds as fair use because, to the extent that it is a close or exact imitation of the original, it lacks any sufficient new message, meaning, or expression that would qualify it as "transformative." Instead, pastiche looks more like an unauthorized "sequel" or "derivative work," the rights in which are reserved exclusively to the copyright holder. Flattery, homage, even idolatry are usually not sufficient justification for pastiche to pass the fair use grade. If you mimic, your motive may not matter. And so unauthorized pastiches of Dr. Seuss works, *Star Trek*, Harry Potter, and other fan fiction have generally not fared well.

"Labor of love" was pure understatement in characterizing my father's reverence for Sherlock Holmes. In his introduction for *Misadventures*, he described his "first meeting" with Holmes when, as a twelve-year-old home ill in bed, he read *The Adventures of Sherlock Holmes* and was hooked. As he put it, he "stood…on the brink of my fate" and "my life's work…[was] born." His enthusiasm for Holmes never flagged. In the celebrated Haycraft-Queen list of cornerstones of detective-crime-mystery fiction, he included *all* of the Sherlock Holmes books—"the complete works"—which my father confessed was "sheer idolatry."

Thus the suppression of *Misadventures* by the Doyle estate was ironic, to say the least. But it was a cautionary tale for me, when asked for permission to publish *The Misadventures of Ellery Queen*. My training and experience as a copyright lawyer do not necessarily influence my views as a copyright heir. I welcome parodies *and* pastiches of Ellery Queen when they represent affection and respect.

And so I celebrate this collection of *The Misadventures of Ellery Queen*, lovingly compiled by Josh Pachter and Dale Andrews. Their book will not incur the publishing or legal misadventures that *The Misadventures of Sherlock Holmes* suffered.

Richard Dannay
New York (NY)
January 2018

THE SINCEREST FORM OF FLATTERY

That there are readers out there who love the Queen canon so much they are driven to invent Ellery tales of their own delights me no end. Imitation, as the saying goes, is the sincerest form of flattery, and has been at least since the saying was coined by Charles Caleb Colton (1780-1832), an English eccentric, art collector, gambler, and all-round clever-boots.

I don't know if my father, Manfred B. Lee—one-half of the Ellery Queen writing team—ever knew the works of Colton, chief among them an anthology of witticisms *(Lacon, or, Many Things in a Few Words: Addressed To Those Who Think)* still available in facsimile over the Internet. But I know Dad's love of the Queen canon, and of the world of literary pastiche in general. *The Misadventures of Ellery Queen* would have tickled him no end.

Rand Lee
Santa Fe (NM)
January 2018

PART I

Pastiches

THE MYSTERY OF THE RED BALLOONS

Thomas Narcejac

(translated from the French by Rebecca K. Jones)

*Thomas Narcejac, together with his long-time collabora-
tor Pierre Boileau, wrote several dozen crime novels from the
early 1950s through Boileau's death in 1989, including the 1954
thriller* D'entre les morts, *which was filmed four years later by
Alfred Hitchcock as* Vertigo. *Prior to the beginning of their collaboration, Narcejac wrote numerous novels on his own. And in
the late '40s, he also wrote numerous pastiches featuring fictional detectives, including Conan Doyle's Sherlock Holmes, G.K.
Chesterton's Father Brown, Dorothy L. Sayers' Peter Wimsey,
Rex Stout's Nero Wolfe, Leslie Charteris' The Saint…and Ellery
Queen's Ellery Queen, which were collected and published as*
Usurpation d'identité. *We are delighted to be able to open this
volume with Narcejac's EQ adventure,* "Le mystère des ballons
rouge." *Written in 1947, it was apparently the first-ever Ellery
Queen pastiche, and this is its first-ever publication in English.*

The telephone rang, pulling Ellery Queen from his reading.

"Hello?… 92nd Street?… All right, Dad, I'll be there in thirty minutes."

He polished his pince-nez, replaced his book on the floor-to-ceiling
shelves that ran the length of the living room, and untied the belt of his
dressing gown.

"Djuna! My grey tweed suit. If Carpenter calls, tell him I'm busy
tonight. Dad needs me for a case that seems rather confusing. No, we
probably won't be home for lunch."

He unfolded a map of New York City on the carpet, got down on his
knees and studied it for a long time before he rose and looked out at the
cloudy sky, which darkened toward the docks. Singing to himself, he
dressed, considering what his father had said.

A red balloon! What a curious coincidence!
He left the house, hailed a taxi, and gave the address.

Sergeant Velie, red-faced and hoarse, struggled with a group of reporters. Ellery gave him an ironic salute and got in the elevator. A policeman opened the grate on the fifth floor.

"To the left down the hall, Mr. Queen."

In the bedroom where the crime had taken place, there was only Inspector Queen, standing beside a covered body. He seemed submerged in meditation.

"Well, Dad," Ellery demanded, "what's all this about a red balloon?"

"I know absolutely nothing," the inspector said, "You have at your feet the Honorable Douglas Percy, forty-two years old, stock broker, killed with a knife to the heart. No clues. He died at about four o'clock this morning. He was apparently surprised by a noise, since he got out of bed, but he put up no resistance. You can see the room is in order. No fingerprints, and the murder weapon has disappeared. No apparent motive. The dead man led an ordinary life—didn't gamble, didn't have a mistress. No indication of who killed him. No one in the building noticed anyone suspicious, no one heard any unusual noises. But we found a red balloon, a child's balloon, out on the balcony."

"What did you do with it?"

"I didn't touch it, El. I thought it would interest you."

Inspector Queen opened the window, and Ellery saw the balloon. It swayed at the end of a long string that had a loop at its other end. The loop had caught on the cleat that held the cord for the exterior blinds. Ellery detached the loop and grabbed the balloon.

The inspector smiled. "Curious, isn't it? That balloon might have floated through the air for miles, but it gets stuck just outside the window of a bedroom where a crime has been committed."

"Why," Ellery said, "do you think it might have floated for miles?"

"Because it's partially deflated. I'm no expert when it comes to balloons, El, but it's easy to see that this one is much smaller than it was originally. I think it blew here from someplace to the west, then lost height and was blown along the front of the building and caught on this window. How else could it have gotten here?"

Ellery readjusted his pince-nez and scratched his head. "Even though it's a little deflated, it's still about ten inches in diameter. Suppose you're right and it slid along the length of the exterior wall, blown by the wind. The string would remain ten inches from the wall. But the cleat is fixed to the wall itself."

The inspector suddenly looked worried. "So you think—"

"I do," Ellery said. "It's a message. The loop couldn't have caught on that cleat by chance. So the balloon was left there on purpose."

"A message?" the inspector repeated. "But why?"

"Correction, Dad," Ellery said calmly. "We should be asking not *why* but *by whom*."

But although they sought the answer all day, their efforts were unsuccessful.

Ellery was awakened by his father at 5 AM.

"Get dressed, El. There's been another murder on 92nd Street. Velie's there now."

"Did he find a red balloon?"

"He sure did!"

The two men tossed back cups of scalding coffee, cursing Djuna, and tumbled down the five flights of stairs.

"I predict," Ellery murmured, "that this Mystery of the Red Balloons is going to cause us some trouble."

Ellery was entitled to his opinion, but the inspector would have preferred him to keep it to himself.

The scene of this second crime was a low-rent residential hotel next to a mechanic's shop. They could see, in a dormer window under the roof, a red balloon tied by a string.

"Body up there?" Inspector Queen demanded of the policeman guarding the hotel's entrance.

The man saluted. "Yes, Chief. In the attic!"

They climbed a narrow staircase that smelled of fried food. Sergeant Velie awaited them on the top floor. He led them into a loft, where a hanging man swayed from a roofbeam.

"Who is he?" the inspector asked.

"An Italian," the sergeant said. "A certain Giuseppe Beppini. He was discovered by the maid who came in to change the linen. Died recently, no rigor yet."

Ellery approached the window. The balloon was identical to the last one. It was attached to a long string, the end of which was wound around an iron rod that had once served as a support for a fire escape.

"There's no doubt!" Ellery murmured. "It wasn't the winds of chance that brought this balloon here. It was left here on purpose."

"So the murderer brought it here?" the inspector exclaimed. "But that doesn't make sense, El! You have to figure that the murderer attached the balloon to the rod, right? And since it's full of helium, he couldn't have inflated it here. So how did he get into the hotel with a helium balloon in tow, without anyone noticing?"

"Slow down, Dad!" Ellery said. "Do we know that Beppini didn't commit suicide?"

They stepped closer to the body.

Inspector Queen smiled. "If he killed himself, El, there'd be a chair or a box here. But the room's empty. So somebody else hanged him. Besides, it looks like the poor guy took a tremendous punch to the jaw."

The inspector pointed out a greenish bruise that covered the left side of Beppini's chin.

"Which leaves us with the balloon," Ellery said. "It has to be some kind of a message. The murderer probably wanted to let someone down on the street know the crime had been committed. So it's likely he inflated the balloon *after* Beppini was dead. It must have happened sometime around dawn, so it should be easy for you, Sergeant, to collect some useful information. The murderer probably came in through the kitchen, if the hotel has one."

"Check it out, Velie," the inspector said, "and send up the manager."

The manager was eager to talk. Giuseppe Beppini worked as a violinist in a dance hall. He knew all sorts of people, and he wasn't up to date with his rent. When asked if the murderer could be someone from the hotel, the manager said no, that was impossible. There were numerous retired residents—they came and went at all hours, and often brought guests home with them. In short, anyone could get into the hotel without being noticed. Beppini lived in a little room on the sixth floor. It hadn't been disturbed. The murderer probably knocked Beppini out, either in his room or in the hall, carried him up to the attic, and hung him. Why? It was a mystery! Velie, however, reported some interesting information. The night watchman slept in the kitchen. He took several naps, most notably between three and six AM, and he hadn't seen anyone in the kitchen.

One by one, the residents were interrogated. Ellery didn't have the heart to help with this tedious task. He left the hotel, secretly irritated with himself.

Why did the murderer leave a message? And what was the link between Douglas Percy and Giuseppe Beppini? Finally, why didn't the criminal camouflage his murders as suicides, which wouldn't have been difficult? He must have *wanted* to draw attention to himself.

Ellery Queen wiped the lenses of his pince-nez. He had an idea. He approached the mechanic's shop and called over a young, oil-stained boy.

"Did you see a car parked in front of the hotel last night?"

"That depends, mister."

"I mean a car that isn't usually in this neighborhood."

"I saw a Lincoln, but it wasn't there long. The driver was badly dressed. He got out, and I saw him go into the hotel."

"Was he carrying a suitcase?"

"No, a hatbox."

"Did he seem to be in a hurry?"

"It's hard to explain. He seemed tired—he was walking slow, heavy-like. I wasn't paying much attention, you know?"

"You didn't see any other cars?"

"Well, yeah! When I was leaving, I saw a Dodge, pulled up right in front of me. I even asked the guy did he want gas, but he didn't. He looked at the hotel like he was waiting for somebody, and then he took off. He was a gentleman, about thirty, bare-headed. I think his hair was black and frizzy. I noticed he had a little white scar on his nose."

"You didn't get his plate number?"

"Jeez, if I got all the plate numbers of all the cars that passed down this street—"

"Had the Lincoln left by the time the Dodge got here?"

"I don't think so."

Ellery put some money in the boy's hand and slowly walked away. He had begun to understand why the murderer had left red balloons in his wake.

Two days later, it was Grace Mitchell's turn to die. Ellery had known her well. She had a charming voice and was a marvelous dancer. Inspector Queen recounted the few facts he knew. The victim had been stunned with a bronze candlestick on which there were no fingerprints. She had not been robbed. Her maid, who slept in the room next door, hadn't heard a thing. A red balloon bobbed against the window. The inspector was pale with rage. Ellery, more taciturn than ever, searched the crime scene without much hope. He did, however, discover something: around the bedroom door's lock were traces of putty. Someone had made an imprint of the lock, which established that the murderer hadn't struck by chance—he'd followed a carefully thought out plan. He knew before he executed Douglas Percy that he would kill Grace Mitchell, because it had almost certainly taken several days to prepare the duplicate key.

Inspector Queen agreed with these deductions and dug into the dancer's past. Ellery, meanwhile, tried to trace the Lincoln and the Dodge, but no one had noticed the tired man with the heavy tread, and no one had seen the man with the scar.

The inspector wasn't happy. Grace Mitchell had been an orphan. She had grown up in misery, had enjoyed a fairly short period of prosperity as a young adult, had fallen back on hard times, and had finally had a successful career launched a year earlier by a theater producer.

"And Beppini?" Ellery demanded.

"He also had his highs and lows," the inspector responded. "He wasn't always a violinist, and he wasn't always called Giuseppe Beppini." He opened his notebook and read aloud: "Teddy Carson, born in Des Moines in 1903. Sentenced to six months, suspended, for theft in 1920. Served a year in 1925, again for theft. Established himself in New York in 1931. For two years, he lived large. He was suspected of participating in the bootleg alcohol trade. Dropped out of sight in 1936. Then he resurfaced, now calling himself Beppini. Since then, he hasn't been in any trouble."

Inspector Queen closed his notebook. "Velie hasn't had much time to work on this. Maybe he could put together a more complete account of the guy's life, but I don't see the need."

"Anything on Douglas Percy?"

"He was easy. He's been a broker since 1933. Before that, he ran a successful law firm, but he had to sell it after some unlucky investments."

"You said Grace Mitchell had a short period of prosperity, Dad. When was that?"

"In 1932."

"That's very curious."

"How so, El?"

"Well, Mitchell, Beppini, and Percy all had money in '32, but in '33, she fell on hard times, Beppini was obliged to leave New York, and Percy took his tumble."

"What do you think it means?"

"I don't know—yet. But it's a link, a detail they have in common. Maybe they knew each other? Maybe they shared some secret?"

"You've got some imagination, El. Now I have a different theory. Suppose a madman killed Percy and Beppini, and then suppose a jealous lover wanted to take revenge on Grace Mitchell. It would have been easy for him to get a red balloon and attach it to her window. Get it?"

"You mean an unrelated criminal decided to mislead us by copying the red balloon from the earlier murders?"

"Yes! The first two balloons suggested a series of crimes and a single criminal. That could have been very convenient for a second killer."

Ellery thought for a moment. His father's theory was seductive and difficult to refute. Maybe they were even dealing with *three* separate murderers. A knife, a rope, and a blunt instrument—three very different weapons. And yet....

Two days later, at seven in the evening, the telephone disturbed the inspector. Sergeant Velie had been notified that, fifteen minutes earlier, a police officer had observed a red balloon on the grounds of Jonathan Mallory's estate. He would send a car to pick up the Queens and deliver them to the Mallory house.

Inspector Queen hung up, pale. Jonathan Mallory. This time, public opinion would catch fire!

Ellery seemed genuinely interested.

"Notice the time, Dad," he said in the speeding car. "The murderer didn't take any precautions. He must have known that this balloon would be seen almost immediately. Why didn't he put it up in the middle of the night?"

"Exactly," the inspector groaned. "The balloon isn't an optical illusion. Some enemy must be out to get Mallory, if he's as rich as they say. Somebody looking to eliminate the competition."

"Is it true he caused the crash of the Pan-American stock market?"

"His firm did. You're not suggesting there's a common denominator between Mallory and Douglas Percy?"

The car stopped in front of a luxurious—to the point of being gaudy—building. Inspector Queen galloped through the garden and the hall. What he saw made him stop short. A fifty-year-old man, leaning on crutches and red-faced with fury, stood on the top step of the staircase leading to the second floor, with a dismayed Sergeant Velie trying in vain to appease him.

"I promise you," Velie stammered, "it's in your own best interests...."

"It's useless," the other man yelled. "Just because some joker had the bad taste to tie a balloon to a tree on my grounds, I won't tolerate a brigade of cops in my home! I will defend myself, sir! If I have reason to make use of your services, my secretary will let you know. But now, I want you to leave!"

"That's Mallory," the inspector whispered in Ellery's ear. He stepped forward.

"Get out of here!" Mallory shouted.

"A murder's going to be committed in this house," Inspector Queen said coldly, "and you have no right to interfere with the actions of the police."

"A *murder*?" Mallory said, mollified. "What's that supposed to mean?"

"You've heard about Grace Mitchell, right? You should be grateful we're here, Mr. Mallory."

The invalid laughed. "All right, gentlemen, do what you have to do! But be sure to give me a full account of your intrusion." He pulled a bell cord hanging against the wall, and a solemn servant appeared. "John, go with them."

He left on his crutches. The right leg of his trousers, stretched by a metal frame, swung gently. Inspector Queen and his son traversed the immense house searching for any evidence. But no one had been murdered, and the inspector—for the first time in his career—was embarrassed.

"Someone's mocking us!" he muttered.

"No, Dad," Ellery said. "I think we're very close. The murderer didn't have enough time to attack Mallory."

"Then why the red balloon?"

"Well, we were wrong about that. The red balloons are put in place *before* the murders, not after. I'll admit I prefer it this way."

"You prefer it?"

"Yes. I'll tell you why soon. For now, it's important to protect Jonathan Mallory."

But Mallory wouldn't listen. When he was informed that the police proposed stationing a guard outside his home, he put up a fight. The inspector tried to reason with him, but Jonathan Mallory was beyond reason. Ellery intervened.

"You're playing the murderer's game, Mallory. He's counting on you to resist us, I'm sure of it, and you're just making it easier for him. But if something happens to you, nothing will keep your competitors from gossiping. Someone might suggest that you killed yourself, that your investments were going badly. We'll downplay that angle, of course, but—"

Mallory's fists clenched on his crutches. "You're no fool, young man," he growled. "And you're right, they would say that."

"Fine, then," Ellery continued, "one of us will spend the night here."

"No," Mallory groaned. "Not you. Leave me one of your best men. If he annoys me, I'll have no qualms throwing him out on his backside."

The atmosphere relaxed. Inspector Queen took advantage of the opportunity to give Sergeant Velie his instructions. He was to install himself in the hall, where he could easily observe the ground floor and the large staircase. Every hour, he would make his rounds. The staff—John, the cook, and the chauffeur—would be locked in their quarters. In case he needed backup, the sergeant would only have to fire his revolver and the officers posted outside the house would immediately respond. The inspector and his son withdrew without Mallory deigning to accompany them.

The house was situated at the back of the lush grounds and was easy to patrol. Inspector Queen, however, could not relax. Despite the four solid officers he had just assigned as guards, he continued to pace the sidewalk with his son.

"What's bothering you, Dad?" Ellery asked.

"There's a devilry in all this that I just don't understand. Why the red balloons before the murders? If the murderer couldn't strike immediately after attaching the balloons—and it seems clear that, today at least, that's the case—then he'd have to come back? That's absurd!"

"But," Ellery said, "the red balloons might be signals, telling the murderer *where* to strike."

"Hmm. So the murderer uses a scout, someone to mark his victims? That's a brilliant hypothesis, El, but it seems awfully risky. And if it's true, a single balloon wouldn't suffice. He'd need a second to signal the correct street and a third for the neighborhood. No, that can't be it. We need to know more about Mallory. Let's go back. I've got a call to make."

Three shots fired, muffled but clearly audible. The inspector swore. His officers swarmed across the lawn, with Inspector Queen and Ellery right behind them. The front door was locked.

"Velie! Let us in! Velie!" the inspector yelled.

There was no sign of life from within. Inspector Queen fired four shots into the lock and the six men crashed through the door. Ellery, in the lead, found a switch and turned on the lights. The men stared, aghast. Sergeant Velie lay sprawled across a chest of drawers, apparently dead. A few feet away lay a young man, his face covered in blood. A dull thump from the upper landing made them raise their heads. They recognized Mallory, arriving on his crutches. He bent over the railing, and his shoulders trembled.

The inspector pointed at the young man on the floor. "There's your murderer, Mr. Mallory. You got lucky." Then, without worrying about the banker, he set to work.

Velie was still breathing. He had been shot in the neck and the arm. The officers rushed him outside and waited for the ambulance. The young man was dead—shot in the heart.

"It's easy to reconstruct what happened," the inspector said. "They fired at each other from close range." He checked Velie's pistol, then looked for the young man's and discovered it on the tile floor, some distance from the body. Two rounds had been fired. It remained only to discover how the man had gained access to the house.

An office window was wide open, overlooking the garden. The inspector saw no visible fingerprints on the windowsill. The grass below was unmarred by footprints. The young man had probably hidden himself in a tree after securing the balloon in a visible location. Then he had somehow entered the office, where he had surprised the sergeant, without leaving any traces on the grass. The inspector didn't see any other possible explanation.

Ellery had remained in the hall. His father told him what he'd seen.

"What you say makes sense, Dad," Ellery said, "but why was the young man's revolver found so far from his body? And why was Velie injured in his right arm and under his right ear?"

Inspector Queen frowned. "If Velie fired first, the young man wouldn't have had time to shoot back, but if *he* fired first, then *Velie* would have been out of commission immediately?"

"Exactly! Which leads me to believe that Velie must have been taken by surprise, explaining why his wounds are all on one side. But since the intruder had the element of surprise on his side, why did he shoot? He wouldn't have wanted to awaken the household. He must have seen us outside the house and known we'd burst in before he could possibly have time to locate and kill Mallory."

"When we can talk to Velie, we'll know more. For now, we need to identify this young man. Maybe Mallory knows him?"

But Jonathan Mallory had never seen the man before, and neither had the servants. The secretary, Bob Seldon, had gone home at 4 PM with Mallory's permission. They would question him in the morning. Mallory seemed dejected. His grim humor had disappeared—he seemed afraid. Inspector Queen promised him that the police would be discreet.

The next morning, they could see clearly that no one had crossed the estate's expansive lawns. The ground beneath each tree was examined with intense scrutiny. From the available evidence, the young man had not been hiding in the grounds.

"You seem satisfied, El," the inspector grumbled.

"Yes," Ellery said, "because I've thought all along that the young man was hidden in the house."

"That just doesn't fly. First off, we toured the house when we got there."

"Yes, but quickly. We weren't searching for a body, or for the murderer."

Inspector Queen shook his head. "I'm in the habit of looking everywhere," he said, "and I tell you that man was not in this house."

"But he had to be, because he couldn't have come in from outside!"

"What about the open window?"

"It could have been opened after the gunshots."

"By whom?"

Ellery adjusted his pince-nez and guided the inspector down the hall.

"Hunker down here, Dad. See where I'm pointing? See that tile?"

"Sure. It's broken."

"Yes, as if a heavy item had fallen on it."

"I'll be damned if I understand where you're going with this."

"I'm going to stand guard tonight."

The inspector jumped to his feet.

"I believe," Ellery said, "the excitement's far from over."

The dead man was identified that day, since the police had his fingerprints and photograph on file. Inspector Queen couldn't help but jerk in surprise when he read the note the messenger handed him. He leapt to the telephone.

"Hello, Ellery? The dead guy's Benjamin Benko... That's right, Slim Vibur's old lieutenant... Velie will be happy to have taken him down, since Benko was so high up in Slim's organization. What's that?... In 1933... Sure I'm sure, because Velie was promoted to sergeant a month after Slim's death."

The inspector gloated: his theory was proving to be a good one. Some years previously, Slim and Benko had specialized in high-profile kidnappings. In just a few months, Slim had amassed an enormous fortune. The Jessie Corton abduction alone had netted him two hundred thousand dollars. Benko had apparently planned to snatch Mallory and hold him for ransom. He must have figured the police would chalk the crime up to the red-balloon killer, and no one would be the wiser.

The inspector smiled. He understood why Ellery had said the excitement wasn't over. Ellery feared that Benko's men would mount an attack, desiring vengeance for their boss. They would be caught in Ellery's trap. Their capture would, to a large extent, mitigate the police's failure to catch the mysterious balloon murderer. Inspector Queen, satisfied by this turn of events, went to visit Sergeant Velie, who remained in critical condition. His wounds were severe enough to require a blood transfusion. He was very weak and unable to talk. His doctor, however, assured the inspector that the sergeant's life was not in danger. Reassured, Queen returned to Jonathan Mallory's house. He found the banker surrounded by suitcases.

"I'm leaving!" Mallory cried. "Since you couldn't keep out the first thug who came into my house, I'm getting out of here. I've had enough!"

"That's your right," the inspector said coldly. "Just don't go far. You'll probably be attacked again before the night is out."

The banker shifted on his crutches. "There are private detectives," he growled.

"Be my guest! I'll just take my leave, then."

"Hold on. You're suggesting that my life is still in danger. Are you sure of that?"

"Listen, Mr. Mallory. When a gangster like Ben Benko is taken out, his men don't just swallow it. They'll have the last word, if we don't intervene. So, here's what I propose. I'll spend the night in your bedroom. Ellery will hide downstairs. Once Benko's goons have been taken care of, you can do whatever you like."

Mallory hobbled back and forth. "I'll give you forty-eight hours," he said at last, "to get rid of these rats. After that, you're barred from my house."

He turned on his crutches and slowly walked away. Inspector Queen made an effort to control himself. Sooner or later, Mallory would pay for his insolence.

Fortunately, Djuna had prepared an excellent lunch, which calmed the inspector's mood. As they enjoyed their chicken and rice, he told his son about the morning's event. "This Mallory's a pain," he concluded. "I'm sorry Velie had to get hurt to protect his millions."

"He's very rich?" Ellery asked.

"So I'm told. When he was fifteen, he hired his first employees. Then, thanks to smart investment, he flourished. In 1932, he made a fortune off American gas. In '33, he founded a wool consortium. If Benko had succeeding in grabbing him, he could have gotten a fortune for Mallory."

"You're assuming his intention was to kidnap Mallory, not to kill him."

"Well, Benko *was* a killer. He's the guy who bumped off Al Renny in '33. You were in California then."

"What strikes me," Ellery murmured, "is the importance of the year 1933. It marks the decline of Percy, Beppini, and Mitchell, as I've already mentioned. Slim Vibur died in 1933, and so did Al Renny. And Jonathan Mallory became one of the wealthiest financiers in the United States in 1933. It's interesting, to say the least."

"It's a coincidence, and that's all it is. Unless you're suggesting there's some connection between these folks, who were all strangers to each other?"

"I don't see one yet, except for the red balloons. Can you tell me why Velie and Slim Vibur's lieutenant met face-to-face last night?"

"Another coincidence. If I hadn't assigned Velie to watch the house, that meeting would never have happened."

"Exactly. But thanks to that little detail—and others, just as bizarre— I find myself wondering...."

Ellery smiled and asked Djuna for a cup of coffee.

"I'm impatient," he said. "I wouldn't be surprised if something truly sensational happens tonight."

Inspector Queen posted two men in the living room and two men on the upstairs landing, and stationed himself near Mallory's front door. Ellery sent one officer to the far end of the hall and hid himself at the foot of the large staircase. The garden and the street were deliberately cleared of surveillance, and the wait began.

To kill time, Ellery reviewed the events that had followed the discovery of the first red balloon. He began to formulate a bold, but plausible, theory. It explained all but two of the important points.

The clock in the entryway sounded the hour.

There was a link between the first three crimes, but it would only make sense if Mallory had been abducted. They had to find the man with the scar. The red balloons were childish.

The roar of an engine grew louder, then stopped. Surprised, Ellery took a step forward. He had not predicted this. He heard the crunch of gravel, and a breeze wafted in from the office. A door creaked. Ellery felt someone pass him in the darkness, but he stayed where he was, gripping his pistol and readying himself to turn on the lights.

Suddenly, a shot was fired. A vase clattered to the ground not far away, shattering into pieces. Ellery threw himself at the switch. Light flooded the hall, illuminating a body. He rolled it onto its back. The man was approximately thirty, with frizzy black hair. There was a small white scar at the corner of his nose. Officers rushed in from all directions, revolvers at the ready.

"He's dead," Ellery said. He pointed at the officer who had stood guard with him. "He took a shot at Fred, and Fred killed him."

Inspector Queen descended the staircase, leading Mallory, who leaned heavily on the bannister.

"That's Bob Seldon," Mallory said dryly. "Now you've gotten my secretary massacred?"

"Bob Seldon knew the secret of the red balloons," Ellery replied.

"You're sure?" the inspector asked.

"Are you saying he was part of the gang?" demanded Mallory.

"Apparently," the inspector replied. "Why don't you go back up to bed, Mr. Mallory, and don't worry about a thing. We'll stay here until morning."

Ellery searched Seldon's clothes, with his father looking on.

"How did you learn, El, that Bob Seldon was part of this business?"

"By chance, Dad. I regret wholeheartedly that he's dead. Fred was too fast—he lost his head a bit. If he hadn't fired, the mystery would now be clear. But maybe this can help us." He opened Seldon's wallet and leafed through the papers inside. An envelope caught his attention. The address had been scrawled in pencil: *93 East 121st Street. Atlantic Garage. Michigan.*

"I see," Ellery murmured thoughtfully. "Seldon didn't know we were here, because he was gone the day before yesterday. This explains everything."

"It does? So what's the significance of the garage and the word Michigan?"

"Patience, Dad! Give me time to confirm a few things. Tomorrow at lunch, I think we'll be set. If reporters ask you any questions, tell them everything you know. The publicity might be helpful."

Ellery started his investigations early the next morning. At 93 East 121st Street, he found a miserable motel on the edge of Harlem. He showed a photo of Benko to the desk clerk, who recognized the man immediately. Benko was known to have shoplifted from a store on Broadway. He received many telephone calls and seemed to engage in a variety of different business. The clerk had seen him once in a fancy car.

"A Lincoln?"

"Might have been."

Ellery searched Benko's bedroom without finding anything. Next, he looked up the address of the Atlantic Garage and wrote it down. He decided it would be useless to visit the garage, though, since it probably housed a dozen Lincolns and it didn't seem to matter which one was the right one. What remained was the word Michigan. Unless Ellery was very much mistaken, there was only one possible interpretation. He went into a pharmacy and called Bill Marsham, an old friend.

"Hello, Bill? I want to sink a bundle into Michigan.... Yes, it's a sure thing.... I was told there could be dividends in the thousands.... What? It's on a downswing? Then forget it, I must have been given a bum tip. If I have to lose my money, I'd rather lose it at the races. Thanks!"

Now he saw the whole picture. The mystery was almost solved. In a matter of hours, Ellery would know if his hypothesis was worth anything. He wiped the lenses of his pince-nez, whistled one of Grace Mitchell's songs, and, with the help of a Woolworth's employee, bought a hat box.

When the inspector returned home, he was not in a sporting mood. The press had given him a hard time, and he was afraid that Mallory—who was connected to a dozen senators, not to mention governors—would retaliate. The inspector had no political ambitions, but he had his pride.

"I left two men at Mallory's," he told his son. "Now that Seldon's out of commission, I figured that would suffice."

"Probably true," Ellery murmured.

Just then, the telephone rang. Inspector Queen seized the receiver, and Ellery could hear a nasal voice, full of exclamations, coming tinnily from the earpiece.

A stupefied expression appeared on the inspector's face. "I'm on my way," he said.

"Another one?" Ellery demanded.

"They just found a second red balloon in Mallory's garden. And Mallory's gone—probably kidnapped and maybe murdered."

CHALLENGE TO THE READER

My readers often tell me, "Give us genuine mysteries. We can guess the solutions too easily!" But detection is not a matter of guessing, of stumbling upon answers by chance. What matters is to be able to name the murderer with complete certainty, after correctly analyzing multiple data points and clarifying issues that, at first glance, may seem impenetrable. You, Gentle Readers, are now in possession of all the clues necessary for a correct solution of the Mystery of the Red Balloons. For once, you are the most-informed party in the case.

So, who killed the broker, the violinist, and the dancer? Who kidnapped the banker? Who distributed those red balloons, and why? Remember, don't guess. Instead, put on your thinking caps and figure it out. —E.Q.

Ellery and his father didn't stay more than five minutes at Mallory's house. The banker's bedroom was in disarray. Torn sheets dragged on the parquet. One crutch lay atop the dresser; the other had fallen behind the bed. Drops of blood splattered the floor. A dagger sat on the nightstand. The officer charged with guarding the upstairs was desperate.

"Why did you abandon your post?" Inspector Queen demanded.

"I was called downstairs! The valet had just found the red balloon, and things got frantic."

"One thing's for sure," the inspector groaned. "The murderer profited from that moment of confusion. He knocked out Mallory, hoisted him onto his back, and hid him, probably in the first-floor washroom. When you returned and found that the banker was gone, you yelled, didn't you, and everyone rushed upstairs? That's when the killer slipped out to the garage and from there to the street."

Inspector Queen's reconstruction of events was easily verified. There were drops of blood in the washroom, and Mallory's little Ford was not in the garage.

"We mustn't lose any more time, Dad," Ellery said. "I know where the murderer's hiding. Let's go!"

He hurried the inspector into the police car they had brought. Ellery drove, lights flashing, sirens blaring. It was, even by New York standards, a riotous journey across town. The car finally stopped in front of the Atlantic Garage. Ellery drew his father around the side of the building. A taxi approached and deposited an old man. They couldn't see him clearly, only that he wore a felt hat and a dark shirt. The man slowly headed for the back of the garage. Ellery and the inspector snuck between two cars, pretending to search the ground for something. They kept their eyes on the silhouette, which stopped near a coupe. The man got into the Lincoln, and the engine roared to life.

"Pay attention, Dad! When he passes us, we have to follow him. Here he comes!"

They moved apart as the Lincoln approached. The car turned, slowly heading for the garage's exit. Ellery tightened his grip on his pistol.

"Hello, Mr. Mallory!" he said. "Are you trying to avoid us?"

"Djuna, another splash of bourbon."

Steam rose from their coffee.

Inspector Queen smiled. "I'm starting to understand," he murmured. "The red balloons are what lost me."

"There I have you at a disadvantage, Dad. I knew that a man with a heavy gait had gone into Beppini's hotel with a hat box. I also knew a young man with a scar at the corner of his nose followed him. So it was fairly easy to figure out the truth. When this case started, I was intrigued by the red balloons. Each of them was a signal. But a signal to whom? Someone brought the balloon, and someone else did the killings. Why?"

"It's simple when you know the answer," the inspector said, "and I feel guilty I didn't see it immediately. The murderer was killing people *he didn't know*. The balloon indicated the location of the person he was supposed to kill."

"That's about the size of it, yes."

"And the man who ordered the murders didn't commit them himself, because he didn't want to incriminate himself."

"Right, for any number of reasons. First, he was physically incapable of fighting or of committing the crimes himself. Second, he was used to having people do his dirty work for him. And, third, he may have been planning to get rid of his hired assassin. None of that got me very far, but then, at Mallory's, the balloon was secured out on the grounds. So how could the murderer have known who the intended victim was? Simple: there *wasn't* one. It was a setup: the killer would collide with Sergeant Velie in the hall and be caught. So it seemed clear that the murderer had been sacrificed. But who could have set him up, if not his Svengali, the brains behind the murders?"

"Very good! And that's how you came to suspect Mallory?"

"No, not exactly. Mallory had a bum leg. I figured he couldn't have gone to the homes of Percy or Beppini. But there was another detail that intrigued me: the year 1933. How could I explain the importance of that year in the lives of everyone involved in this melodrama? Some of them were left impoverished, some closed out the year enriched. I had to reconcile those two polar opposites. Who lost? Percy, Beppini, Grace Mitchell. Who gained? Mallory and Sergeant Velie."

"Velie? How's that?"

"He was promoted to sergeant in 1933. And that gave me a glimpse of the solution. Two gangsters were wiped out in 1933, Al Renny and Slim Vibur. Now, who were the people killed by our mysterious murderer? To name them in order: Percy, Beppini, Mitchell, almost Velie, and then Benko, Slim Vibur's lieutenant. Suppose that the first three were ruined by the death of Al Renny. That would require us to assume that they were part of his gang. But we've already agreed that Benko was sent to his death by his puppetmaster. It began to seem as though Slim Vibur's heir had used Benko to annihilate the survivors of a rival gang, and then sacrificed Benko. That made sense, but I was still stuck with a serious difficulty. The instigator of all these executions couldn't have known that Benko would collide with Velie. Luckily, I was reminded of something Mallory said. When you offered to stay with him, he responded, *No, leave me one of your best men.* He knew you'd give Velie the assignment. And Velie—the officer who had killed Vibur—was his target. At that moment, everything became clear. The murderer was Mallory, and Mallory set up the red balloon on the grounds of his own house to bring in the police. He couldn't get to Velie, so he brought Velie to him."

"But he said he didn't want police protection."

"Play-acting! That obliged us to accept his conditions and leave Velie in the hall. It was very clever play-acting, Dad. But Mallory made a mistake: he fired at Velie."

"You think?"

"I'm sure of it. Velie was attacked by Benko, who was armed with the dagger we found in Mallory's bedroom. You think Benko would have gone to the house without a revolver? He wasn't that stupid. Then Velie fired and killed Benko. But Mallory intervened and wounded Velie, then threw the revolver down the hall, cracking one of the tiles. Finally, he went into the office, opened the window so we'd believe Benko came in through the garden, and picked up Benko's dagger in passing. One conclusion presented itself: Mallory's legs both worked just fine. So *he* was the man with the heavy gait seen by the garage employee. Mallory was leading a double life. Sometimes he played the role of a crippled banker, and sometimes he traveled in disguise, in the notorious Lincoln, which allowed him to transport the red balloons without danger. When he feared discovery, he hid them in a hatbox. He would go to the houses of his victims at times when he knew they wouldn't be home to leave his signal, and Benko would follow soon after."

"But the last red balloon?"

"I'm getting there. Once I knew it was Mallory, I figured he'd try to disappear as soon as possible in some spectacular way. Didn't we warn him about another kidnapping attempt?"

"That's true. I told him myself how he could escape. I'm getting old, El!"

"No, Dad. It's just that Mallory was smart. I expected things to turn out this way, once Seldon showed up. I didn't have time to intervene. Seldon had discovered Mallory's double life and knew about the Lincoln. Seldon—who was missing, I imagine, because he was trying to verify certain hypotheses and conduct his own investigation—heard a noise. He thought he'd fallen into Mallory's trap. He fired first and foolishly headed downstairs. I'll regret that for the rest of my life. But it's thanks to him I was able to unravel Mallory's diabolical plan. The meaning of the note in his wallet was clear, except for the word *Michigan*. But I finally remembered another of Mallory's remarks. Think back: when he decided to accept our protection, I showed him that his disappearance would inevitably lead to financial chaos. He accepted my point of view remarkably quickly. Had I unwittingly said something important? Mallory had prepared himself for the upset his kidnapping would cause—an upset that, in the end, would benefit him. But Michigan shares were well-rated."

"Well reasoned, El! If the price went down, that would prove Mallory was laying the groundwork to buy the shares back on the cheap."

"Exactly! And a simple telephone call confirmed it. Once I made that call, the Mystery of the Red Balloons was no longer mysterious. Mallory must have been related to Slim Vibur—"

"They were brothers! He admitted it immediately after you left."

"Very well. Then Mallory, who'd been enriched by his brother, dreamed of vengeance. Above all, he wanted Velie. He set up this whole series of crimes so that Velie could ultimately be shot in his home—and so that he himself, protected by the police, would appear to be completely innocent. Then, by an unexpected stroke of good luck, he arranged things so that his vengeance would pay double—because no press is bad press, he knew that his disappearance and triumphant return would considerably increase his financial position. Knowing the message it would send, I bought a red balloon myself, brought it into Mallory's house concealed in a hatbox of my own, and hung it in the grounds. This challenge from an unknown enemy who obviously knew his secret terrified Mallory, and he fled. Where would he go? First to a hotel to transform himself, and then to the Atlantic Garage to get the Lincoln. So all we had to do was wait for him at the garage and arrest him when he showed up."

"Son, you never cease to amaze me. I—"

A series of explosions sounded in the smoking room, and the inspector set down his cup so abruptly that his coffee splashed onto the table.

Ellery laughed. "It's Djuna, Dad! He's amusing himself by popping the balloons I bought this morning. I wasn't positive Mallory would take flight right away, so I bought a dozen of them!"

DYING MESSAGE

Leyne Requel

Those not already familiar with Leyne Requel's "Dying Message" may well find themselves—as they read it—wondering what it's doing in the pastiche section of this book. We understand—and have ourselves wrestled with the proper placement of this story. It contains elements of humor, which could justify calling it a parody. But in other respects it structurally resembles a pastiche. "Then where," we hear you ask, "is Ellery Queen?" When "Dying Message" was first published in EQMM in 1966, Frederic Dannay provided an explanatory note at the end. So, too, will we. For now, we ask you to trust us: we'll meet again at story's end, where all will be explained.

The shrilling of the telephone in a certain Manhattan apartment disturbed the slumbers of three people. It was Jandu, the houseboy, who struggled into wakefulness to answer it, and even he was without his customary cheerfulness as he groped for the offending instrument.

A voice spoke urgently from the other end, but Jandu was firm. No, he could not disturb Mr. Requel. The voice urged some more, and then the phone was taken gently from Jandu by Leyne Requel himself. That gentleman, minus his pince-nez, listened intently, startled wide-awake by what he heard. He reached for pad and pencil, scribbled down an address and directions, and was soon racing into his clothes, heedless of a protesting Jandu. The third sleeper, Requel's father, merely rolled over when the phone rang, and so did not hear the story until later....

The sun had just risen over the sleeping village of Scundermere when Leyne drove through at an indecent pace toward the lake. He screeched to a halt by the signpost, consulted his notes, and hurried on as fast as the dirt road permitted. Spying a hunting lodge through the trees, Leyne pulled into the dirt track, jumped from his car, and headed for the door of the lodge.

A State Trooper stopped him, and he was still trying to persuade that doughty individual to let him in when the local Chief of Police, hearing heated voices, came out.

"What is it, Oattes?" he asked.

"Sir," replied Trooper Porter Oattes, young pride of the State Police, "this feller wants to butt in."

Leyne hastened to explain. "I'm Leyne Requel—"

"Say no more," exclaimed the Chief. "I used to work with your old man on the New York police force. I'm Carson Pellicott, and I'm proud to know you. Oattes, this is a good man to have around." To Leyne he said, "C'mon in. I'll fill you in if you like—or do you know all about it?"

"All I know," said Leyne, "is that an old friend called me in the wee hours of the morning and said he'd be arrested for murder if I didn't do something pronto. So here I am. I don't know a thing."

"Hmmm," said Pellicott. "Would your friend be Spence Cuttinson, by any chance?" Leyne's expression was all the confirmation he needed, and the Chief went on thoughtfully. "I don't see what you can do. Cuttinson *must* have done this killing. We found his footprints—and only his—where the murder was committed. *And* he was the one who 'found' the body out in the summerhouse, on his way to do some pre-dawn fishing. *He* says. And if that ain't enough, the victim wrote out Cuttinson's initials before he died. Looks to me like that clinches it."

"Who else was here?"

"Only the owner of this place, Kit Heller—he's a theatrical producer—and the man who was killed, Vic Hemitt, a shady lawyer from New York."

"Where are Heller and Spence now?"

"Cuttinson is in the kitchen. Heller took off. I know," Pellicot raised a hand. "It looks suspicious, but Heller left a note saying something important had come up and he'd be back. He could have gotten a phone call, though no one heard any. But that's not the point. The point is—"

"Hi, Leyne," interrupted a tragic voice from the doorway. Leyne looked and could not believe his eyes. Spence Cuttinson was normally a bouncing individual whose spirit was never dampened. Evidently, however, suspicion of murder had worked a change. Now he was haggard, and even his voice was a hollow mockery.

"The trouble," Spence said wearily, "is that Hemitt seems to have accused me in his last moments. I don't understand it, and I can't explain it."

Leyne was thinking furiously. "How are you so sure," he asked Pellicot, "that some unknown person didn't come along and do it?"

The Chief of Police sighed. "There's a small summerhouse out back, a one-room affair with one door and two windows. The ground around it is so muddy that no one can get near it without leaving prints. Well, we can see where Hemitt went out to it—to the door—but no one else went anywhere near the door. There was one set of tracks up to each window, and I'll swear both sets were made by different pairs of shoes—but *both* pairs belong to your friend."

"The awful thing," Spence cut in, "is that I think so, too. I did make the tracks going up to the window on the side nearest the house. That's when I went for a fishing rod I'd left out there. When I saw the light I went up to the window to see what was going on. I could tell at a glance that Hemitt was dead, and alone, and I could see the bullet hole, so I came back and called the police. I didn't want to go in and touch anything, or walk around outside, for fear of messing up clues. Little did I realize," he concluded wryly, "where the clues I was so careful to preserve were going to point!"

"And," said the Chief, "there's another set of prints going up to the other window, and a spent cartridge on the ground outside. The murderer went up to that window and shot his victim through it, all right, and I'd take my oath he was standing in Cuttinson's shoes at the time. We found that pair by the back door of the lodge, and your friend identifies 'em. I've sent casts of the prints, along with the shoes, to the lab, but I don't think there's much question. Your friend's guilty as sin."

Seeing the protest in Leyne's eyes, the Chief added, "Yes, Heller's about the same size and weight as Cuttinson, and he *could* have pinched the shoes and worn 'em to divert suspicion. But that don't explain the initials the victim wrote when he was dying."

"Couldn't Heller have gone in through the window and written the initials himself?" asked Leyne.

"No, sir. That window was stuck—open a slit, just enough to poke a gun muzzle through. The other window ain't been opened for years. You can take it from me, it was Hemitt that wrote *SC*."

Leyne's silver eyes narrowed. "Let's try another tack. What was the connection between these people, and why would someone want to kill Hemitt?"

"Blackmail," Pellicot answered promptly.

"Oh, come," Leyne exclaimed. "Don't ask me to believe that Cuttinson had a guilty secret, too! Spence, old pal, what have you been up to? What are you doing with this crowd, anyhow?"

"That's simple enough," replied Cuttinson. "I know Heller only slightly, but I have a client who's making a deal with him to back a show he's planning to produce. Hemitt was Heller's lawyer, and he asked us both to come up here and work out some of the details of the contract. I thought I'd get in some fishing, too. Hah!

"But I'll tell you this. If I didn't know that Hemitt wrote my initials after he was shot—and he *couldn't* have thought it was I outside the window; there's no earthly reason—I'd say now that Heller set up this whole weekend to frame me for the killing. Since the motive's supposed to be blackmail, it wouldn't prove anything if they can't show a connection between me and the dead man."

"Not much doubt about the blackmail," Pellicot said. "Hemitt's room was searched, but I mean thoroughly, by someone looking for something. We've searched, too, and didn't find anything, so I guess Cut—the murderer found what he was looking for."

"Right," said Leyne. "But Hemitt could just as easily have been blackmailing Heller, who could have searched the room while Spence was asleep.

"Spence has a spotless reputation," Leyne went on. "I've never known him to say or do anything dishonest. Therefore, I'm going on the premise that he didn't do this and is telling the truth. That means there's another explanation for those initials—there must be."

He hoisted his lean frame out of the chair. "Well," he said, with more cheerfulness than he felt, "I'd like to have a look at those confounded initials."

Chief Pellicot accompanied him, leaving Oattes in charge. The two men made their way to the summerhouse, a small structure a few hundred yards from the lodge.

On the way Leyne inspected the footprints, now added to by the boots of the State Police. They told precisely the story he had heard.

The summerhouse still contained the unpleasant spectacle of the dead man. He might have been an unprepossessing figure in life, but in death he was pitiful. Slumped in a chair that had been drawn up to the table, his body faced the slightly open window away from the house, his head twisted toward the other window, so that the bullet hole in the forehead was clearly visible from the spot where Spence said he had discovered the crime.

Hemitt had apparently spent his last moments before the shooting without any suspicion of danger. He had come out to the summerhouse equipped with a crossword puzzle, which he was about two-thirds through, and at the side of the table was a book. It seemed more than likely that he had made an appointment to meet someone out here, and had provided himself with amusements until the other person should appear.

The pencil with which Hemitt had been doing the puzzle had dropped to the floor, but what he had written last was not part of the crossword. A large *SC* had been irregularly scrawled across the diagram, and it certainly looked like the shaky writing of a dying man.

"Well, Mr. Requel," asked the Chief, "what do you think?"

"I admit it *looks* incriminating," agreed Leyne, "and the meeting in the summerhouse implies a certain secrecy. But logic dictates that there must be another explanation for the *SC*. Hemitt must have had a good idea of who might murder him—the person he had an appointment with—but my conclusion is that he tried to leave a clue that would escape the murderer's notice, or that the murderer wouldn't understand."

They were interrupted by some State Troopers who had come to remove the body. One of the Troopers had two reports to make. First, the lab had declared positively that the shoes and the footprints matched; second, the New York police (in the person of none other than Steve Geileran—Leyne's father's right-hand man), stated that Vic Hemitt was a known blackmailer.

"Look, Mr. Requel," Chief Pellicot said, not without reluctance, "I've got to arrest your friend unless you can give me some other reason for those initials."

"Let me have an hour," Leyne urged. "One hour more or less won't matter."

Pellicot agreed, and they walked to the door. Leyne spotted two men hanging about behind the trees. He jerked his head toward them, eyebrows raised in question. Pellicot said, "Names are Ferdinand Arcey and Dean F. Belmer. They ain't suspects—we know where they were all last night—but they're involved in some way. I can't make out how, and they won't say a word, but I'm sure they're partners in crime."

With this Pellicot departed, while Leyne settled himself in the summerhouse for a siege of concentrated thinking. He sat at the table, his chin propped on his hand. Absently he nibbled his knuckle. The minutes ticked by.

He glanced idly at the part of the crossword with which Hemitt had evidently spent his last moments on earth. A six-letter horizontal word meaning "weapon" appeared to be the last word filled in. Vertically, the definition—numbered *50*—was "a set of implements or tools," in three letters.

Leyne shook his head and examined the book. It was called *Scenes of India*, and his eyebrows rose. The title began with *SC*. Hemitt might have meant to write more before he died. Leyne inspected the book minutely, but he found nothing helpful.

Suddenly he sprang to his feet. How blind he had been!

He hurried back to the lodge. Spence Cuttinson looked up with a ghost of hope in his eyes, the Chief with curiosity and skepticism.

"Pellicot," Leyne asked triumphantly, "what's a three-letter word meaning 'a set of implements or tools'?"

A look crossed the old Chief's face that has crossed the faces of other men who do not know Leyne Requel well. Cuttinson managed to say in a strangled voice, "Do you mean 'kit'?"

Leyne beamed. "Exactly! Isn't that the first name of our elusive host, Kit Heller? It's also the crossword clue Vic Hemitt was working on when the murderer cut his puzzling short. *And it's number fifty down!*

"You still don't see? If a dying man tried to write *50*, but scrawled it so shakily that it trailed off before he finished, it might well look like *SC*.

"And, you know," Leyne concluded with a smile, "it just had to be Kit Heller."

"What do you mean?" asked Cuttinson.

"Why, Kit Heller is the perfect name for the killer."

EDITOR'S NOTE—CHALLENGE TO THE READER

An old proverb, elaborated on by Plutarch and Thucydides, tells us that history repeats itself. A true variation—thus giving us a new proverb—is that mystery repeats itself. So here is Mrs. Norma Schier (to use her real name) pulling the wool over our eyes....

Leyne Requel = Ellery Queen

And if "the killer" and "Kit Heller" (perfect name for "the killer" indeed!) is the only anagram that Leyne Requel himself spotted, the great detective is indeed slipping. [A]ll the proper names in the story are anagrams—but, of course, you knew that all along, didn't you? For example:

Scundermere = murder scene
Porter Oattes = State Trooper
Carson Pellicot = local Inspector
Spence Cuttinson = innocent suspect
Vic Hemitt = the victim
Jandu = Djuna
Steve Geileran = Sergeant Velie

There were other clues, too—a plenitude of giveaways. This addendum is headed CHALLENGE TO THE READER—a phrase coined by Ellery Queen, and a hallmark of both E.Q. the author and E.Q. the detective. The title of the story, Dying Message, *is a creative approach which, if not invented by Ellery Queen, certainly has become one of Queen's trademarks, and is more associated with E.Q. than with any other mystery writer. And the use of the same name for both the author and the detective also points inescapably to Ellery Queen, the only modern mystery writer who uses this double device.*

And still that is not all. Mrs. Schier has added a bonus of two clues—which, if you unscramble them, earn you a special commendation. Remember those two silent, skulking characters in the story revealingly called "partners in crime"?—Ferdinand Arcey and Dean F. Belmer. Anagrams again, and two red herrings standing for the two creators of Ellery Queen—Frederic Dannay and Manfred B. Lee to whom, in Mrs. Schier's own words, she "is enormously indebted; they have won my undying gratitude for reading pleasure these many years, to say nothing of my gratitude as an author for their wonderful editorial help and encouragement."

F.D., M.B.L., and E.Q. are equally grateful to you, Mrs. S.—and who will be next in your anatomy of anonyms and anagrams?

The italicized "Editor's Note" that appears above was written by Frederic Dannay and published in the July 1966 issue of EQMM, *immediately after the story. (It's telling, by the way, that the apostrophe in "Editor's" appears* before *the "s," a solid indication that the magazine was edited by Fred Dannay alone, while Manny Lee was busy with other things.)*

"Dying Message" was the fourth anagram story Norma Schier contributed to EQMM, *following tales presented as by "Norma Haigs" (Ngaio Marsh), "Cathie Haig Star" (Agatha Christie), and "Handon C. Jorricks" (John Dickson Carr). Six more pastiches would appear in* EQMM, *and then Mrs. Schier wrote five more for the Mysterious Press's 1979 hardcover collection,* The Anagram Detectives.

THE GILBERT AND SULLIVAN CLUE

Jon L. Breen

*Author's Note: I got my mystery writing start as a parodist.
A loyal reader of* Ellery Queen's Mystery Magazine, *I knew the
editing half of EQ, Fred Dannay, loved parodies and pastiches,
and, after he had bought three from me, he invited me to take
a shot at Ellery Queen. The resultant story, "The Lithuanian
Eraser Mystery," published in the March 1969 issue, featured
E. Larry Cune (a very strained parody name!) and was based
on the early Ellery of the pure-puzzle days. Thirty years later,
with both of the Queen collaborators long deceased, Edward
D. Hoch and I were invited to contribute new stories about the
character, pastiches rather than parodies, to commemorate the
seventieth anniversary of* The Roman Hat Mystery, *the first
EQ novel. Since then, Dale Andrews has inventively evoked an
Ellery who ages in real time, but both Ed and I followed the
lead of Dannay and Manfred B. Lee who (with only occasional
exceptions) set their stories in the present day, with Ellery stay-
ing more or less the same age from decade to decade. While
I still like "Lithuanian Eraser," I wanted to be represented in
this anthology by "The Gilbert and Sullivan Clue" for several
reasons. With increased attention to character and theme, it
attempts to capture the more roundly developed Ellery of the
late thirties and after. And I liked the idea of bringing together
three examples of successful but sometimes rancorous artistic
collaborations: W.S. Gilbert and Arthur Sullivan, of course; the
fictitious comedy team of Joe Dugan and Ozzie Foyle, whose
parting of the ways suggests several real-life counterparts; and,
behind the scenes, the Ellery Queen team themselves, who were
known to compare their rocky relationship to that of Gilbert and
Sullivan. (I also liked the chance to write new lyrics for "I've
Got a Little List.")*

The voice on the telephone said, "How are you, Ellery?"

Gazing at the Hollywood Hills from his insanely luxurious hotel suite, Mr. Ellery Queen answered honestly, "Worn to a nub by the pressures of the treadmill, racked with guilt at stealing money for doing nothing a roomful of word-processing chimpanzees couldn't do as well, terminally bored by sunny weather, and ready to return to the restful chaos of New York City. Who is this?"

"Same old Ellery," his caller laughed. "It's Gil Castberg." Castberg was a Hollywood agent, a snappy-dressing cheapskate with more high-powered clients than Southern California Edison. "Sounds like you need to get away. When are you leaving for the Big Apple?"

"I'm here till Wednesday, when for reasons too complicated to explain I must needs take one more meeting and do one more lunch before returning to civilization."

"Nothing to occupy you till then?"

"Apart from plotting the murder of a twenty-two-year-old studio executive who never heard of Dashiell Hammett, nothing."

"How about a cruise? As my guest."

"That's kind of you, but where to?"

"Nowhere."

"Sounds perfect."

For two days and three nights in January, said Gil Castberg, the smallish but luxurious ship *Sea Twin* would cruise the California coast, beginning and ending in San Pedro, offering champagne, entertainment, and no ports of call. A lady friend for whom Castberg had procured a separate cabin had sent regrets at the last moment.

The headline entertainer on the cruise was to be an old Castberg client, Ozzie Foyle, once of the comedy team of Dugan and Foyle but for the past ten years a single. Ellery had done the second or third version of the script for the team's last film together, a detective comedy, but nothing of his had wound up on the screen. The producers had decided such frills as fair clues, sensible motivation, and plotting logic undermined their concept.

"So why did Dugan and Foyle break up the act, Gil?" Ellery inquired, sipping Mumm's Cordon Rouge under a grey sky on the deck of *Sea Twin*. A half hour out of San Pedro, the sea was already choppy.

The agent shrugged. "Who knows with these artistic types? They never did get along, and Ozzie wanted to stretch his wings. He signed up for six weeks of *Waiting for Godot* at a little theater in Hollywood, working for Equity scale. Dugan was on vacation. Funding came through suddenly for a *Star Wars* parody that would've been the perfect follow-up to their detective flick, but they'd have had to fly to Canada immediately to start shooting. Foyle refused to pull out of his stage engagement. Dugan got pissed, called his partner a pretentious poser, and took a walk. Ozzie was just as happy. He'd saved his money and wanted to do more serious stuff. *Godot*'s an entree into high culture for low comedians. Bert Lahr played in it. Chico Marx."

"I thought Groucho was Foyle's idol," Ellery remarked.

"Well, Groucho loved Gilbert and Sullivan, but he wasn't the specialist Foyle's become. Appears in productions all over the country. Again, not much money, but he's happy and fulfilled."

"And still rich."

"It doesn't hurt."

"Is Foyle still your client, Gil?"

"No, we parted company. Still friends, though, or I wouldn't be here."

"What became of Joey Dugan? I haven't heard much of him since the team split."

"Neither have I. Neither has anybody," said a querulous voice behind Ellery. Swinging around, he beheld a familiar lanky figure leaning against the deck railing. The sad-eyed hound-dog features of Joey Dugan, the skilled straight man of the Dugan and Foyle team, looked more lugubrious than ever. "Actually, my career went just where this tub is going, right, Gil? A voyage to nowhere. Hiya, Ellery, good to see you. Wish we'd'a shot your script, I love a good mystery, but these days you gotta blow stuff up. That's the key to a good gross. My partner, typically, overdid it. Blew up Dugan and Foyle so he could pander to the opera crowd."

"I wish I could get you boys back together," Gil said.

"There are a few slight barriers." Joey Dugan enumerated them on his fingers. "One, my former partner is suddenly allergic to anything that appeals to an audience without tuxedos and lorgnettes. Two, my former partner probably has *Mikado* and *H.M.S. Pinafore* engagements up the wazoo five years into the new millennium. Three, by now most fans think Dugan and Foyle are about as cutting edge as Laurel and Hardy or Abbott and Costello. Four, I can't stand to be in the same room with the little bastard. But I guess a great agent like you can overcome minor things like that, huh, Gil?"

"Is that the point of this reunion?" Ellery asked. "You want to get them back together?"

"If I thought I could," said Gil. "But it's no reunion. I didn't even know Joey was going to be on the cruise."

"Sadie wanted to come. I figured what the hell, I got nothing better to do, and this ship may not be the *Queen Mary*, but it's big enough I can avoid running into Foyle for three days."

Ellery said, "You two worked so well together. Did you hate each other all that time?"

"Naw, not till the second week. The little creep thinks he's a genius, thinks he was the whole act because he was the funny one. But he knew how important my part was, just wouldn't admit it. Ozzie Foyle would always go that little bit too far, add that one last unnecessary frill, milk a gag just a beat beyond where the laugh peaked. I could rein him in."

"The straight man never gets his due," said Gil. "Show-biz tradition."

"Sure. Take Bud Abbott. Brilliant performer, criminally underrated. It's good George Burns got some appreciation in his last years. Gracie was great, sure, but George was the key to that act. Well, gotta go meet the wife. See you guys around."

As Dugan loped off, Gil Castberg muttered, "Sadie's on board."

"Is that a problem?" Ellery asked.

"It makes it all the more important those two guys stay out of each other's way. The break-up of Dugan and Foyle had more to do with Sadie than Samuel Beckett."

Across the empty swimming pool, Ellery noticed a young woman in a long raincoat looking pensively out at the Pacific.

"Lovely girl," he said softly.

"Yeah," Castberg agreed, "but she tries so hard to hide it. Has to in her position. That's Rainbow McAllister, Ozzie Foyle's assistant."

A couple of hours later, after a nudge to the maitre d', Ellery found himself at a table for two in the dining room with Rainbow McAllister. ("Hippy parents," she explained.)

"So are you part of the Dugan camp or the Foyle camp?" Rainbow asked over the sorbet course.

"Neither."

"Good. There must be hundreds of people on board who never even met Dugan or Foyle, but every time I turn around I see some of the old crowd."

"I understand you work for Foyle."

"His personal assistant. I answer his mail, read the scripts that come over the transom, that kind of stuff. His wife Amanda's jealous as hell, so I also have to keep out of the way as much as I can."

"And do your best to look like Little Orphan Annie?"

"Not hard, I'm afraid. The funny thing is, I'm not the least bit attracted to Ozzie Foyle, and God knows he's not attracted to me."

"If he's a straight male, I have a hard time believing that last part. So tell me about the old crowd, as you call it."

"At that table to your left are four of them. The skinny guy who looks like an accountant is Ozzie's accountant, Fred Breedlove. No sense of humor, but nice. The huge African-American with the earring is Dale Washington, known professionally as Daddy Trash. He's a rap singer who loves Gilbert and Sullivan, go figure. The short crew cut is Marlon Crandall, old pal of Ozzie's on the comedy-club circuit, now raking it in as a TV evangelist—I think he's funnier doing that than as a standup. The one with the gray hair is Herman Gable, Ozzie's accompanist, forty and doesn't look a day over seventy. Oooh, look at that."

Ellery was already looking. A six-foot blonde in a revealing gold gown was striding across the room, seemingly oblivious to the masculine eyes following her. She passed a shorter, older, darker, and heavier woman who, Ellery suspected, probably had cut an equally striking figure twenty years ago. The women acknowledged each other with glares.

"The blonde," Rainbow whispered, "is Amanda, Ozzie's trophy wife, his third."

"He's been married three times?"

"Four times, but that's his third *trophy* wife. The other one is Sadie Dugan, Joey's wife. They say she and Ozzie had an affair once, but it was before my time."

After several more courses of Japanese-themed nouveau cuisine (pretty but sparse), Rainbow agreed to accompany Ellery to the ship's impressive tiered showroom to see Ozzie Foyle's one-man performance. Their table far to one side afforded a good view of the stage and an even better one of the glittering front row. Daddy Trash and Marlon Crandall sat at a ringside table with Amanda Foyle and Fred Breedlove. Gil Castberg was seated a few tables away with a young woman Ellery didn't recognize. Surprisingly, Joey and Sadie Dugan also had ringside seats. Given what Dugan had said about his old partner, could he even stand to watch him perform?

"This is quite a crowd," Rainbow whispered. "There's an L.A. County supervisor and his wife at that table next to Dugan, and the guy with them may back a Broadway show Ozzie hopes to get off the ground. The girl with him would like to be in the show."

Every seat was filled when Ozzie Foyle came on stage at ten o'clock. The short, cherubic-looking comic bowed to the ovation, did a few cruise-ship jokes to more laughter than they deserved, and began a rapid-fire Gilbert and Sullivan medley, with selections from *Trial by Jury*, *H.M.S. Pinafore*, and *The Pirates of Penzance*.

When Foyle brought out an oversized, dangerous-looking samurai sword and started brandishing it with clownish clumsiness, the audience knew what was coming: Foyle's theme song from *The Mikado*, in which

Ko-Ko, the comic Lord High Executioner, tells what he would do in the event he actually had to carry out an execution. In long-honored theatrical tradition, new lyrics had been freshly minted for the occasion.

"As someday it may happen that a victim must be found, I've got a little list, I've got a little list—"

A fresh outburst of applause covered up the second line. Herman Gable, Foyle's frail and wasted-looking piano accompanist, vamped for a bit while the comedian beamed and bowed, waiting for the ovation to subside.

"A group of fellow voyagers who might as well be drowned: they never would be missed, they never would be missed. There's the exercising ingénue who runs six miles a day, the glum computer expert who drones on of Y2K, the posturing politicos who won't say what they mean, the philanthropic patron who loves every other scene, the pierced and tattooed rapper who's just waiting to be dissed: they'd none of them be missed, they'd none of them be missed!"

Several good-natured smiles and guffaws from the front-row targets—the girl with the potential angel must have been the exercising ingénue given her whoop of delight—greeted this first verse.

"The parasitic agent who lives royally off your toil, and the rich evangelist: I've got him on the list! The fickle fans who ask you, 'Weren't you once Ozzie Foyle?' They never would be missed, they never would be missed!"

Comic turned preacher Marlon Crandall looked like a man who resented the crack but was determined to be a good sport. Gil Castberg smiled convincingly. But laughter was less general now, not because of the more personal nature of the attacks—most of those in the crowd wouldn't get them anyway—but because Ozzie Foyle's manner had changed. No longer good-humored, he seemed to be putting the lines across with genuine venom. Even those not targeted were feeling uneasy, without knowing why.

"The former partner whining 'cause he cannot get a job, the tennis player sobbing 'cause she cannot hit a lob, the broad who married money but divorces poverty, who'd come into your cabin for a price upon the sea, that superior freeloading detective novelist: I don't think he'd be missed, I'm *sure* he'd not be missed."

"Why the attack?" Ellery murmured to his companion. "I'm not freeloading off *him*."

"And that sniveling accountant, who says the money's gone, a math contortionist: I've got him on the list! That love-starved married lady who will vanish with the dawn: no more will she be missed, she is no longer missed!"

Foyle was shouting the lines more than singing them, and the audience sensed a great talent in full meltdown. A pained-looking cruise director had stepped tentatively onto the stage as if to interrupt Foyle, but the comedian held him off with a gesture.

"There's that wife who spends my money in exchange for jealous glares, that bad piano player who snorts cocaine all he dares, those patronizing toadies that we call an entourage, those unrepentant roadies with their halfwit badinage. All who would drain my genius of its reason to exist: they damn well won't be missed, and I have…them…on…my…list."

Foyle gave an ironic bow. There was no applause, just stunned silence. The stage lights dimmed, the houselights came up, and Joey Dugan bounded onto the stage with the apparent intent of throttling his former partner.

"I've had all I'm going to take from you, you little bastard!" Dugan roared. The shorter man stood his ground, as Dugan was restrained by a burly waiter. Several other bodies—ship's crew and passengers—insinuated themselves between them.

Rainbow said softly, "Out of character."

"Who? Foyle, you mean?"

"Oh, no, Ozzie didn't surprise me. I've seen his tirades. But for Dugan to go postal like that…he's cynical, sarcastic, sure, but always in control."

"I didn't catch all the allusions," Ellery admitted.

"Well, I'm the sobbing tennis player," Rainbow said wryly. "Thought I'd be playing at Wimbledon by now, not gofering for Ozzie Foyle. The love-starved married lady is probably Mrs. Dugan—that'll be what set Dugan off, more than the crack about him. The broad who married money—well, there are so many, how can I narrow it to just one? I'm a little tired, Ellery. Shall we call it a night?"

After Ellery returned to his cabin, the gentle rocking of the ship sent him off to sleep surprisingly quickly. When the ringing of the telephone interrupted his slumber, he glanced at his watch and saw that it was 3 AM.

"Mr. Queen, this is Captain Badger speaking." The crisp British tones had an uneasy edge. "I'm sorry to interrupt your rest, but there's an awkward matter I'd like your help with. It's, ah, well, it's murder actually."

"That *is* awkward, Captain, I'll agree. Who's been murdered?"

"Mr. Ozzie Foyle. His wife, returning to their suite rather late, found his body stretched out on their bed. There's quite a lot of blood. It looks like a stab wound in the back. It's, ah, really horrible, and I need your advice."

"Put into the next available port and turn the case over to the local police."

"Well, yes, that, of course, but given your proven expertise in these matters, I thought perhaps…you do have a reputation as a detective. They call you Maestro, don't they?"

"Only Sergeant Velie, who works for my father, and in light of some of my failures, I've always found the expression rather ironic."

"Well, ah, in any case, couldn't you just have a look?"

"I guess so," Ellery said, with feigned reluctance. "What's Foyle's cabin number?"

"Suite 1B. On the deck above you. I'd be obliged if you didn't mention what's happened to any other passengers."

As he was dressing hurriedly, Ellery heard a tapping on the door of his cabin. Had the impatient captain sent an escort for him?

Opening the door, he found a short, fat, bald man in an expensive gold-dragon robe standing in the doorway, smiling apologetically.

It was Ozzie Foyle.

"Can we talk a minute, Ellery? I heard you moving around in here, so I knew I wasn't—is something wrong?"

"Come in, Ozzie. I regret to inform you that you're a dead man."

"Hey, I know I got a little rough in my act tonight, but nobody's come after me yet."

"Don't be too sure. Somebody they think is you has been found dead in your cabin. Why weren't you there? And who took your place?"

"Ellery, is this a joke? Did I sign on for a murder-mystery cruise without knowing it?"

"It's serious. Tell me what's been going on this evening."

The comedian scratched his bald head. "I had a fight with Amanda after the show. I was trying to apologize for the act. I wasn't myself. Those lyrics just sort of came out."

"Lyrics don't just *sort of come out* in that kind of perfect meter. Those were premeditated insults."

Foyle shook his head. "No, no, they were all in fun. It wasn't the words, you know. It was the delivery. If I sang them the usual way, you know, light, people would see I was only joking. But I've been taking this new medication. It's supposed to help my crazy mood swings, but sometimes I think it brings them on instead. That's why I sang those lines the offensive way I did. Do you think I'd want to offend a guy like Gil Castberg, who did a lot for my career, or my accountant, Fred Breedlove, a terrific guy, good sport even if he doesn't get the jokes, or Herman, my accompanist, who hasn't put anything but his asthma inhaler in his nose for ten years, or my wife, who's very sweet when she's not terrorizing my assistant, or a swell writer like yourself? Did I ever tell you, by the way, I wish we'd shot your script? Dugan was against it, but he has no taste at all."

"Ozzie, the person who thinks he killed you may have been one of the targets of your *Mikado* parody."

"There was no motive for murder in that song, Ellery. Till that pathetic whiner Joey Dugan came after me, I didn't realize what I was doing. By then, I wanted to apologize to everybody, even Dugan, but I got escorted back to the cabin by three big crew members who kept telling me everybody should sleep on it. When my wife came back, like I said, I tried to apologize but she wouldn't hear of it and we had a fight and she stormed out. I just wanted to sleep then—I'd had a drink, and I shouldn't mix that with the medication—but I didn't want to be there in the cabin when she came back. Better we both cool off a little, right? So I looked for somebody who'd loan me their cabin for a few hours. I found Gil Castberg in the lounge, apologized about the song. He took it well. Gil's a good sport. I said I was looking for a place to sleep. He said he thought he had something lined up for the night—a girl, I guess, you know Gil—and anyway, he wouldn't need his cabin. Use hers, I guess. So he gave me his key."

"And did you give him yours?"

Foyle looked blank for a moment. "I suppose I did. I don't really know why. He wasn't going to sleep there. Unless he was sleeping with Amanda." With automatic comic timing, Foyle paused and said, "That was a joke." Another pause. "Wasn't it?"

Ellery did not laugh. "Ozzie, stay in this room. Don't communicate with anyone else, and don't let anyone in but me. You may have given somebody a motive in that song without even knowing it."

"Dugan wouldn't kill me. He doesn't have the spine for it. You know, he never appreciated me. Always thought he was the straw that stirred the drink. Now a straight man is important, but who was getting the laughs? And who made a career for himself as a single? Not Joey Dugan."

"Ozzie, stay here. Please."

When he reached Foyle's suite, Ellery was met at the door by the dapper but shaken Captain Badger.

"Mr. Queen, is it true the murderer always returns to the scene of the crime?"

"A stupid murderer might, I suppose. Why?"

"Just moments ago, while my officers and I were, ah, securing the murder scene, someone came dashing down the passageway and threw that through the door."

The captain pointed. Soiling the white carpet of the opulent suite's sitting room was the huge samurai sword Foyle had used as a prop. Its tip was bloodied.

"Deuced considerate of the killer to bring us back the weapon, eh?" the captain said with forced nonchalance.

"Did you get a look at him?"

"No, one of my officers gave chase, but the fellow was not to be found."

"You haven't touched the sword?"

"Certainly not. We'll leave it where it lies. Would you care to view the body, Mr. Queen?"

"Please." *And find out who it is*, Ellery added to himself.

They looked into the bedroom over a length of red ribbon spanning the doorway in lieu of a crime-scene tape and adding an incongruously cheery touch. The body lay face down on the bed, covered by a dressing gown with a springing tiger on its back.

"Mr. Queen," said Captain Badger, "in the excitement I nearly forgot to tell you. The victim is not Foyle."

"Who is it?"

"Gil Castberg, Foyle's former agent. He was wearing one of Foyle's dressing gowns, so Mrs. Foyle mistook him for her husband. And so, apparently, did the murderer."

Ellery took in as much of the murder scene as he could from the doorway. There was plenty of blood from the wound but not much other sign of struggle. The scene had an oddly staged look about it. A large book lay open on the bedside table, neatly undisturbed. Ellery peered at it from a distance.

"I recognized that book at once," said the captain. "A very fine illustrated edition of Gilbert and Sullivan's operettas. I'm a bit of a bibliophile, Mr. Queen, as I believe you are as well."

"The book is open to the first page of *Utopia Limited*," Ellery observed. "Do you know if that play contributed to Foyle's repertoire?"

"I rather doubt it. One of the team's lesser works, in fact."

"Why would the book be open to that play?"

"A dying message?" the captain ventured.

"Hardly. Even if Castberg could have left us a clue in his dying moments after that stab wound, I don't imagine he could have done it so neatly. Has anyone been in the room?"

"Mrs. Foyle took a couple of steps in, recoiled at what she saw, and called the bridge. The ship's doctor did nothing beyond assuring himself the victim was beyond help. Then we put up the ribbon, as you see."

"Obviously the room and the weapon must be untouched until the police can come on board. In the meantime, you and I can begin an investigation. I'm afraid we'll have to wake a few people up."

"Starting with Mr. Joey Dugan?"

Dugan proved to have an alibi. His well-attended poker game had broken up a few minutes *after* the body of Castberg had been discovered. Most of the other targets on Foyle's little list, including rapper Daddy Trash, accountant Fred Breedlove, pianist Herman Gable, evangelist Marlon Crandall, and Ellery's new friend Rainbow McAllister had retired to their cabins, alone, hours earlier. When Castberg's date for the concert was located, her testimony was particularly interesting: they had had a pleasant chat, but certainly had no carnal plans for the evening.

When Ellery returned to his own cabin, he found Ozzie Foyle waiting anxiously. "Who was killed, Ellery? What happened?"

"I think you know the answer to that, Ozzie. Why did you and Joey Dugan put aside your differences and plan Gil Castberg's murder?"

Ozzie gaped at him. "I couldn't have killed him, Ellery. I was here with you when…" Ozzie realized his slip a little late.

"When what, Ozzie?"

As the *Sea Twin* neared San Pedro, its return a couple of days early, Ozzie Foyle and Joey Dugan were in discreet custody in Captain Badger's office, resigned to being turned over to the police. Ellery and the captain listened to Foyle's story.

"He deserved to die. Actors are simple people, you know, gullible, not good with figures, wrapped up in their art. Who knows how many of his other clients Gil Castberg swindled? You know, I killed him, really. Joey's an accessory at best. I'm the real murderer here, Ellery."

"I'm a full partner, damn you," Dugan retorted. "It's just like you to hog all the credit."

"Sometime after we broke up the act, Fred Breedlove figured out that Gil Castberg had been systematically cheating us for years. He kept all the records for the team and was constantly draining off money for himself, way beyond his commission, which was big enough. We were doing so well in those years, we didn't notice. If either of us ever questioned anything, Castberg would put the blame on the other one. I was sure Dugan was running up needless expenses."

"And I thought Foyle was," said Dugan. "It made me hate him more than I did already."

"We never talked about business," Foyle said. "We never talked about anything except the act."

"And we fought about that," Dugan agreed.

"Castberg sailed too close to the wind, though. Things got dangerous for him. He knew he'd be found out soon, unless he could prod us into dissolving the partnership. That stuff about the sudden call from Canada to start shooting our sci-fi movie during my run in *Waiting for Godot* was all orchestrated by Castberg, designed to break up the team. And it worked. He knew just the right buttons to push to make us go after each other and stay on good terms with him. So we split up, him crying crocodile tears while breathing a sigh of relief and thinking his game wouldn't be found out."

"When Breedlove did find out, Ozzie and I got together again," Dugan said, "united against a common enemy. For Ozzie, it was all an ego thing."

"Hell, it was a humanitarian thing, ridding the world of a scumbag."

"Yeah, sure. For me, it cut more deeply. Castberg had ruined my career."

"So you got it together one more time and plotted Castberg's murder," Ellery said. "Ozzie would do an over-the-top offensive show to make himself an obvious target for murder. You, Joey, would be so incensed you'd have to be physically restrained from publicly killing your partner. He'd murder Castberg with the samurai sword at a time when you had a perfect card-playing alibi. Then, while he was talking to me and had an equally strong alibi, you'd come charging down the corridor to deliver the samurai sword to Captain Badger and his officers. Each of you was alibied for one part of the crime. A perfect collaboration, one last time, all the while convincing the world you hated each other."

"So how'd you get on to us?" Foyle demanded. "I thought it was a great plan."

"It was like something out of a Charlie Chan movie," Ellery scoffed.

"Well, yeah, as a matter of fact, it was. But still, what did we do wrong?"

"For one thing, your story about trading rooms with Castberg didn't wash. I could see it if he really was planning to spend the night somewhere else, but I couldn't believe he'd go into your cabin and put on your robe and sleep in your bed when your wife might be coming back at any time, which she did. How *did* you get him to put on the robe, by the way, Ozzie?"

"He always admired my robes. I got him to come to the suite on a pretext of talking business. He liked the robe, and I invited him to try it on. Piece of cake."

"Another thing that bothered me was how this cruise came about. How did Castberg happen to be on the cruise in the first place, and why was such a notorious cheapskate so quick to offer a free cruise to me on the spur of the moment? He couldn't have been paying for it—if he were, he'd be demanding a refund from the cruise line, not inviting me. I was indignant about that line in your *Mikado* parody about my freeloading, because, though I *was* freeloading in a sense, it wasn't off you. But if you gave Castberg his tickets, in a sense I *was* freeloading off you. Your inviting Castberg could have been quite innocent, I realize, just as the presence as your guests of Daddy Trash and Marlon Crandall could be innocent. But what was your old partner, the man who couldn't stand to be in the same room as you, doing on the cruise anyway? And why did Joey Dugan act so out of character in his rushing-the-stage tirade after your act? It just didn't add up, unless you were cooking something up together.

"With all that, however, I still might not have figured it out without the deliberate clue you left me, Ozzie."

"What deliberate clue?" Joey Dugan demanded.

"The book on the side table. Gilbert and Sullivan, like Dugan and Foyle, accomplished great things together despite strong personal differences. Ozzie, you left that collection of libretti open to one of their more obscure works, *Utopia Limited*. And what is significant about *Utopia Limited*? *It was the operetta Gilbert and Sullivan completed* after *they had dissolved their partnership and been induced to collaborate one last time*. Leaving that book open as it was told me that the murder of Gil Castberg was Dugan and Foyle's *Utopia Limited*."

"You did it again," Joey Dugan said, more sadly than heatedly. "Always that last bit of gilding to make the goddamn lily droop, that last drop of milk out of the gag. A clue that implicated us, just to show how clever you are. How could I ever have worked with you all those years, Foyle?"

Ozzie Foyle leaned over to his partner and said in a stage whisper, "It'll help with the insanity defense. You know we'll never be convicted. You know what juries are like nowadays. Face it, Dugan. I'm always thinking of the act."

OPEN LETTER TO SURVIVORS

Francis M. Nevins

Author's Note: In 1968, I shook hands for the first time with Fred Dannay. One of Fred's abiding concerns was bringing new blood into the genre, and each monthly issue of EQMM *contained at least one short story by an author who had never published a mystery before. He must have encouraged almost everyone he met to try writing for him. After we had come to know each other a bit better, he certainly encouraged me. I slaved over a story for two months and finally mailed it to him. Its inspiration was a line from one of my favorite Queen novels,* Ten Days' Wonder, *and I was sure he'd like it. A few weeks later, sipping brandy in his living room, he ripped my story apart with a surgical precision that I soon came to realize was more than justified by the sheer unadulterated silliness of what I'd writ-ten. Then we began to build the story up again. He taught me what I should have done—not in so many words but indirectly, by emphasizing the wrong steps I'd taken and leaving it to me to make them right. I spent the next couple of months rethinking and rewriting that story from first word to last. Finally, in fear and trembling, I sent him the revised version, and in turn he sent me a contract. There's more I'd like to say, but I'll wait until you've finished reading the story. See you on the other side!*

"...there was the case of Adelina Monquieux, his remarkable solution of which cannot be revealed before 1972 by agreement with that curious lady's execu-tors...."

ELLERY QUEEN, *Ten Days' Wonder* (1948)

The book was conceived only in part, the rest of it was still strug-gling for conception inside him. A large and vicious neighborhood cat, some lines from Jung, a long wait in the subway station in the stifling post-midnight hours of torrid summer, were all parts of the organism fighting for birth. But something was missing, some vital element. And when he realized that what he and the book needed was total immersion in the postwar international nightmare, he picked up his phone and called Burt Billings, who was his attorney, his friend, the attorney for Adelina Monquieux.

The indomitable, the inimitable, the incredible Adelina—or, to use her professional name (though she had never married), Mrs. Monquieux, pronounced Mon-Q, not monkey. She was the last of an asset-studded line and the foremost political analyst of the generation. Her gargoyle face with its luminously intelligent eyes had made the cover of *Time* three years earlier, soon after Hiroshima; the artist had sketched endless cameos of death within the tangles of her unkempt henna hair.

The feature story in *Time* had chronicled her travels through Europe and Asia during the Thirties and most of the war years, the disenchanted brilliance of her many books and articles on international politics, and her unrelieved pessimism about mankind. After Hiroshima and Nagasaki, she had written an essay boiling with humane fury titled "God Damn Us Everyone," had changed her will so that most of her wealth would be left for the care of the bomb's victims, and had retired to the family estate to brood and write.

Billings called back within an hour: the great lady would talk with him the following Sunday at noon.

He drove out of the city early Sunday morning, the cloudless sky like blue glass promising thick heat before noon. He had spent Saturday rereading the *Time* story and leafing through some of the woman's books. He had learned that she lived on the estate with the three orphans of World War I whom she had adopted as her sons and with a niece who did her secretarial work. He had learned that she had come to believe that no man can govern a modern nation-state without raining hideous atrocities on his own people and on his country's neighbors. He thought he had detected a certain oscillation in her between an idealistic anarchism in the Thoreau tradition and a Swiftian disgust with the entire race. All in all a fascinating woman, combining a large fortune with a desolate philosophy, a dazzling mind with a dumpy body. He looked forward to the meeting with relish.

At eleven, he spun the new '48 Roadmaster off the Taugus Parkway, and the wheels crunched gravel up the steep slope of the drive, which was only five miles beyond where that gas-station attendant had said the turnoff would be. Then suddenly he had crested the peak, and a lush cool bed of forest spread below him, with a squarish block of stone seeming no larger than a child's toy in a wide clearing near the center.

Fortress Monquieux.

He descended.

From the radio speaker, a voice intoned headlines. Civil war in Greece. Blockade threat against Berlin. Crisis in Czechoslovakia. The infant state of Israel struggling for survival. Truman denounces Stalin. Stalin condemns Truman. *God, what a world*, he thought. *Maybe Adelina's right: who would choose to be born?*

On such gloomy reflections he maneuvered the Roadmaster along the curves of the descent and through the tangled green tunnel of forest, finally through a stone archway and into the parking circle at the side of the Fortress. He pocketed his keys and strolled past time-faded classical sculptures in beds of ill-kept greenery. His wristwatch read 11:26, and he hoped he wasn't unconscionably early.

Half a minute after his ring, the massive front door opened, and he was ushered in by a tall, well-built fellow in his early thirties with crisp dark hair. Over shirtsleeves the man wore an expensive-looking summer-gray dressing gown, monogrammed X at the breast. "Hello and come in," he invited. "I am Xavier Monquieux, and I've read most of your books at least twice."

"Delighted to hear it. You must be one of Mrs. Monquieux's foster sons."

"Right," Xavier said. "And if you'll step in here"—he led the way into a high-ceilinged room of immense size, filled with books and over-stuffed furniture—"you can meet my brothers. This is Yves, and this is Zachary."

Two more tall, well-built fellows in their early thirties stepped forward from the mahogany bar, each with crisp dark hair, each with a gin-and-tonic in his hand, each wearing an expensive-looking summer-gray dressing gown over shirtsleeves. They were as close in resemblance to Xavier and to each other as three prints of the same photograph. Only the gold letters of their monograms distinguished them: one wore a Y, the other a Z.

"I hadn't realized you were identical triplets," he said inanely and accepted a light scotch-and-water from Yves.

"Monozygotic is the technical word, or at least it was when I was in med school," Yves corrected. "Identical down to our fingertips. No one but Adelina can tell us apart, and God knows how she does it. We're biological rarities, but it's sort of fun, switching on dates and things like that."

"And speaking of girls, *mon frère*," Zachary cut in, "the young ladies ought to be here any minute, so perhaps we should get into our trunks and make sure the liquor cart's stocked up. It was very nice to have met you, sir, and after you've talked to Adelina I'm sure we could find a bathing suit your size, if you'd care for a dip." And Zachary and Yves bowed themselves out of the room, the sound of their feet becoming audible a few moments later when they ascended a staircase.

"No sense of the finer things," Xavier clucked disapprovingly. "Imagine preferring a swim to a chat with a famous mystery writer. I'm afraid bookishness has rubbed off only on me. Most of these are mine," he added, sweeping his hand to indicate the crammed shelves.

"Do your brothers have any passions of their own?"

"Oh, yes—we don't have to work for our keep, of course, but all of us got enough boredom in the military during the recent war to ever want to sit around doing nothing again. Yves had a year of medical school before he was drafted and may go back some day, and he's also an amateur concert violinist. Zach is a fanatic stamp collector, and he has secret dreams of being a Hollywood star. If you'll excuse me, I'll go downstairs and tell Adelina you're here." He moved lightly out of the room.

Like most writers and many readers, the guest had an insatiable urge to inspect the contents of all bookshelves that chanced within his eye. He was glancing over a large hand-rubbed cabinet devoted to the modern European novel, with Mann and Sartre and Silone well represented, when a feminine cough behind him gave notice that he was no longer alone. A tall blonde in beige was inspecting him through heavy-rimmed glasses, as though he were a signed first edition of something curious.

"Aunt Adelina apologizes," she said, "but she's tied up in a chapter of her memoirs and won't be free for another little while. I'm Marie Dumont, her niece several degrees removed or something like that. Also her secretary and all-around drudge. She asked me to amuse you for a few minutes."

She said nothing more for about thirty seconds, as though she had no idea how to amuse a male guest. Then, "I understand you want to sort of pick her brains for political atmosphere on a book you're doing? I think you might get more mileage out of her crazy will—you know about that, don't you? When Aunt Adelina dies, the three boys each get half a million outright and the income from another half million held in trust. The remaining twenty million or so after taxes will build and support a hospital to take care of the children we bombed in Japan. But—and here comes the catch—if the safe in her office downstairs is opened by anyone, for any reason, sooner than twenty-four years after her death, all the hospital money is immediately transferred to the Flat Earth Society."

"That *is* a strange will," he commented politely, although something about its terms had already begun to gnaw at him and he was not sure what. "What's in the safe that would lead her to protect it that way?"

"Even I'm not sure, and I've been her secretary for twelve years. It's in the manuscript of her memoirs, which she calls *Open Letter to Survivors*, that's all I know. She's writing it in longhand, you see. When she's not actually working on it, the manuscript is kept in that safe, and the safe is always locked, whether she's working on the book or not. Only she and I and her attorney know the combination. When you think how much of the inside history of the past thirty years must be in those pages, how governments might topple if the secrets leaked out—well, you can see why she takes such precautions."

"Do you inherit anything under the will?"

She shrugged. "A few hundred thousand, I think. Not enough to make up for twelve years of stagnation in this place."

"You could have left."

"You can't put yourself out of the center of a whirlpool," she said. Which he cynically constructed as: *you don't throw away free room and board and a guaranteed two or three hundred thousand.* "Well, I think she may be done by now, it's almost noon. Let's go down to her office and see."

And she led him along a vast foyer full of Victorian statuary and ancestral portraits and down a steep spiral staircase that ended in the center of a sort of anteroom. A functional secretarial desk, piled with papers and folders, stood against the far wall. A few comfortable chairs, occasional tables holding wrought-iron lamps and current magazines, strategically placed smoking stands—it reminded him somehow of a prosperous dentist's waiting room.

Marie Dumont knocked on the door to an inner office, then poked her head in. "Ready yet?"

"Please show him in," he heard a deep rich voice reply, and a moment later he stood before her teakwood desk in the center of the big windowless room. On the wall to his left, hanging above the squat and forbiddingly shut steel safe, was a tranquil landscape in oils. Adelina Monquieux was seated in a red-leather armchair behind the desk, her henna hair in wild disarray, her spectacles askew on her Roman nose, looking like an intelligent gargoyle.

"I'm so pleased to meet you," she said, touching a thick loose-leaf binder of tough material filled with paper—the only object on the desk except for the blotter, an old-fashioned fountain pen, a small table lamp, and a wicked-looking letter opener. "I'm through writing for the day, and my pen has gone dry, anyway. It will take me just a few minutes to read my morning's stint, and then I will be glad to give you all the time you desire. Tell me, do you think our survivors, assuming we have any, will appreciate reading the truth about our time?"

She asked the question with mixed bitterness and resignation, as if being witness to three decades of international politics had burned into her the inevitability of man's greed and stupidity and corruption. When she smiled at him, it was like the grin he had seen on the faces of the dead.

It was only after he had closed the door gently behind him that he realized he had not said a word to her.

The silence in the anteroom was oppressive, and he needed to make conversation. He turned to Marie Dumont, who was seated at her own desk. "Does she do all her writing in there?" he asked, not really concerned to know.

"Ever since she inherited the house and had the basement done over. It's a perfect workroom—soundproof, no windows, no distractions, and that door is the only way in or out. Even the bathroom is outside here."

She suddenly gestured up to one of the windows and he heard the noise of splashing and gay squeals coming, he gathered, from the swimming pool. "The girls must have arrived. Peaceful sounds like that drive Aunt Adelina to distraction when she's working, even though she must have been in a dozen air raids in Europe. That's why she had her office soundproofed. By the way, did you notice the English country scene above the safe? That was painted by Churchill."

They both looked up as light footsteps sounded on the spiral stairs and one of the triplets appeared, barefoot and wearing only dark-blue swim trunks. He did not break stride but went right to the inner door, tossing a casual "Have to see Adelina for a minute" over his shoulder.

The triplet gave a perfunctory knock on the inner door and entered, shutting the door behind him. The cuckoo clock on the wall above Marie Dumont's desk announced that the hour was noon. The wooden bird had just cuckooed his last and retreated behind his tiny door when the big door opened again and the triplet walked out and over to the staircase and mounted.

"I wonder what that was all about."

"I don't know," Marie replied. "But I think Aunt Adelina must be through by now. I'll check."

She knocked lightly, stepped in, closed the door, and in less than a minute was back, her face sick-white.

"My God, she's dead," she whispered hoarsely.

A wild thought seized him, and he knew what had disturbed him about the will: *If she died with the manuscript still on her desk, what good is that crazy twenty-four-year clause? It will protect not the manuscript but just an empty safe.*

He rushed into the office. Adelina Monquieux lay sprawled in her chair, staring sightlessly through spectacles still askew. Blood ran from her heart. The manuscript of *Open Letter to Survivors* was not in sight, and the safe was tight shut: he breathed relief.

Then he noticed that the wicked-looking letter opener was not in sight either.

The cuckoo made five noises and popped back into his slot. The body of Adelina Monquieux—according to the medical examiner, she had died within a minute after the blade had entered her—had been removed, and, when it left, most of the police technicians had left, too. The office and anteroom had been searched thoroughly, and the letter opener had not been found. A few plainclothesmen still roamed the rooms and grounds haphazardly. Cody, the cigarillo-chewing Taugus County detective in charge, crushed his butt into a smoking stand disgustedly.

"What a cool customer we are dealing with, amigo," he said. "I wish I'd had him in my platoon behind Kraut lines in Normandy! He just walked right past you and the girl, stabbed the old lady to death with one blow of the letter opener, marched out past you again with the weapon, calm as you please, and went out to mingle with the girls at the pool. That, amigo, is a man with guts."

"And with a shrewd sense of psychology," the mystery writer added. "He figured that, with my brief exposure to the triplets, I couldn't tell them apart, and he must have known from experience that Miss Dumont couldn't, either."

"That," Cody exploded, "is the hell of it. A big whodunit writer like you, a guy who's cleaned up umpteen cases for the New York force, and you can't even tell me what was the monogram on the killer's bathing suit, an X, a Y, or a Z."

"What bothers me more is that the letter opener that killed Mrs. Monquieux is missing. Why did the killer take it? To deprive us of his fingerprints? But why didn't he simply wipe his prints from the weapon right there in the office? Why did he take the much riskier step of removing the knife from his victim and carrying it past two witnesses in the anteroom? Was it impossible or impracticable for him to follow the safer course? Again—why?"

"Very clever, Mr. Genius," Cody snorted. "But changing the subject don't fool me. You didn't notice what monogram the killer was wearing."

"I don't think it would mean anything even if I did. We can't assume the guilty one didn't simply get hold of a monogram belonging to one of his brothers and sew it over his own, or even wear one of his brothers' bathing suits. By the way, what was the result of that test for bloodstains your technician performed on the three dark-blue bathing suits in the household?'"

Cody waved a paper from the sheaf on his lap. "Absolutely no dice. My man examined 'em inside and out, and not a trace of a bloodstain. None of the old lady's blood splashed onto the killer's trunks. No, we can't solve this one the easy way, amigo. He killed her with one stab, so we'd have no bloodstains. And he's one of triplets, so for all practical purposes we got no one who saw him!" He cursed while taking out another cigarillo.

"Well, we can at least be thankful that Mrs. Monquieux put her manuscript back in the safe before he walked in and killed her. After all, it was much too thick for the killer to have walked past us with it unnoticed, and there's no way he could have destroyed it in the office itself—even the toilet is out here. So it's got to be back in the safe, and whatever Adelina Monquieux knew will stay under wraps for twenty-four years. Adelina? Pandora would have been a better name. By the way, you will keep a guard on that safe overnight till Mr. Billings and the truck come for it?"

"Damn right I will, I—hey, what's the matter with you?"

For the distinguished *litterateur* across from Cody had suddenly risen and was pacing angrily.

"Scars," he muttered. "Look, the brothers mentioned to me this morning that they were all in the service during the war. Didn't any of them get wounded or scratched or marked somehow, even if only in a tattoo parlor? Can't we eliminate one or even two brothers on the ground that neither Miss Dumont nor I saw any marks on the killer?"

"Hell, no," Cody grunted. "Those boys spent their war in a nice safe psychological testing laboratory stateside. Y'see, they've got something between 'em that the eggheads call tele*pathy*—identical twins and triplets have it fairly often, so I'm told—and the Army had some crazy idea of finding out what causes it and using it to help spring Allied troops from enemy POW camps. The whole thing fell through, of course; there's no way of teaching that stuff to someone who ain't got it in the first place. Hell, if God wanted people to read each other's minds, He wouldn't have given us vocal cords. Hey, what's got you now?"

"Don't you see? If each of the triplets can read the thoughts of the others, why can't we simply *ask them* who is the murderer?"

"Oh," Cody rumbled. "Reading your own storybooks again, hey, amigo? Well, first of all, to give you the kinda reason you enjoy, we couldn't rule out that the one guilty brother and one accomplice brother weren't framing the third innocent brother. Second, that tele*pathy* stuff can't be used in court, anyway. And third—hell, except for the war, I've lived in this community for thirty-seven years. I know those boys. I know they've done everything together their whole lives long. I know as well as I know I'm sitting here that all three of them were in on this murder. They drew straws or some such thing to see who'd do the actual dirty work. But you try to prove that in a court of law, amigo. You storybook writers don't have the first idea in the world the problems of a working cop."

His respect for Cody soared once the truth of a conspiracy among the brothers had sunk home. How could he not have seen it? From the moment he had rung the bell, every word and every action of those three smiling affable brothers had been as carefully calculated as a Broadway stage performance. Dressing identically, speaking with virtually identical modulations, each one doing or saying nothing that would stamp him as an individual in the mind of their guest. He had been manipulated like a puppet, and he didn't like it. He stoked his pipe furiously.

Uselessly.

As the sun set, he growled a goodbye to Cody and slunk out to his car and drove out of that monstrous valley through a tunnel of darkening forest and mocking bird cries….

Next day, he read of the murder in the papers, noting idly the news that Adelina Monquieux's private Pandora's box had been crated up by her executors, the law firm of Billings & Krieger, and transferred to a chilled-steel bank vault in the city. *Open Letter to Survivors* having been made doubly inviolable, he tried to dismiss the whole Monquieux affair from his mind as a fiasco.

It was not until two months later that he saw what he should have seen while Adelina's body was still warm.

What triggered it was a piece of research. He had gone to the County Medical Association Library to look up some data on childbirth that he needed for his own novel aborning; his serendipping eye had wandered from childbirth to infants and from infants to twins and to the precise differences between monozygotic and fraternal twins.

And there it lay, buried in a mountain of medical jargon but unmistakable as a gold nugget in a coal pile.

Monozygotic twins, being genetically identical in every respect, are identical in fingerprints also.

His mind took that fact and raced with it.

Three minutes later he was out of the library with a slam of the door and the glares of several peeved medicos behind him.

He dashed into his apartment and dialed Billings & Krieger, demanding to speak to Mr. Billings at once on a matter a thousand times more urgent than mere life-and-death. When he had the attorney on the line, he was brief and to the point. "Burt, can we use your office tonight for a conference on the Monquieux case?"

Billings sounded puzzled. "What's up? Why my office?" Then, after a moment, "Hey, you haven't solved the murder, by any chance, have you?"

"In one way, I think I have, in another way no… I'm sorry, Burt, that's all I can say now. Eight o'clock all right with you? I'll need both you and Mr. Krieger, in your capacity as executors. And I'm going to have Cody there, too—you remember him? Thanks a million, Burt, see you at eight." He hung up and placed a call to Cody, who agreed to attend the meeting.

Shortly after dinner, he made an excuse to go out, leaving the dishes to his long-suffering father, and paced the neon-washed streets, marshaling his thoughts, until 7:45, when he hailed a cab. Ten minutes later, he stepped into the offices of Billings & Krieger. Burt and Cody were already present, and James B. Krieger, who looked like a starving mouse, came in shortly. Introductions were exchanged, hands shaken, chairs pulled up to the conference room's long table.

He began by explaining the fact of identical fingerprints in monozygotics. "Of course, the great bulk of mystery stories—my own included, I blush to say—have spread the impression that each set of prints is unique, that no one's prints are the same as any other person's. The man in the street accepts without question that every man's prints are exclusively his own, but, as I've indicted, it's just not so. Therefore, we must conclude—of course we can verify this with no trouble at all—that Xavier, Yves, and Zachary Monquieux have identical fingerprints. Now, what follows from that?

"First, it reminded me that all three brothers must be aware of this fact; for it was Yves, talking to me, who used the word monozygotic, and even used the phrase 'identical down to our fingertips,' which is quite literally true.

"Secondly, it satisfied me that we had completely misinterpreted the whole matter of the missing letter opener. We had assumed two things: A, that the person who took it out of the office was the murderer; B, that possibly his motive was to deprive us of his fingerprints, which for some unknown reason he could not simply wipe off on the spot. We now know that B is a completely false assumption: all three brothers know their prints are identical and know, therefore, that their prints would be of no use to us. So the killer's reason for taking away the knife could not have been what we thought it was. Gentlemen, can any of you suggest another reason?"

Silence. Cody chewed his cigarillo.

"Nor can I. In fact—and I kick myself for missing this two months ago—not only had he no reason, but it was *physically impossible* for the killer to have taken the letter opener with him!

"Marie Dumont and I observed the killer walk out of his victim's office, and he certainly wasn't holding the opener in his hands. Could he have concealed it in his clothes? Well, he was wearing only a bathing suit; the letter opener might have been slipped inside the suit. But you told me, Cody, that there was not the slightest trace of a bloodstain on any of the three dark-blue pairs of trunks that could possibly have been worn by the murderer—*inside or out*. Certainly if he had carried out that bloody weapon inside his trunks, you *would* have found traces. Conclusion: the murderer did not, because he could not, take the weapon away."

"Then what happened to it?" Cody demanded. "Because my men searched that office with a fine-tooth comb and it sure as hell wasn't there!"

"Patience, Cody, patience. Now, let's tackle the problem from another direction. Who had the opportunity to hide or remove the opener between the time I spoke to Mrs. Monquieux a few minutes before her death and the time Marie Dumont and I entered the office shortly after her death and learned that the opener was missing? When I phrase it that way, you can't miss it. *Only one person* set foot in the office during that brief interval. And that was Marie Dumont, who you'll recall was alone in there for almost a minute before she stumbled out to announce that her aunt was dead.

"Now, can the wings of reason bear us any higher? Yes, indeed," he assured his listeners. "Let's go back to your question, Cody—what did she do with the weapon? With me standing right outside the door, would she have concealed it in her clothes and taken a chance she could safely get rid of it later, with the police shortly to invade the premises? Not if she had a safer option, she wouldn't. Was there a safer option in that enclosed office?

"Yes, there was—a *safe*-er option, if you'll pardon the pun. Your men searched the entire office, Cody, but in view of the Monquieux will and of your plausible but false conclusion that the killer had taken the opener away with him, you didn't dare tamper with the safe, to which, I remind you, only Mrs. Monquieux and Miss Dumont and you, her attorney, Burt, knew the combination.

"And since that safe was under police guard until your truckers removed it to the bank vault, Burt, I'll wager that letter opener is in the safe right now."

"My God," Billings muttered.

"But why would she have hidden the murder weapon like that?"

James B. Krieger squeaked.

"If you mean her motive—whether she's in love with the murderer, or hopes to extort money or marriage out of him—I don't know, and its exact nature doesn't affect my analysis. But in a general way her motivation is clear: she intended to protect the murderer. Now, what is presupposed by such intent?"

Again silence.

"Don't you see that it presupposes *she knew which of the triplets* is the murderer?

"Now, did she know prior to the murder itself? Hardly, or she would never have revealed as much information to me as she did. Then she must have learned the truth *after* the murder. But then she had less than a minute, alone in that office, to see the truth, to make a decision, to hide the letter opener in the safe, to return to the doorway. It must have been something instantaneously apparent that revealed the truth to her.

"At this point, gentlemen, we are driven to speculation, but speculation solidly based on facts. Fact: your medical examiner told us, Cody, that Adelina Monquieux lived for perhaps a minute after being stabbed. Fact: Mrs. Monquieux's fountain pen had gone dry shortly before her death, so there was no usable writing implement on her desk. Fact: we don't *know* that it was Mrs. Monquieux herself who put away the manuscript of *Open Letter to Survivors.*

"Hypothesis: In the last moments of her life, Adelina Monquieux—the only person on earth who could tell those brothers apart—pulled the knife from her body and slashed into the tough material of the binder of that manuscript the initial—that's all it would take to identify him—of her murderer. X, Y, or Z. This is what Marie Dumont saw when she entered the room. And to protect the murderer she had to conceal that manuscript cover. And, being forced to open the safe to place the damning manuscript cover inside, she decided it would be safer to conceal the opener there also. She was counting on being able to remove both objects from the safe later, but circumstances and your truckers, Burt, frustrated her.

"Any questions, gentlemen?"

Cody was now sweating, as if from the strain of following the analysis. "Thank God you lawyers moved that safe to where we can still get at the evidence!"

Billings stared at him as if he had mumbled babytalk. "But you *can't* get at it," he pointed out. "Mrs. Monquieux's will provides that the safe cannot be opened for any reason until the twenty-fourth anniversary of her death. If you violate that provision, the hospital for atom-bomb victims will not be built. How many lives is it worth to you to procure your evidence, your *hypothetical* evidence?"

Cody went down fighting. "Can't that will be broken? Hell, this isn't the kind of a situation the old lady had in mind when she made that crazy will."

"You can try to break it in the courts," Krieger said. "My considered opinion is that you won't succeed. And our duty as executors under the will, and as human beings, is to stop you."

Billings nodded. "Something even worse, Cody. Suppose the courts *did* rule that the opening of the safe by the police would not defeat the hospital bequest. If the analysis we've just heard is correct, the opening of the safe would disclose proof positive that the safe had *already* been opened, immediately after our client's death. And that prior opening would be beyond the court's power to ignore. The end result being God knows how many dead war orphans, and a windfall for the Flat Earth Society."

Cody leveled a long series of curses at the law. No one in the room was hypocrite enough to contradict him.

"Well, as a professional writer," ventured the only professional writer present, "my hands aren't tied by that will. Why can't I publish my analysis of the case and at least let them know that I know, and maybe make them do something insane like attempting to silence me?"

"You want a million-dollar libel suit slapped against you?" Billings boomed. "You forget you've got no solid evidence—not a shred!"

They sat in silence.

When he could take no more of it he rose, stretched his drained and aching body, and trudged wearily to the door. "I'm not in my dotage yet," he said, "and neither are they. I can wait; and after all, by waiting, we make sure the great bulk of the Monquieux estate goes to a decent cause. But I swear, Burt, that I will be there when you or your successor opens that safe twenty-four years from now. I'm going to see with my own eyes whether or not I was right....

"Gentlemen, I'll see you in 1972."

Author's Afterword: I wrote this story more than 45 years ago. Ellery Queen was still a household name back then, and many readers of the time would have spotted most of the countless Queenian motifs with which my tale was studded. Today, I'm afraid very few without the specialized interest of this anthology's audience would recognize the origins of the X-Y-Z theme, the dying-message clue, the Iagoesque manipulations, the Alice in Wonderland*-like will (Lewis Carroll was always a favorite of Fred's), and so much more. How many contemporary readers will catch the oblique references to Queen's masterpiece,* Cat of Many Tails *(1949)*, or the attempt to replicate the intellec-tual excitement of a Queen climax? Without the giveaway in the opening quotation, how many could even name my nameless detective?

Incidentally, the biology in the story also owes something to Alice in Wonderland. *Today (though not necessarily in 1948) there's a scientific consensus that both heredity and environment contribute to one's fingerprints, from which it follows that the prints of monozygotic siblings are similar but not identical. But which of us hasn't ever made a mistake?*

I can't believe I've lived to see one (or, if you count Fred Dannay and his cousin and collaborator Manfred B. Lee sepa-rately, two) of the most important authors of my formative years fall into obscurity. Will this anthology help return to Ellery the prestige he deserves? Will e-books or some other high-tech medium we haven't yet dreamed of restore the author(s) and character to the central position they enjoyed for years before I was born and for much of my lifetime? Many of us are trying to achieve that goal. I see this anthology as a step in the right direction.

THE REINDEER CLUE

Edward D. Hoch

"The Reindeer Clue" was for years a mystery within a mystery. It appeared originally in 1975 as a Christmas offering in The National Enquirer *and was long regarded as the last short story ever written by Ellery Queen. But it was in fact a pastiche, albeit an authorized one, devised and written by the legendary Ed Hoch. In an interview that appears on Kurt Sercu's Ellery Queen website, Ed explained its pedigree: "It was Fred's agent, Scott Meredith, who contracted for the Christmas story, possibly without Fred's initial knowledge. I felt honored that Fred wanted me to write it. Four years after Manny's death, he simply did not want to undertake the task himself." This story, then, is unique among our Queen pastiches: an Ellery Queen story so Queenian that, for decades, it successfully masqueraded as an original.*

"Ellery!" Inspector Queen shouted over the heads of the waiting children. "Over here!"

Ellery managed to work his way through the crowd to the entrance of the Children's Zoo. The weather was unusually warm for two days before Christmas, and the children didn't mind waiting.

If the presence of a half-dozen police cars stirred any curiosity, it was not enough for anyone to question Ellery as he edged his way forward.

"What is it, Dad?" he asked, as the inspector closed the wooden gate behind him.

"Murder, Ellery. And unless we can wind it up fast, there are going to be a lot of disappointed kids out there."

"Are they waiting for Santa Claus?" Ellery asked with a grin.

"The next best thing—Santa's reindeer. It's a Christmas tradition here to deck the place with tinsel and toys and pass one of the reindeer off as Rudolph."

Ellery could see the police technicians working over the body of a man sprawled inside the fence of the reindeer pen. Off to one side, a white-coated man kept a firm grip on the reindeer itself as the police flashbulbs popped. Another white-coated man and a woman were standing nearby.

"Who's the dead man?" Ellery asked. "Anyone I know?"

"Matter of fact, yes. It's Casey Sturgess, the ex-columnist."

"You've got to be kidding," Ellery exclaimed. "Sturgess murdered in a children's zoo?"

The old man shrugged. "Looks like he was up to his old tricks." Sturgess had been the gossip columnist on a now-defunct New York tabloid. When the paper folded, he'd continued with his gossipy trade, selling information in a manner that often approached blackmail.

Ellery glanced toward the woman and two men. "Blackmailing one of these?"

"Why else would he come here at eight in the morning, except to meet one of them? Come on—I'll introduce you."

The woman was Dr. Ella Manners, staff veterinarian. She wore straight blond hair and no makeup. "This is a terrible thing, simply terrible!" she cried out. "We've got a hundred children and their mothers out there, waiting to see the reindeer. Can't you get this body out of here?"

"We're working as fast as we can," Inspector Queen assured her, motioning Ellery toward the two men.

One, who walked with a noticeable limp, was the zoo's director, Bernard White. The other man, younger than White and grossly overweight, was Mike Halley—"Captain Mike to the kids," he explained. "I'm the animal handler, except today it's more of a people handler. Our reindeer is tame, but it's still a big animal. We don't let the kids get too close to it."

The inspector motioned toward the body. "Any of you know the dead man?"

"No, sir," Bernard White answered for the others. "We didn't know him, and we have no idea how he got in here with the reindeer. We found him when we arrived, just after eight o'clock."

"You all arrived at once?" Ellery asked him.

"I was just getting out of my car when Captain Mike drove up. Ella followed right behind him."

"Anyone else work here?"

"We have a night crew to clean up, but in the morning there's only the three of us."

Ellery nodded. "So one of you could have met Casey Sturgess here earlier, killed him, and then driven around the park till you saw the others coming."

"Why would one of us kill him?" Ella Manners asked. "We didn't even know him."

"Sturgess had sunk to some third-rate blackmailing lately. You all work for the city, in a job that puts you in contact with children. The least hint of drugs or a morals charge would have been enough to lose you your jobs. Right, Dad?"

Inspector Queen nodded. "Damn right! Sturgess was shot in the chest with a .22 automatic. We found the weapon over in the straw. One of you met him here to pay blackmail, but shot him instead. It has to be one of you—he wouldn't possibly have come into the reindeer pen before the place opened to meet anybody else."

Ellery motioned his father aside. "Any fingerprints on the gun, Dad?"

"It was wiped clean, Ellery. But the victim did manage to leave us something—a dying message of sorts."

Ellery's face lit up. "What, Dad?"

"Come over here by the body."

Ellery passed a bucket that held red-and-green giveaway buttons inscribed "I saw Santa's Reindeer!" He ducked his head under a hanging fringe of holly and joined his father by the body. For the first time, he noticed that the rear fence of the reindeer pen was decorated with seven weathered wooden placards, each carrying eight lines of Clement Clarke Moore's famous poem, "A Visit from St. Nicholas."

Casey Sturgess had died under the third placard, his arm outstretched toward it.

"He could only have lived a minute or so with that wound," the old man said. "But look at the blood on his right forefinger. He used it to mark the sign."

Ellery leaned closer, examining two lines of the Moore poem:

> Now, Dasher! now, Dancer! now, Prancer and Vixen!
> On, Comet! on, Cupid! on, Donner and Blitzen!

"Dad, he smeared each of the eight reindeers' names with a dab of blood!"

"Right, Ellery. Now you tell me what it means."

Ellery remained stooped, studying the defaced poem for some minutes. All the smears were similar. None seemed to have been given more emphasis than any other. Finally, he straightened up and walked over to the reindeer that was drinking water from its trough, oblivious of the commotion.

"What's its name?" he asked the overweight Captain Mike.

"Sparky—but for Christmas we call him Rudolph. The kids like it."

Ellery put out a gentle hand and touched the ungainly animal's oversized antlers, wishing that it could speak and tell him what it had seen in the pen.

But it was as silent as the llama and donkey and cow that he could see standing in the adjoining pens.

"How much longer is this going on?" White was demanding from the inspector.

"As long as it takes. We've got a murder on our hands, Mr. White."

He turned his back on the zoo director and looked at his son. "What do you make of it, Ellery?"

"Not much. Found anyone who heard the shot?"

"Not yet. The sound of a little .22 wouldn't carry very far."

Ellery went back for one more look at the bloody marks on the Moore poem.

Then he asked Ella Manners, "Would you by any chance be a particularly good dancer, Doctor?"

"Hardly! Veterinary medicine and dancing don't mix."

"I thought not," Ellery said, suddenly pleased.

"You got something?" his father asked.

"Yes, Dad. I know who murdered Casey Sturgess."

CHALLENGE TO THE READER

Who killed Casey Sturgess, and how did Ellery know?

Sparky the reindeer looked up from its trough, as if listening to Ellery's words. "You see, Dad, there's always a danger with dying messages—a danger that the killer will see his victim leave the message, or return and find it later. Premeditated murderers like to make certain they've finished the job without leaving a clue. You told me Sturgess could only have lived a minute or so with that wound."

"That's right, Ellery."

"Then the killer was probably still here to see him jab that sign with his bloody finger. And are we to believe that in a minute's time the dying Sturgess managed to smear all eight names with his blood, and each in the same way? No, Dad—Sturgess only marked *one* name! The killer, unable to wipe the blood off without leaving a mark, smeared the other seven names himself in the same manner. He obliterated the dying man's message by adding to it!"

"But, Ellery—which reindeer's name did Sturgess mark?"

"Dad, it had to be one that would connect instantly with his killer. Now look at those eight names. Could it have been Donner or Blitzen? Hardly—they tell us nothing. Likewise Dasher and Prancer have no connection with any of the suspects. Dr. Manners might be a Vixen and White could be a Cupid, but Sturgess couldn't expect the police to spot such a nebulous thing. No, Dad, the reindeer clue had to be something so obvious the killer was *forced* to alter it."

"That's why you asked Dr. Manners if she was a dancer!"

"Exactly. It's doubtful that the limping Bernard White or the overweight Captain Mike are notable as dancers, and once I ruled Dr. Manners out as well, that left only one name on the list."

"Comet!"

"Yes, Dad. The most famous reindeer of all might be Rudolph, but the most famous *comet* of all is surely Halley's Comet."

"Captain Mike Halley! Somebody grab him!"

Moments later, as the struggling Halley was being led away, Bernard White said, "But he was our only handler! We're ready to open the gates, and who's going to look after the children?"

Ellery glanced at his father and smiled broadly. "Maybe I can help out. After all, it's Christmas," he said.

THE BOOK CASE

Dale C. Andrews and Kurt Sercu

Authors' Note: "The Book Case" appeared in EQMM*'s Department of First Stories in May 2007, and went on to take second place in the* EQMM *Readers' Choice Awards that year. Editor Janet Hutchings introduced it as follows: "Dale Andrews ... and Kurt Sercu ... are longtime Ellery Queen fans who first met on-line through* Ellery Queen, a Website on Deduction, *which is run by Mr. Sercu. Both attended the EQ Centenary Symposium in '05, where they met in person—outlining this intricate story on a train they both took after the event."*

Prologue

A chilly March wind whistled through the open window of the apartment, rustling the papers on the desk and puffing the white corn-silk hair on the old man's head. He raised a thin arm, sheathed in a coat of tweed, to his brow and absentmindedly smoothed his hair back into place. The old man scanned the letter lying on the desktop in front of him before pulling a blank sheet from a stack of note pads. He scrawled a short sentence on the pad, reached for an envelope, addressed it and then sealed the note inside. He dropped the envelope into a box on the corner of the desk, and then turned to the pretty young red-haired woman patiently reading a book in the leather chair across the room.

"I think that will do it for today, Nikki. Can you see that these are posted?"

Part 1: Reunions

Detective Harry Burke shifted his weight as he waited for the elevator. His bum right knee ached, and he wondered—not for the first time—if maybe he was getting a bit old for all of this. He eyed his younger partner ruefully. Stanley Santos, with his pegged slacks, turtleneck and short-cropped mousse-spiked hair, was the future. Not a transplanted aging Scotsman like him, staring down a rapidly approaching retirement and the pension that might let him live almost comfortably somewhere, but not here.

Surely not *here*. West Park Towers was everything he disliked in the New York City of this new century. Excess masquerading for taste, money for refinement and dignity. This is what happens in a world that exalts Trump. Sure, the marble floors squeaked, the rooms expanded through the placement of mirrors. But where was the soul? Where was the New York he had fallen for, decades ago? The bustling, cramped city to which he inevitably returned? It might be somewhere, but it wasn't here. The elevator arrived, and he and Santos stepped in.

The apartment on the thirty-sixth floor was more of the same. Harry sniffed as he walked through the living room, with its spare furniture and its neatly displayed Oriental art. But this time Harry did not sniff in disdain. He sniffed, instead, in anticipation of that smell, the smell that always recurred in his line of work. The unmistakable coppery smell of death.

Harry and Santos entered the study, and, across the room, in a pool of blood sprawled on top of a desk, were the remains of Dr. Jason Tenumbra. In front of the desk was more blood, splattered in pools toward the doorway, where a brass-and-ebony electrical clock lay on the floor, unplugged, its hands frozen at eight-thirty.

Harry pushed past the three policemen and the coroner to approach the desk, a single sheet of glass supported by chrome saw horses. He surveyed the contents of the desk—a flat-screen computer display, a wireless keyboard, a wireless mouse. Tenumbra was face down in the middle, hands pulled up under his chest.

"What do we know?" Harry asked.

"We know," Santos answered, "that Dr. Jason Tenumbra was a successful graduate of Johns Hopkins, an M.D. in psychiatry with postgraduate training in oncology from New York University. He was well-off, too—formerly married to Janiel Friedman, who runs the Friedman and Norr department-store chain.

"Tenumbra didn't show up at his office this morning. His appointments didn't begin until the afternoon, but, when the lunch hour passed and no one could reach him by phone, his staff contacted the concierge desk. A building employee entered the apartment with a passkey—actually, a magnetic entry card—and found the body. He called us as soon as he was done being sick."

"Any witnesses?"

"Nope. But the concierge screens all visitors. We're getting the list once they can dump it off the computer. Judging by the blood on the floor and the clock, it looks like Tenumbra may have lunged after the murderer. But then he must have returned to the desk, where he died."

Squinting, Harry eyed the bookcase behind the desk. "What the hell?"

"Yeah," Santos replied. "I for the life of me don't know what that is all about."

Both men gazed at the bookcase. While the books on either side of the desk were neatly arranged, spine to spine, the volumes directly behind the lifeless body of Dr. Tenumbra had all been pulled from the shelf. They lay piled haphazardly on the floor.

From across the room, one of the uniformed policemen approached. "The coroner is done with the initial forensics. They say we're free to check out the body."

As the officers turned the body over, two things were evident to Harry Burke. The first was the silver scalpel protruding from the bloody center of Tenumbra's throat. The second was the small sheet of paper, barely visible, clasped in the bloody death grip. Harry gingerly pried apart the fingers of the corpse and unfolded the paper. "Son of a bitch!" he exclaimed, wide-eyed.

"What? What is it?" asked Santos, but already Harry was on his knees examining the pile of books.

"Son of a bitch!" he repeated. "Goddammit, of all people!"

Santos bent over the desk to examine the paper. At the top was a date, March 21, 2005. Below that, one sentence was scrawled: "I have received your inquiry, but I have no books that I wish to sell." Across the top of the note, finely embossed, was the name "Ellery Queen." Only then did Stanley Santos look down at the books scattered on the floor. Each bore the same name: "Ellery Queen."

Santos shook his head, perplexed. "Who the hell is Ellery Queen?"

The sunlight was already dwindling when Harry and Stanley Santos heard the soft knocking. A uniformed officer opened the door, and into the room walked an ancient but remarkably erect man dressed in tweeds. He supported himself with a cane in his right hand, and a young woman—late twenties, Santos thought (he had an eye for that particular detail)—lightly supported the old man on his left. Stanley glanced at his partner, who stared wide-eyed at the couple.

Harry Burke watched the old man's approach in amazement. He was ancient. The gait was halting, and the old man seemed to move only through sheerest will power. Harry offered his hand. "Ellery," he said, "it's been a long time."

"That, Harry," replied the old man, "it has." At the sound of the old man's voice, Harry Burke was lost in a second wave of astonishment. The voice was unchanged, unbowed by the years.

"Dad told me years ago that you had returned to this side of the pond," the old man continued, "and I knew you joined the force here. I understood why you didn't renew our acquaintance...."

"Those times were tough on me," Harry agreed. "The way they ended...."

Santos momentarily wondered what was up with his partner but then dismissed this idle curiosity. Who really cared? "Mr. Queen, maybe you two can catch up on old times later. We could have handled this over the phone, as I told your"—he paused, searching for a word—"companion."

"Ms. Porter is my assistant, Officer—?"

"Santos," Stanley replied. "Stan Santos. And it's Detective. As I told Ms. Porter when I called you, we're investigating a murder you may be involved in." Santos held up the blood-stained note, now protected in a plastic zipper-locked bag. "Do you recognize this?"

Ellery stared at the note, left eye squinted almost shut. "I do, indeed," he replied. "It's one of my notepads, and the writing is mine." Turning to Nikki, he asked, "When was it that we sent this out?"

"One week ago," Nikki answered. She turned to Santos. "I help Mr. Queen with his correspondence. A little over a week ago, we received an inquiry from a Dr. Jason Tenumbra who, I believe"—and she glanced around the room nervously—"you told me is the victim. Dr. Tenumbra said he was a collector of books, particularly detective first editions. He inquired whether Mr. Queen would be interested in selling copies of certain books that Mr. Queen wrote many years ago."

"What, detective stories?" Santos asked.

Ellery raised an eyebrow. "Actually, he was interested in some nonfiction writings of mine, analytic works concerning mystery literature."

"Any idea why Tenumbra would have had the note in his hand when he died?"

"None whatsoever," replied Ellery, "but I can almost certainly assure you that, at whatever time he did in fact die, Ms. Porter should be able to corroborate that I was either napping, working on sudoku puzzles or swallowing medicine. That's about all I do nowadays."

"There's something else," Santos said, and he gestured toward the pile of books, still scattered behind the desk in the study.

Supported by Nikki, Ellery crossed the room to the pile of books. "First editions," he muttered. "Tell me, the volume under that one"—he gestured to the left—"is that *The French Powder Mystery*?"

Nikki bent down to examine the book. "Yes," she said, "and it has a dust jacket."

Ellery turned and gazed at the rest of the library, still neatly shelved. "Dr. Tenumbra was an organized fellow," Ellery observed. "His library is grouped alphabetically by author. So the volumes on the floor—the Queen works—were shelved between the Poe collection and the Ruth Rendell/Barbara Vine works."

Ellery turned back toward Santos and Harry Burke. "I have no idea why these books are on the floor. But I can hazard a pretty educated guess as to where Dr. Tenumbra acquired them. There are virtually no remaining copies of *The French Powder Mystery* with an original dust jacket. I personally know of only two. I have one. This, quite possibly, is the other. Is there an inscription inside the front cover?"

Santos gingerly picked up the red volume. Flipping it open he read: "To Djuna, with continuing admiration and thanks, Ellery Queen." Santos turned back toward the old man and his young companion. "Do you mind telling me who Djuna is?"

"Djuna worked for my father and me decades ago, when he was little more than a boy. He was an orphan. We supported him and eventually sent him off to school. I used Djuna, or someone much like Djuna, as a character in my early novels. This was always a source of pride to him. He loved the books and the analytic process. I retired from writing in 1971, and from editing in 1982, but when I was still writing I always sent Djuna an inscribed first edition of every book in which Dad or I appeared as characters."

"Maybe we need to talk to this fellow," Santos muttered.

"That," replied Ellery, "would be difficult. Djuna and his wife died in the late 1980s. I suspect these books must have been acquired from their estate." The old man's eyes drifted, perhaps sadly, toward the ceiling. "I don't know why, but Dad and I lost touch with Djuna and his family a long time ago. After graduating from Columbia, Djuna opened a West Side restaurant that eventually grew into a chain. He was a workaholic, as were we. He didn't marry until the mid 1950s, when he was already in his forties. Djuna and his wife were unable to have children, but they eventually adopted two newborns, I think in the late 1960s. Quinn eventually became a doctor, Elise is a professor of English at Columbia."

Harry Burke looked up sharply. "Wait a minute," he exclaimed, and stepped back into the living room. Returning, he handed a pad of paper to Santos. The top sheet bore the inscription: "Dr. Jason Tenumbra, Dr. Quinn Djuna, Consulting Psychiatric Services."

Santos' eyes met Burke's. "Yeah. Apparently they were partners. Another thing," Harry continued. "I was just on the phone with Tenumbra's office. Dr. Djuna wasn't due in the office until this afternoon, and now *he* hasn't shown up, either. The office can't raise anyone on his phone. His apartment is two blocks from here, and I was just about to send a couple of uniforms over."

"Let's do this ourselves. I'm starting to have a bad feeling," Santos muttered.

"That," said Ellery, "would make at least two of us. If you could slow the pace a little, perhaps Ms. Porter and I might be permitted to tag along?"

Dr. Quinn Djuna's apartment building was much more to Harry Burke's liking. Old and solid, 1930s New York. No concierge here, just a resident manager who grudgingly informed them that, if entry to Dr. Djuna's apartment was required, his sister—Professor Elise Djuna—had custody of the spare key. She had already been called by the precinct and had been informed of both Tenumbra's murder and the need to locate her brother.

Harry Burke therefore was not surprised when an attractive dark-haired woman in her late thirties, dressed bookishly in slacks, an oxford shirt and a twill jacket, anxiously approached them in the lobby. Before she could speak, Ellery placed a gentle hand on her forearm. She looked at him, at first uncomprehending, but then her eyes widened in shocked recognition.

"Elise," Ellery said, "do you remember me? Ellery Queen? I am afraid it's been a good many years."

"Mr. Queen…Ellery—what are you doing here?"

"I suspect," replied Ellery, "that I am either helping out the authorities or getting in their way." He cocked his head to one side, narrowed his eyes appraisingly, and smiled. "Your father would have been proud. You have grown into a splendid young woman."

"Not as young as all that." She paused and smiled. "I'm glad you're here. I'm a bit frantic. I've been trying to reach Quinn since yesterday, and then I received the call to meet the police here. I don't know what this is all about, but I'd do anything for my brother. He's all the family I have left. I owe him my life. If anything has happened to him—"

Santos broke in impatiently. "Right now, if you don't mind, we need to get upstairs."

The elevator deposited them in a long hall carpeted in frayed Oriental patterns. At the end of the hall, Elise fumbled for a key and opened an apartment door, revealing a large, comfortably furnished living room. As they stepped inside, Ellery's eyes widened, and he shared a glance with Harry. This time they both smelled it. Copper.

A fast survey revealed the source. In the bathroom adjacent to the apartment's single bedroom, in a tub filled with rose-colored water, was the body of Dr. Quinn Djuna, both wrists slit. Ellery sighed, closed his eyes and pinched the bridge of his nose, just as Elise screamed.

Part 2: Out of Retirement

Days later, Harry Burke found himself in front of the still-familiar brownstone on West 87th Street. The disconnect was surreal. For a period of a few hectic weeks, many years before, he had practically lived here. Harry sighed, squared his shoulders, and climbed the stairs to the front door.

Inside the apartment, the feeling of disconnect remained. The room was virtually unchanged. Over the fireplace, the Thiraud portrait of Ellery and the inspector still stared with eyes that reached every corner of the room. And there, next to the portrait, was Ellery—Harry could still find the face of his friend in this old man, but his aspect now also reminded him of the inspector.

"Harry, it's good to see you again," Ellery smiled from across the room, beckoning Burke to a chair as Nikki retreated to the kitchen for coffee. "I take it you and your partner have made some progress?"

"Actually, Santos and I don't see eye to eye on much of anything, and this case is no exception. I'm here officially, but also on my own."

Ellery raised an inquiring eyebrow, and Burke continued. "As far as Santos is concerned, this case is finished. It's a simple murder/suicide, and he may be right. It turns out that Dr. Djuna had a motive to kill Dr. Tenumbra and a reason to take his own life as well. Dr. Djuna was engaged to a well known Long Island socialite, Rhonda St. Regis. That engagement ended rather badly several weeks ago, and it was Dr. Djuna's partner, Dr. Tenumbra, who was, shall we say, the third side of the triangle.

"Tenumbra's collector proclivities extended beyond detective novels. Over the years, he was quite the ladies' man. He spent the last few months pursuing his partner's fiancé. St. Regis might have been one in a string to him, but she was apparently a lot more to Dr. Djuna. Djuna was already prone to depression. After the breakup, he fell apart. The office staff report that he and Tenumbra quarreled openly during the last few weeks, and Djuna became increasingly unglued."

"So," Ellery interjected, "you have motive. What about opportunity?"

"In spades. Both doctors occasionally saw patients in the office Tenumbra maintained at his apartment. So Djuna had his own electronic key to the apartment—easy access whenever he needed it. And the coroner sets the time of death for both Tenumbra and Djuna sometime between eight and ten Sunday night, completely consistent with a murder followed by a suicide. The stopped clock on the floor of Tenumbra's apartment indicates that he apparently died around eight-thirty, which is consistent with the autopsy findings. Finally, and this sort of seems to cement it, Dr. Djuna incontrovertibly took his own life. The coroner says that the cuts to his wrists, the knife found next to the bathtub, the fact that there were no signs of any struggle, are all consistent with suicide. As far as Stanley Santos figures it, that closes the book on the matter."

Ellery smiled. "But you are still troubled?"

"You bet. My book's still open. Or maybe I should say *your* books are still open, and lying on the apartment floor. I can't get that out of my head. What were the books doing on the floor? And why did Tenumbra have that note from you crumpled in his hand?"

Harry shuffled through his brief case and handed a piece of paper to Ellery. "This is the list of the books—in chronological order, based on publication date. I assume, from the other volumes in Tenumbra's library, that this is also how they were shelved on his bookcase."

Ellery scanned the neat rows of titles, Nikki peering over his shoulder:

The Roman Hat Mystery	*Cat of Many Tails*
The French Powder Mystery	*Double, Double*
The Dutch Shoe Mystery	*The Origin of Evil*
The Egyptian Cross Mystery	*The King is Dead*
The Greek Coffin Mystery	*Calendar of Crime*
The American Gun Mystery	*The Scarlet Letters*
The Siamese Twin Mystery	*QBI: Queen's Bureau of Investigation*
The Chinese Orange Mystery	*The Glass Village*
The Adventures of Ellery Queen	*Inspector Queen's Own Case*
The Spanish Cape Mystery	*The Finishing Stroke*
Halfway House	*The Player on the Other Side*
The Door Between	*And on the Eighth Day*
The New Adventures of Ellery Queen	*The Fourth Side of the Triangle*
The Four of Hearts	*Queen's Full*
The Devil to Pay	*A Study in Terror*
The Dragon's Teeth	*Face to Face*
Calamity Town	*The House of Brass*
There Was an Old Woman	*QED: Queen's Experiments in Deduction*
The Murderer is a Fox	*Cop Out*
The Casebook of Ellery Queen	*The Last Woman in His Life*
Ten Days' Wonder	*A Fine and Private Place*

"Interesting," Ellery murmured, "all of the novels and all of the original short-story collections."

"But none of the farmed-out books, like those spy novels," Nikki added. "Who was that character? Tim Corrigan?"

"Mike McCall," Ellery sniffed. "I never should have let Fred and Manny talk me into those licensing arrangements. No, the only works here are the novels and collections that I actually wrote. I wonder, Harry, if I might hold on to this list?"

"Be my guest. And there's something else you might be interested in. We got this from the concierge." Harry pulled a second sheet from his briefcase. "This is the list of visitors to Tenumbra's apartment on Sunday and the times they checked in."

Ellery took the paper and read: "Janiel Friedman, 7:15 PM; Tabitha DuVal, 7:47 PM; Rhonda St. Regis, 8:18 PM."

Nikki glanced back at Harry. "Well, Ms. Friedman and Ms. St. Regis we know. But who is Tabitha DuVal?"

"This gets sort of sick," Harry responded, somewhat embarrassed. "Tabitha DuVal is an actress. She's in her mid-twenties, but she's already pretty well known—she's been in a number of well received shows on Broadway. But for our purposes she is—or more properly *was*—the last in the long string of women Tenumbra pursued."

Ellery couldn't stifle a smile. "The last woman in his life, eh? So, in the course of one hour, Tenumbra was visited by his former wife, the woman who jilted his partner for him, and another woman he was already after?"

"Exactly. Tenumbra may have been brilliant, handsome and rich. But he was also, it would appear, an undeniable cad."

"Tell me," Ellery asked, "do we know when each of these ladies *left* the building?"

"No, and there's the rub. Guests check in, but there's no record of when they leave."

"So any one of these three women could have still been in the building at the time of the murder," Ellery mused. "Well, Harry, you've gotten my attention. If you don't mind the company of an aged companion, I think maybe we should pay a visit to each of these ladies. But first perhaps we should set the stage just a bit. Nikki, can you see if Elise Djuna is free for lunch today?"

They were already seated in a dark restaurant on Amsterdam Avenue, tucked into the shadows of Columbia University, when Elise Djuna was shown to their table.

"How are you bearing up?" Ellery asked, as she seated herself between Nikki and Harry.

"As well as can be expected, I suppose. Thanks so much, Ellery, for the flowers. Quinn would have appreciated that. And thank *you*, Harry. You've been most kind and patient with me."

Harry Burke twisted in his seat uncomfortably. "I'm sorry about Santos. He can be a bit brusque."

"And I apologize as well," interjected Ellery, "because I am afraid we also have some questions. But let's at least wait until after lunch."

Later, over coffee, Ellery cleared his throat and began. "Elise, as I said, there are some things we need to discuss with you. The police have just about closed this case as a murder/suicide, and they may be right. But there are still some troubling aspects to the matter."

"How can I help?" Elise asked.

"Perhaps with some background," replied Ellery. "As Nikki explained on the telephone, my interest—and I think I can speak for Mr. Burke as well—was piqued by the fact that Tenumbra had a note from me in his hand when he died and the matter of those books on the floor."

"Well, I suppose I can shed a little light at least about the books," Elise responded. "When our father died, the books—and everything else—were left to us. Quinn and I were still students at Columbia. Not much was left in the estate after the restaurants were sold. We ultimately helped to finance our education by selling off all of Dad's personal belongings, including his library."

"Is that how your brother met Tenumbra?" Harry asked.

"No. Actually Quinn and I had both seen Jason professionally over the years. So we each had known him before. Quinn had been treated for depression ever since childhood. He worked out a lot of issues with Jason. And the process was, I'm certain, what prompted Quinn to pursue a career in psychiatry. So when we needed to sell the library, we already had an obvious potential purchaser. Jason prided himself on his mystery collection and probably paid us a good deal more than the library would have brought at auction. He was a big fan of yours, Ellery. He used to say he wanted to have a first edition of every book that had your name on the spine."

"So both you and your brother were close to Dr. Tenumbra?" Ellery observed.

"Well, yes and no. Jason was brilliant, but not a very nice man. I've barely seen him over the years. Quinn admired Jason, and they practiced together, but Jason was a master at manipulation, and vain and lecherous to boot. No woman was safe from his advances unless she rejected him authoritatively and early on. That's what I did. After that, he lost interest in me, and I never had any interest in him. But, over the years, I watched what he did to Quinn.

"Quinn was always sort of timid, a bit unsure of himself. That's why I thought it was so great when he and Rhonda became engaged. Rhonda is a bit of an airhead, but she seemed fun and gregarious, and she really brought Quinn out of his shell. It was disgusting when Jason began pursuing her. It might have been just another conquest for him, but it broke Quinn to lose Rhonda." Elise sighed. "I'm an English professor. I don't know anything at all about psychiatry. But I really thought that Quinn was stronger. I had no idea of the effect that the breakup must have had on him—until he tried to call me the night he died."

Ellery's eyes narrowed. "Did you in fact speak with him at that time?"

"No, I wasn't at home when he called. He left a voice message, though, around seven-thirty Sunday night. He sounded distraught and said he needed to speak with me. I kept trying to call him back, but all I got was his answering machine."

Ellery reached across the table for Elise's hand. "One last thing, Elise. Did you know that, at the time of his death, Dr. Tenumbra was involved not only with Rhonda St. Regis but was also apparently pursuing someone else"—he fumbled for a scrap of paper in his coat pocket—"a Ms. Tabitha Du Val, a Broadway actress?"

"No, I didn't. But it hardly surprises me. Jason Tenumbra never changed. He was always chasing skirts." Elise squared her shoulders, composing herself. After a few seconds, she smiled and looked back across the table. "If that's all, Ellery, I'll thank you for lunch and be off."

She pushed her chair back and, at the same time, a bit awkwardly, Harry Burke stood as well.

Ellery and Nikki eyed the detective as Burke blushed.

"Ms. Djuna," he stammered, "has agreed to show me a new collection in the rare books section of the Columbia University library this afternoon."

Ellery smiled and waved dismissively. "We'll catch up with you later, Harry."

As the two left, Nikki raised a quizzical eyebrow. Ellery smiled back and said, "Getting back to business, Ms. Porter, where does all this leave us?"

"Well," Nikki responded, "it leaves us with the police theory, your books on the floor, your note, and three women, each of whom was in Tenumbra's apartment just before he was killed."

"Precisely," replied Ellery. "We know how to proceed, don't we?"

Nikki hesitated for a moment and then looked squarely into Ellery's eyes, her concern evident. "Do you think you're up to this?"

Ellery sighed, and his voice sounded older when he replied: "I really don't know. Let's just take it one day at a time, shall we?"

The executive offices of the Friedman and Norr department-store chain, in the tradition of the 1930s, were located on the top floor of the flagship Manhattan store. Ellery, Nikki and Harry Burke waited in a sparsely furnished anteroom until a door across the room eventually swung open and a young woman in tailored linen announced that Ms. Friedman would see them now.

Janiel Friedman rose as they entered her corner office. Tall and slender, dressed in a pinstriped business suit, she looked every bit the executive. In her mid-fifties, hair long and wound back in a French twist, she personified her reputation as the "Queen of 42nd Street." Gracefully, but with business-like precision, Friedman gestured for Ellery, Nikki and Harry to be seated. "Gentlemen, madam, what can I do for you?" she asked.

It was Harry who began. "As you are aware, Ms. Friedman, the police are investigating the murder of your ex-husband, Dr. Jason Tenumbra."

"Actually," Friedman interrupted, "I am *not* aware of any such fact. I have already spoken with Detective Santos by telephone, and I understand from him that the police investigation is concluded. Furthermore"—and her eyes rested on Ellery and Nikki—"I was not aware that even on-going police examinations are conducted by task forces that include private citizens."

Harry bristled. "The fact that Detective Santos may have called you on the telephone has no bearing on this visit, which is, I can assure you, part of the police investigation. My name is Harry Burke. I am a detective with the New York City Police Department. I am senior to Detective Santos, this investigation is most decidedly still open, and I will either speak with you now or later before a grand jury. That choice is yours. As for my companions, this is Mr. Ellery Queen and his assistant, Ms. Nikki Porter. Mr. Queen has a long-standing relationship with the NYPD but, in any event, their presence here today is *my* decision, not *yours*." Harry took a deep breath and forced a smile. "Now, may we continue?"

Friedman allowed herself a slight sniff. "Certainly, but please be direct. I have a very busy schedule."

"According to the building's concierge," Harry continued, "you signed in to visit Dr. Tenumbra at exactly seven-fifteen. We would be very interested in hearing what brought you to the West Park Towers that evening."

"I had an appointment with Jason. He was supposed to sign some legal documents."

Ellery raised an eyebrow. "From your use of the word 'supposed,' are we to surmise that Dr. Tenumbra did not in fact sign those papers?"

With a slight slump of her shoulders, Friedman nodded. "He did not." She turned to face Ellery. "It seems quite irrelevant to what you are investigating, but I suppose it won't hurt to explain matters. Friedman and Norr is an old-line establishment. When I say 'old-line,' I don't mean old-fashioned or conservative. What I mean is that, in an era of conglomerate control of merchandising, we buck the trend. Other department stores' personalities exist only insofar as they serve the whims of the conglomerate owners. That has never been the case with Friedman and Norr, which always has been privately owned. However, during the past few months we are—or I suppose I should say have been—in the midst of a hostile takeover bid from Federated Department Stores."

"Pardon my ignorance," Ellery interjected, "but how could that be if the store's ownership is privately held?"

Janiel Friedman sighed. "Our stores were founded by my grandfather, Davarian Friedman, and his partner, Jacob Norr. My grandfather owned sixty percent of the stock; Norr owned forty percent. Those percentages have persisted to this day. The Norr stock is voted by a trust established for Jacob Norr's grandchildren. I am the sole heir of my grandfather's stock, and I vote his shares. Or at least I did."

"You did?" Ellery asked.

"This is a bit complicated," Friedman continued. "As part of my divorce settlement with Jason, he received half of the earnings from the stock, although I continued to have voting control, with one exception."

"I sense," said Ellery, "that we are about to hear about that one exception."

"Yes, I am afraid you are. My divorce decree with Jason provides that, in the event of a proposed sale of the Friedman stock, Jason could vote half the shares. This was to protect his damned interest rights against a sham sale. To make a long story short, the Norr trustees are enamored of Federated Department Stores' buyout offer. Normally, I wouldn't care what the Norr family wanted to do, since their forty percent holdings are a minority interest."

"But not," Ellery murmured, "when there is the possibility of Jason Tenumbra voting fifty percent of your shares in favor of a different outcome."

"You have articulated the nub of my problem, Mr. Queen. I needed Jason's agreement to vote against the takeover. Typical of Jason, he agreed—but only in exchange for one hundred thousand dollars. My meeting with Jason was for the sole purpose of consummating that agreement. I arrived at his apartment with a cashier's check and an agreement authorizing me to vote all of my shares in the takeover attempt. He was supposed to sign it that night."

"But a problem arose?" Ellery queried.

"You might say that. When I arrived, Jason told me that he had thought about it and decided he had sold out too cheaply. Something about a new Lamborghini that had caught his fancy. We argued, but he was insistent. The price, he announced, was now two hundred thousand. I tried to reason with him. If Federated Stores acquired all of the stock, I would get the proceeds of the sale, and then Jason's income from the stock would have ceased. But Jason would hear none of that—he just smiled and shook his head as I talked. When I ran out of steam, he said, 'Janiel, this isn't about logic, it's about extortion. I have something you need.' In the end, I swallowed my pride. I wasn't going to lose the stores for another measly hundred thousand dollars.

"Anyway, the bastard refused to sign, because all I had with me was a cashier's check for *one* hundred thousand dollars, not two hundred thousand. He wouldn't take my word that I would get him the rest the next day. So I left the apartment. In total, I couldn't have been there longer than fifteen minutes."

"I wonder," said Ellery, "whether you could tell us what you did afterwards?"

"Afterwards?"

"Yes. Did you in fact arrange for the additional hundred thousand dollars?"

Janiel Friedman looked uncomfortable. "Well, as it turns out, I did nothing. My visit with Jason was on Sunday. I couldn't very well call my attorney that night. But on Monday, by mid-day, I had been informed of Jason's…demise. At that stage, there was no reason to draw another check. The stock was again mine to vote."

Janiel Friedman lapsed into silence. After elongated seconds, she spoke again. "Look, after I left Jason's apartment, I went home, poured myself a stiff drink, cursed the bastard and went to bed. I wouldn't kill anyone, not even that scumbag, for a mere two hundred thousand dollars. That's the truth, and that is also all I am saying. I wish you good fortune in your investigation, since good fortune, if it leads to the truth, can only remove me from your list of suspects. But for now, gentlemen and Ms. Porter, I have business to attend to." With that, Janiel Friedman pushed a button on the side of her desk, summoning her assistant to usher them out of the office.

The marquee over the Majestic Theater several blocks from Times

Square announced the imminent opening of *American Heroes*, a "bold and rollicking musical salute to the comic-book superheroes of the 1940s." Harry, Ellery and Nikki walked through double doors and into the vestibule of the theater. A guard, lounging on a straight-back chair tipped back against the wall, rose, intent on blocking their entrance. But once Harry explained that they had an appointment with Tabitha DuVal, he waved them into the theater.

The dressing rooms were in a musty warren of halls, scenery and stage equipment tucked behind the stage. Harry Burke tapped gently on a door that bore the name "DuVal," and it swung slowly open. Across the small room, a slender blonde in black tights and a cape sat in a director's chair, hunched over a script. She looked up. "Mr. Burke?"

"Yes, Ms. DuVal. And this is Mr. Ellery Queen and Ms. Nikki Porter."

Tabitha DuVal flashed a quick smile. "We're a little short on chairs," she said, eyeing Ellery with some concern.

"We're fine," Ellery assured her, resting on Nikki's arm.

"We don't want to take any more of your time than necessary," Harry began. "I know you're in rehearsals. But, as I explained on the phone, we want to discuss certain matters relating to the death of Dr. Jason Tenumbra."

"I'll be glad to tell you anything I can, but I actually don't know much. I mean, I was sorry about what happened to Jason, but I didn't know him all that well."

"The concierge records at his building indicate," continued Harry, "that you visited Dr. Tenumbra's apartment at around 7:45 on the night of his death."

"I was there, all right. I sort of thought it was on business, but it kind of didn't end up that way. This musical we're working on, it's not fully capitalized. I mean, do you know what it takes to open a musical on Broadway? I've got a share in this one, as well as a role in it. I met Jason through the producer—Jason said he was interested in investing in the show. He was pretty well known among the cast and crew. Apparently he hung around the stage lights a lot. Anyway, he started showing up during our rehearsals. He was a really charming guy, ultra suave. Serious older hunk, if you know what I mean. He was talking about investing half a million dollars, but then he kept putting it off.

"The money is really important to us. We're still two weeks from opening, and we're basically busted. So I pushed Jason quite a bit, and finally he asked me to stop by his apartment that Sunday. He promised he'd have a cashier's check for a hundred grand as a first installment."

"Didn't a Sunday-night business appointment seem a little strange?"

Nikki asked incredulously.

Tabitha's smile receded. "Look, I don't know what you're implying, but, yeah, I guess I thought maybe it wasn't just business—sort of 'business plus,' maybe. Look, I'm single, unattached, and this is New York. Jason could have been a great catch. I mean, the West Park Towers is to die for."

"Perhaps," observed Ellery.

"I didn't mean it that way. Anyway, I showed up at his apartment around a quarter to eight. He made drinks and immediately started hitting on me. I'd try to talk money, and he'd change the subject and finger my blouse. At first I sort of went along. But then I was like, exactly where is this going? So I pushed him away and said flat out, what about the money? And Jason comes right back and says he's not going to invest anything, he's got something else he's interested in. Some car. So I sort of blew up at him. Things were getting kind of tense, when all of the sudden the phone rings. Jason answered it, looked a little distressed, and then told me his fiancé was on her way up.

"Well, that floored me. No money for the show and a fiancé to boot. So, I'm still tearing into Jason, but all the while he's bustling me back toward the bedroom, telling me to play it cool. I told him I wasn't doing anything wrong, *he* was the one playing all the scams, and what was this about a fiancé, anyway? I mean, where did *that* come from? But he just kept shushing me and pushing me back toward the bedroom. So, what could I do? He closed the door, and I sat down on the bed and fumed.

"Well, I didn't end up waiting very long. I could hear this woman's voice in the living room, screaming. A couple seconds later, the bedroom door bursts open, and in storms a really angry lady holding my glass in her hand. I guess she saw the two cocktail glasses in the living room and sort of added things up.

"Anyway, I'm like *how is all this happening to me*, and then I sort of blew up again and started yelling at her and at Jason for having gotten me into the middle of their damned mess. The woman was clawing at me, but I got past her and stormed out the front door. That was the last time I saw either of them. But I can tell you this—when I left, Jason was fine. I mean, he was really going at it with this fiancé woman, but they were both very much alive."

"And you left the building immediately?" Ellery asked.

"What do you think? I'm going to hang around in the hall to see what *else* can go wrong?"

There was a tap at the door to the dressing room, and a man with a script under his arm looked in. "Your number's up in five minutes, Tabitha."

She turned toward Harry inquiringly.

"I suppose that's all for now, Ms. DuVal, but we may need to speak with you again."

"Before you leave," Ellery asked, "I wonder if you could tell us just a little about your new show."

Tabitha, already headed for the door, stopped and turned back to Ellery. "Like I said, assuming we even make it to opening night, it's a musical, set in 1944. The characters are all based on Marvel comic-book superheroes."

"And you play—?"

"Sharon Shannon Kane."

"Ahh," replied Ellery. "Sharon Kane. She was Spider Queen, wasn't she?"

Rhonda St. Regis' apartment building, a lingering bastion of an earlier age, sat squarely in front of Central Park, defying encroachment with a dowager stubbornness that had calcified over seventy-five years of pre-eminence. Ellery therefore was not surprised when a uniformed attendant operated the elevator that deposited them on the thirty-ninth floor.

St. Regis' apartment was a study in elegance. Expansive views of Central Park, overstuffed wool and leather chairs and couches, Chippendale end tables, and deep Persian carpets all conveyed the impression of a living space at home with itself.

And equally at home was Rhonda St. Regis, who greeted them in the vestibule and glided to what Ellery suspected was her accustomed throne, a wing-backed chair in a corner of the living room. As a maid in a black-and-white uniform straight out of a *New Yorker* cartoon placed a tray containing a teapot and four teacups and saucers on a walnut-and-brass coffee table, St. Regis smiled across the expanse of her domain.

"As I told you on the telephone, I don't know what—if anything—I can add to your investigation. I already explained to Mr. Santos that, when I last saw Jason, he was alive and kicking. Kicking, quite literally. But it is, as they say, your nickel, Mr. Burke."

"Well, it's really rather simple," Burke replied. "We know that you were one of three people who, according to building records, visited Dr. Tenumbra on the night of his death. We need to know everything about your visit."

Rhonda St. Regis eyed Burke. "Well," she began, "I arrived at Jason's apartment unannounced, just after eight. I decided, on a whim, to surprise him. Jason and I had been seeing each other for some time, although it had been a clandestine relationship until the week before his death. But by the night of my visit we were no longer a secret. I reveled in the fact that I was free to just drop in on him, without going through all the shenanigans that had been the hallmark of our prior arrangements."

"The prior secretive nature of your meetings was, I take it, occasioned by your engagement to Dr. Quinn Djuna?" Ellery asked.

The question hardly flustered St. Regis, who continued, "Quinn was a dear man; a dear but intense man. Looking back, everything just happened too fast between us. He was so certain that we were preordained for each other that I suppose I got caught up in it. But, almost from the moment that I accepted his proposal, I had second thoughts. I realized that I had been carried to that point by momentum but little else. And always, hovering in the background, there was Jason. He'd be there with a smile or a kind word. Very suave, self assured, never pushy. Eventually I opened up to him about my feelings—maybe *lack* of feelings would be more precise—toward Quinn. He would respond with his own questions, you know, the way psychiatrists do, and, as I continued to reach out to him, well, one thing just led to another. Shared coffee progressed to shared dinners, shared evenings to shared nights. Each morning, when I woke up beside him, there would be a wave of guilt, and I would resolve to try to work things out openly. But for weeks I didn't know what to do.

"Then Jason proposed. He was so eloquent. He told me that he felt terribly about what he was doing to Quinn, but that he and I were soul mates, that we couldn't allow the opportunity to live our lives together to slip through our fingers. Even then, I had to take some time to think. As you probably know, my family was quite wealthy. As an only child, I inherited everything. I've always been careful in relationships. I have to be sure people are interested in me, not in my money. But Jason was so warm, so understanding. He seemed to have no interest in the St. Regis inheritance. And, finally, I sort of looked inside myself and said, *okay, this time it's real*.

"Once I decided that, I knew I had to come clean with Quinn. I met with him and, as gently as I could, I broke the news. He took it even worse than I had expected. He cried. He begged me not to leave him. I explained that it takes two to make a relationship, that it's not a one-way street. And then he started cursing Jason. I told him that it really couldn't be Jason's fault, that if it had really been right between us there would never have been a Jason. But he wanted none of it.

"Jason told me afterward that Quinn just got worse and worse. The two of them were arguing in the office, in front of patients. Jason said they were going to have to break up their practice—we even talked of how I might advance Jason the necessary funds to buy Quinn out.

"I'm telling you all this because you might as well know my state of mind when I entered Jason's apartment that night. Finally, everything was right. I was absolutely at the top of my game until I saw that damned cocktail glass, with lipstick on the rim, in Jason's apartment. Then my world just crashed. What I had been guarding against all of my life had happened. The man I thought I was in love with was just another cad."

Ellery, Nikki and Harry Burke watched silently. As Rhonda St. Regis went on, her voice rose an octave and doubled in cadence. A red flush crept up her neck.

"No one," she continued, "can get away with that with me. I stormed into his bedroom, and there's this young blond wisp of a thing, sitting on the edge of the bed, like she belonged there. And then, can you believe this, *she* starts yelling at *me*. I tried to grab her, but she bolted for the door. I was calling Jason all the ugly names I could think of, and through all of it he's whining, 'I can explain, I can explain.' Finally I just yelled, 'You bastard, explain *this*.' Then I kneed him in the groin and stomped out of the apartment.

"That's it. That's the full story. When I last saw Jason Tenumbra, he was lying on his study floor, surrounded by his damn art work and damn books, grabbing his damn crotch and howling. He might not have been feeling that great, but he sure as hell wasn't dead."

As the threesome entered the elevator, having left behind a still-fuming Rhonda St. Regis, Harry's cell phone rang. When Harry finished the call, he turned to Ellery. "That was Santos. He wants us to meet him as soon as we can at Tenumbra's place."

Jason Tenumbra's apartment was in the midst of being cleaned and straightened when Nikki, Ellery and Harry were escorted into the study by Stanley Santos, who bore a smile that Ellery took for smug. Arranged on the glass desk, now sparkling clean, were several items. Santos stopped at the desk and turned around to face the others.

"Mr. Queen, during the last few weeks I read a couple of your books. They were okay for their time. Pretty good stuff. After I read a few, I decided you might enjoy hearing the solution to this case at the scene of the crime. That's something I could picture you doing. Of course, *you* might have filled the room with possible culprits, but I'll dispense with that, since, as I told you from the beginning, there is no Hitchcock ending here.

"What I did want to demonstrate to my partner, and to you, is that— as good as your so-called deductive approach used to be—there just isn't much need for it any more. While you folks were tromping about town interviewing everyone you could think of, I did what modern detectives do. I gathered the physical evidence, sent it off to the lab, and waited for the results. And the results, my friends, tell the whole story. We live in an absolutely marvelous scientific age."

Santos turned to the table and, with a flourish, picked up a small leather case. "Exhibit One," he said, passing the case to Harry Burke. "This is a set of scalpels we located in Dr. Djuna's apartment. Look at the inscription embossed on the inside cover."

Harry opened the box and read: *"To Quinn, best wishes as you embark into the field of medicine, Jason Tenumbra."*

"That box was kept in a small display cabinet in Djuna's living room. And look again—see anything missing?"

The box contained four scalpels of varying sizes. A spot that could have held a fifth was empty.

"Exhibit Two," Santos continued, picking up a scalpel from the glass desk top. "The murder weapon. Not only does it fit into the open space in the carrying box, it is a precise match to the other four scalpels. Same metallic alloy. The boys in the lab verified it, and we were even able to trace it back to the manufacturer, using the serial number on the underside of the box. So, what do we know? We know that the weapon that murdered Dr. Tenumbra was a knife he had given to Dr. Djuna. Surprise, surprise!"

Santos dripped another smile before turning back to the desk for a plastic card the size of a credit card. "Exhibit Three, the magnetic entry card that gave Dr. Djuna uninhibited access to Dr. Tenumbra's apartment. The card was left in the middle of Dr. Djuna's desk in his apartment. So there was no reason to worry about the names on the concierge list. With this card, Quinn Djuna could bypass the list completely. And, what's this?" asked Santos, feigning surprise. "Why, there seems to be a blood stain on the back of the card.

"So, let's see, Mr. Queen, what do we have? We have motive: Dr. Djuna had been jilted by his fiancé after he had been cuckolded by his partner. We have opportunity: Dr. Djuna had free access to the apartment with that bloodstained card. And we have means: Dr. Djuna's own scalpel, found at the scene of the crime."

"Impressive," murmured Ellery.

"Oh, that's not all," Santos continued. "I saved the best, the very best, for last." He turned back to the desk and picked up the final object, a typed report held together by a black clip. "This is the forensics report on the blood from the scene of the crime. Actually, it's *two* reports, because it turned out there were two different blood types on the floor of the study."

Santos gestured back to the desk. "The blood on the desk matched Tenumbra's blood. Plain and simple." Santos turned back to the front of the desk. "But the blood out there"—he gestured toward the door—"and the blood we found on the carpet, as well as that smudge of blood on the electronic entry card? That wasn't Tenumbra's blood at all. It seems that the murderer must have been cut during the struggle, and there were very good samples of that second blood type. So, what can I tell you about it?

"Let me spare you from plowing through a long report. We'll start with some general observations, and then we'll move to the specifics. As you know, even blood work can't positively identify who the blood came from. All that DNA analysis can do is establish the odds, and they're usually astronomical, that the blood came from a particular person. But there is one thing, one very special thing, that *any* blood test can tell you with absolute certainty. It can tell you the sex of the person who produced that blood. All male blood has an X and a Y chromosome. Not so with the ladies." He winked at Nikki. "The ladies have two X's.

"I bet you can see what's coming," he continued, smiling patronizingly at Ellery. "The blood in front of the desk and the blood on the entry card—in other words, the blood that was not Tenumbra's—was the blood of a male. Shows up clear in the analysis: X's and Y's all over the place. Of course, all that does is rule out about fifty percent of the population. But guess what? Surprise again! It rules out *everyone* you three have been wasting your time interviewing the past week—every one of those ladies. None of them could have done it. It's scientifically impossible.

"But, as I said, we can also move from the general to the specific. We know more than the fact that the murderer was a man. The test also shows that the blood in front of the desk and on the entry card—again, the blood that is not Tenumbra's—is in fact a perfect match to Dr. Quinn Djuna, which makes him the murderer, just like I told you from the start."

"*Very* impressive," Ellery muttered, nodding.

Harry, however, still looked unconvinced. "What about the books?" he asked.

"Will you forget about the damn books?" Santos exploded. "This is not about the books. They don't matter."

"I see," Ellery said, "that they have been returned to the bookcase."

"Yeah," replied Santos. "It seems that, while Tenumbra brought in a lot of money, he spent a lot more. Recipe for fiscal disaster. Apparently he died in the red, both actually and metaphorically. The family has scheduled an auction here to sell off his Oriental art and his library. They've been pushing us to get the place back in order before the high rollers show up."

Ellery got to his feet, his joints protesting. He wished, not for the first time, that he could exercise over his ancient body the control he still wielded over his mind. Haltingly, he walked across the room to the wall of books. They were, as he remembered them, tightly shelved, spine to spine. He fingered the volumes of Catherine Aird at the beginning of the collection. Then he walked stiffly to the end of the library and knelt on creaking knees to examine the Emile Zola volumes snugged tightly against a bookend. He straightened, returned to the middle of the collection, and stared at his own volumes. And then his eyes widened, and he gasped. Between the end of the Queen collection and the beginning of the Ruth Rendells, there were approximately eight inches of blank shelf.

"Thank God," Ellery whispered. "The light. It hasn't failed." He laughed out loud, and Nikki, Harry Burke and Santos turned to look at him, uncomprehending.

"Of course," Ellery marveled, and he laughed almost giddily now. "It's Poe! Poe had the answer all along!"

Part 3: An After-Dinner Chat

The dinner dishes in the Queen apartment had been cleared, and Ellery, Nikki, Harry Burke and Elise Djuna sat over steaming cups of coffee. With some exasperation, Harry interrupted what had been light, if strained, after-dinner conversation.

"Look, Ellery. That was a great dinner, but I ended up suffering through it. You've been playing coy ever since yesterday. You promised to let us in on that epiphany you had at the apartment, and I for one am on the edge of my seat."

"I admit," Ellery responded, "that I have been taking my own sweet time on this. As I grow older, I find that I have slowed down a bit. But that's not entirely due to the aging process. It's also because experience has taught me that with knowledge comes responsibility, and with responsibility comes the need to step back and ponder a little sometimes.

"Where to begin? I used to start, as Detective Santos noted, by gathering the suspects. But as I grew older I found that sometimes managing all those people is a chore in itself, one that gets in the way of clean explication. Sometimes it is better just to talk the matter through with friends.

"The physical evidence summarized yesterday by Mr. Santos is impressive. And ultimately we must return to it. But what has always, I believe, troubled my old friend Harry was the pile of books on the floor. Certainly that's what coaxed me into the fray.

"It seems safe to conclude that my books were swept to the floor either by Dr. Tenumbra—who, due to the absence of blood on the volumes, would have to have done this before he was stabbed—or by the murderer. And the meaning of the pile of books would vary depending on who put them there. Presumptively, if Tenumbra left the books on the floor, he did so to identify his murderer, but, if the murderer moved the books, it would have been for a different reason, no doubt to deflect our attention in the wrong direction.

"Let's first assume that the books were moved by Tenumbra. What could he have been trying to tell us? This is always a problem with dying clues: they are all too often murky. Was Tenumbra trying to tell us that the murderer was somehow associated with the word 'queen?' If so, this is no help. Every single person who had access, or may have had access, to Tenumbra's apartment that night has some obscure connection to that word. Janiel Friedman is proud to be known as the merchandising 'Queen of 42nd Street'—the phrase is even used in advertising for the Friedman and Norr chain. Tabitha DuVal is about to appear on Broadway as a character who, to avenge injustice, becomes the Spider Queen. And Rhonda St. Regis? Well, 'Regis' derives from the Latin 'regina,' meaning 'queen.' And of course Quinn Djuna is easily linked to the Queen books that were originally his father's.

"In sum, this possible clue leave us with nothing. If all of the references to 'queen' are obscure, and if each suspect can be identified by at least one such reference, how could Tenumbra have concluded that a pile of my books would lead us to the culprit? The answer is that he could not.

"Equally puzzling is why *all* of the books were removed to the floor. Wouldn't just one book convey the same message? I must admit that, until yesterday, none of this made sense to me."

"So what changed yesterday?" Harry asked.

"I'll come to that. But first let's focus for just a minute on the books themselves. I think we can learn a great deal about Tenumbra from those volumes, and from other things we know."

"I'm puzzled, now," Nikki interjected. "We already know that the Queen books were the volumes you sent to Elise and Quinn's father over the years. If that library was acquired, in total, by Tenumbra, how can it tell us anything about him?"

"It is true that Tenumbra acquired Djuna's library," Ellery replied. "But remember that Djuna only had an interest in the Queen books in which Dad or I appeared, and those are the only books I sent him. They were all on the floor, but there were two other volumes there as well, *The Glass Village* and *Cop Out*. While I wrote those books, they were never in Djuna's library. Why? Because Dad and I were characters in neither of them. So Tenumbra must have acquired them elsewhere.

"We also know that Tenumbra had contacted me to find out if I would be interested in parting with copies of my non-fiction analytic volumes, books that were not otherwise in his library. Finally, we know that Tenumbra was completely uninterested—and in this regard I applaud his taste—in any of the ghostwritten Queen volumes: the Mike McCall and Tim Corrigan works, and the other paperbacks that bore my name but that I really had nothing to do with."

"I don't see where this gets us if all the books he had were in fact on the floor," Harry groused. "And what does it have to do with Poe?"

"It has everything to do with Poe. We know from Poe that the best place to hide a book is on a bookcase. This is just the obverse. The best place to hide the *absence* of a book is in the context of an *empty* bookcase."

Harry rolled his eyes. "Look, Ellery, I'm trying to stay with you on this, but it's making no sense at all. Absence of *what* book? All your books, except the ones you wouldn't sell to Tenumbra, were on the floor. You already said that."

"No. What I said was that Tenumbra was a collector of books that I had written, and that this was true regardless of whether Dad and I were characters in the books. All that I knew, but it told me nothing until yesterday when I saw, for the first time, my books *replaced* on the bookcase. As you all observed, the books by other authors were shelved tightly, ending with a bookend after the last Zola volume. But when the Queen library was reshelved, in the middle space it previously occupied, there was a blank space of approximately eight inches after the last Queen volume.

"When I saw that, I understood everything. The books on the floor could not be the dying message. They were red herrings, misdirecting us not toward someone, but away from something. The real dying clue, what the murderer couldn't allow us to find, was no longer there. This may become a little clearer if we move from Poe past Queen and examine the next set of books in Tenumbra's collection."

"What next set of books?" Harry asked in exasperation.

"The books that, alphabetically, immediately follow the Queen collection: the first editions of Ruth Rendell's works. Tell me, Harry, did you notice anything telling about those volumes?"

"No. And I am so confused now that I'm just going to shut up and let you work this through to the end."

"And we are almost there," Ellery replied. "The Ruth Rendell books are informative because *all* of her works are there. By this, I mean all of the books she authored both under the name Ruth Rendell and under her *nom de plume*, Barbara Vine. And the Vine books are shelved together with the rest of Rendell's works.

"When I saw that, it was immediately clear what must have happened, particularly in light of what Mr. Santos had just told us. Not only did I know which of my own volumes were missing, I also knew which of those particular volumes Tenumbra must have grasped and pulled from the shelf while grabbing my note to him in his other hand. Tenumbra left a clue to the identity of his murderer, and at the same time did his best to ensure that I would be called upon to interpret his dying message."

Ellery gazed across the room at his guests. "There were only four of my works of fiction that were not on the floor of Tenumbra's apartment: the books I wrote under the pseudonym of Barnaby Ross." Ellery was quiet for a moment. His eyes now looked as old as his years, and sadder. "I think you expected this, Elise."

Silently, Elise Djuna nodded and pulled two volumes from her purse: *The Tragedy of X* and *The Tragedy of Y*. Each was stained with blood, and on the cover of the first volume, roughly sketched in the blood of the dying Jason Tenumbra, was an O with a cross at the bottom. "I knew you'd figure it out, Ellery," she said. "So I brought the books with me. I have no interest in prolonging this."

"Wait a minute," said Harry, knowledge and anger welling up in equal parts. "I don't like where this is headed. But in any event, you're wrong. Remember the DNA analysis? Elise can't have had anything to do with this."

"Of course I remember the DNA analysis," Ellery replied. "But unfortunately DNA has *everything* to do with this. Blood is, in fact, the key."

Ellery locked eyes with Elise. "What was it? Leukemia? Hodgkin's?"

In a small and resigned voice, Elise answered, "Leukemia."

Now it was Nikki's turn to be perplexed. "Ellery, I'm lost. What's this all about?"

"Like everything else in this case, it's about blood. Blood and books. We knew from the very first day that both Elise and Quinn had previously been patients of Dr. Tenumbra. Elise told us that. And we also knew—again from Elise's own words, when she was explaining the nature of Quinn's recurring bouts with depression—that she herself was utterly unfamiliar with psychiatry, something no one who had personally struggled through psychiatric analysis would have said. Therefore, her consultations with Dr. Tenumbra must have had nothing to do with psychiatry. But we also know that Tenumbra at some point had another specialty: oncology. When Elise told us that Quinn saved her life, she meant it literally. Quinn saved her with his blood. Djuna and his wife adopted Elise and Quinn, but Quinn was, in fact, your fraternal twin, wasn't he, Elise?"

She nodded.

"How could you have known that," Nikki asked, "and why would it matter?"

"It was the only logical answer. The best and most reliable cure for leukemia—or for Hodgkin's disease—involves a bone-marrow transplant, and the best match for a donor transplant is, predictably, a sibling. In order to effect a remission, the recipient's blood and bone marrow is literally eliminated through radiation treatment. Bone marrow from the host—in this case Quinn—is injected. The transferred marrow then begins producing blood, blood that eventually replaces the recipient's blood. And the new blood cells are identical in all respects to those of the donor. Elise, in fact, owes her life to the fact that she has the blood—and the identical blood DNA—of her brother Quinn. While Santos was correct that the blood of a female would have only X chromosomes, Elise's veins pulse with Quinn's blood. Blood that carries—like that of all males—both an X and a Y chromosome.

"And that is what Dr. Tenumbra, her treating physician, knew and tried to tell us. He no doubt saw that Elise was bleeding during the attack, and he knew that she, not her brother, was his killer. In his dying moments, he grabbed those two volumes and drew on the cover of one the universal medical symbol for 'woman.' He was literally telling us that—while the second blood type we would find in the apartment was that of a man, with both X and Y chromosomes—the murderer was in fact a woman. A woman with X and Y chromosomes.

"Like all dying messages that are not facially self-evident, this one had some obscurity to it. But Tenumbra ensured that that obscurity would be unraveled by also grasping my note in his dying grip. He knew that dying messages have always been somewhat of a specialty of mine. By dying with my note clutched in his grip, he ensured, as best he could, that I would become involved in deciphering this one."

"But then why did Quinn take his own life?" Nikki asked.

"Quinn took his life out of depression, and over the sorrow he experienced in the breakup of his engagement," Ellery answered. "But what we did not realize earlier was that Quinn's suicide must have preceded Dr. Tenumbra's murder."

"How can you say that, when the coroner could only establish that the two men were killed during the same two-hour period?" Harry Burke asked, and Ellery noted that he was now holding Elise's quivering hand.

"Harry, we know it because of the blood. We assumed from the beginning that the clock on the floor of Tenumbra's study, the one frozen at eight-thirty, likely resulted from Tenumbra tripping on the clock's electrical cord. But now, as Mr. Santos has so conclusively demonstrated, that is not possible. No one in Tenumbra's condition could have reached the clock without leaving a blood trail. Yet we know that the only blood found on that side of the desk was that of the murderer. So it was the murderer who unplugged the clock. And we also know," Ellery continued, "that this was a deliberate, not an accidental, act."

Ellery glanced around the room and again was met only by stares.

"We know this," he sighed, "because the murderer obviously had the time to arrange the other aspects of the room. If there was time to remove the Barnaby Ross volumes and to sweep the rest of the Queen volumes to the floor, there was also time to right the clock. Unless, that is, the murderer *wanted* us to find the clock on the floor—in fact planted it, to misdirect us as to the time of the killing.

"I imagine"—and Ellery looked toward Elise—"it went something like this. You stabbed Tenumbra. As he lay mortally wounded, perhaps you even taunted him a bit, explaining that you were free to kill him without fear, that you would never be caught, since the blood evidence you were leaving behind would, upon analysis, identify your brother as the killer. Assuming Tenumbra was dead or dying, you left the room, probably to clean up. When you returned, you found Tenumbra, now dead, sprawled on his desk. But to your probable horror, you also saw that he had those two Barnaby Ross volumes grasped in his bloody hand. Worse yet, we now know he had managed to scrawl yet another clue, the universal medical sign for woman, on the front of one volume.

"You are your father's child. You grasped immediately that this clue, if deciphered, could identify you as the murderer. So what did you do? You pulled from the bookcase the four books I wrote under the Barnaby Ross pseudonym—*The Tragedy of X*, *The Tragedy of Y*, *The Tragedy of Z*, and *Drury Lane's Last Case*—and set them aside to remove from the apartment. Then you swept the remaining Queen volumes to the floor in order to obscure what was missing from the collection. Finally, you pulled the cord of the clock from the wall and set the dial back, probably by an hour, thus indicating that Tenumbra's death occurred earlier than it in fact did. What you didn't find was my note to Tenumbra, clasped almost invisibly in his other hand.

"But even if that is not precisely how it all transpired, we do know for a fact that Quinn's death had to have preceded Tenumbra's. Elise, it was obvious that your brother meant everything to you. You've told us as much in your words as in your actions. You would have never framed him with his own blood, with the blood he donated to you to save your life, had he not already been dead. In fact, you killed Tenumbra only *because* your brother was dead, which you discovered yourself when, unable to reach Quinn by phone, you went to his apartment, used the same key you used the next day to let us in, and found his body.

"And then, I suppose, the rest just fell into place. You took Quinn's scalpel, took his entry card for Tenumbra's apartment, where you killed Tenumbra to avenge your brother. Afterwards, you returned Quinn's entry card to his apartment, and then simply waited for the police to discover the two bodies, the latter one with your own assistance, and accompanied by, I should add, a most convincing scream.

"You were shocked to see me the next day outside Quinn's apartment. But that shock did not result simply from the fact that we had not seen each other in years. It was a reaction of fear. You and your family knew my work even better than Tenumbra did. You knew that my life has been dedicated to unraveling perplexities, and particularly dying messages. You knew, in short, that I might prevail where the police would not. That even with the Barnaby Ross books removed, I might still figure out what that pile of books was all about. In fact, that's why you suggested early on that Tenumbra wanted to acquire, in your words, *every book that had my name on the spine.*

"That statement, as we now know, was demonstrably false and an attempted misdirection itself. If Tenumbra wanted to acquire copies of *all* books bearing the Queen name, it's true that the Barnaby Ross books would not have been included, but all of the franchised books—the McCall and Corrigan potboilers that, while farmed out, purported to have been written by Ellery Queen—*would* have been included, since they had my name on the spine. And, of course, your statement is incompatible with what we know about Tenumbra's collection. Look again at the Ruth Rendell collection. It contains *all* of her works, including those written under the Barbara Vine pseudonym."

Still clasping Harry Burke's hand, Elise Djuna looked up. "You're right, Ellery. And you're also right that I always feared that you'd eventually piece this together, the moment I saw you standing in the lobby of Quinn's apartment."

Elise turned to Harry, tears beginning to form in her eyes. "Harry, I'm so sorry to put you through this. I really do care deeply for you. And I had hoped, hoped against hope, that I could pull it off. It didn't matter so much before. When I did this, for Quinn, there was only me. I could have faced the future, not easily, but satisfied that what I did was completely justified. I hope you understand that it's completely different, now that I've found you. I'm just so sorry."

She brushed a tear from her cheek. "I knew it would come to this. That's why I brought along the Barnaby Ross books. I was willing to play the game of logic with you, Ellery, but I'm not about to continue fighting after checkmate."

Ellery continued to stare across the room. "There is one thing I'm still curious about. I know that you had Quinn's entry card, but how did you manage to approach Tenumbra in his own apartment?"

"That was easy," Elise replied. "I called Jason after I discovered Quinn's body and told him I was finally willing to part with some books from my own collection." From her purse, Elise pulled three more volumes: *The Detective Short Story*, *Queen's Quorum: A History of the Detective/Crime Story*, and *In the Queen's Parlor*. "When Jason knew I was willing to sell those books, he greeted me with open arms."

Ellery shook his head in amazement. "Of course. The same books Jason Tenumbra tried to acquire from me."

Elise squared her shoulders and looked directly into Ellery's eyes. "I guess it's time for you to call the police."

Ellery took a deep breath. "As I told Harry yesterday," he finally said, "I needed to think this matter through for a while. In my earlier years, it seemed to me that, once I'd solved a crime, it was not for me to judge whether punishment was deserved. Issues of justice, I always thought, were for the criminal justice system, not the detective. But I am older now. Perhaps wiser, but most certainly older."

He rose shakily. "Thank you for coming tonight, Elise. I'm sorry for what you've been through." Ellery reached across the table for her other hand. "I always greatly admired your father."

Then he turned to Burke. "As for you, Harry, you're a member of the NYPD and you can do as you wish, but personally I remain retired. I'm not calling anyone."

"It's funny you should phrase it that way, Ellery," Harry replied. "I gave notice of my own retirement this morning."

Ellery eased back into his chair, stretching ancient joints. "You know, Nikki," he said, "I think we should cap off this evening with some single malt. And perhaps"—he glanced across the room at the humidor—"perhaps I'll even have a nice evening pipe."

"I think," responded Nikki, "we can do the single malt, but after that you're going to bed."

Ellery Queen's ancient gray eyes narrowed in mock anger. "You know, Ms. Porter, you are the latest in what is now a long line of hard-nosed and obstinate women. This all started with your grandmother: first she invented her own name, then she refused to give it up, and then she passed it along to two more generations of self-assured, stubborn redheads. Who do you think you are to deny Ellery Queen a well-deserved evening pipe?"

"I know precisely who I am," Nikki responded. "And as I said, after that drink it will be time for bed, Grandfather."

Authors' Postscript: Readers interested in the back story of Ellery's friendship with Harry Burke should read Face to Face *by Ellery Queen, originally published in 1967 and available in hard copy and as an e-book from Amazon.*

PART II

Parodies

TEN MONTHS' BLUNDER

J.N. Williamson

Gerald "Jerry" Neal Williamson wrote over forty novels and countless short stories, earning a reputation principally as a master of horror and science fiction. He received the lifetime achievement award from the Horror Writers of America in 2003, and edited the primer How to Write Tales of Horror, Fantasy & Science Fiction *(Writers Digest Books, 1987). Notwithstanding all of this, his first published work was in fact a Sherlock Holmes pastiche, "The Terrible Death of Crosby, the Banker." He is represented here by his one and only Ellery Queen riff, a story positioned strongly on the parody side of the ledger.*

When Celery Keen walked into the back room of the old pawnshop, with its array of weapons spread across the wall and its owner crumpled on the floor, he found his father the inspector glowering at a motley trio of men.

Sergeant Realie leaned one of his seven-foot-wide shoulders against the door, which caved in, and growled, "Look out for that there rug, Mr. Keen, sir."

"Ah," said Celery brightly, falling to his knees and running his silver eyes across the rug. "Splendid! Either an Axminster or an original Jacquard. As it nears the maximum of a hundred and twenty-eight tufts to the square inch, the probability resides with the former."

"I only meant that it was a throw rug, and I was afraid you'd slip on it," growled Sergeant Realie, as he pried his shoulder out of the door. "I know how hard it is for you to see with them pants-nays pinchin' your sinuses."

Celery clucked like a chicken—one of his better impressions—and stood up. "Ah, Dad, I see you are interrogating the suspects. Please don't forget Dr. Samuel Johnson: 'Questioning is not the mode of conversation among gentlemen.'"

The inspector said peevishly, "'Lo, son. You been hittin' the Bartlett's again?"

"Just a small solution," Celery declared.

"That's all I'm looking for," said the aged inspector, glowering for practice. "This case is in your line."

"Ah. Indeed?" Celery's silver eyes glittered. "Splendid. Tell me, have you identified yonder *corpus*?"

"Yonder *corpus* is Orebaugh Christy, owner of the pawnshop."

"So! *Corpus* Christy. Is he from Texas?"

"What do you make of the message on the wall?"

Celery's sharp sensitive sensible silver gaze scrutinized the wall. "Ah! The word FAN—in Christy's own blood!"

As he spoke, Celery whipped a tape measure and a large magnifying glass from his pocket. Then he trotted noiselessly around the room, sometimes stopping, occasionally kneeling, and once lying flat on his face (when he tripped on the throw rug). The other men in the room were irresistibly reminded of a pure-blooded, well-trained foxhound. At last he stopped.

"Tell me, Dad, what have you found out about the array of weapons on the wall above the bloody word?"

"This old man Christy was a real eccentric. Only interest he had in life was his collection of guns."

"A splendid display, too." Celery's thin nostrils began to quiver. "Colt single-actions, muskets, fowling pieces, breech loaders, shotguns and rifles, even blunderbusses and derringers."

"Nice job of reading the signs, son. Now help me with the questioning. These three characters here are Christy's only friends: Righty Dugan, Angelo Angelissimo, and Lefty Bilphrick."

"Indeed. You, Mr. Dugan," began Celery, inserting Turkish tobacco into his portable hookah. "May I ask how you happened to lose your left arm?"

"I turned around in a subway at rush hour."

"Are you married?"

"Naw, I'm a nut for night baseball. Lefty here, he was my hero."

"Commendable. We'll get to Lefty in a moment. You, Mr. Angelissimo. How did you happen to know the late Orebaugh Christy?"

"I happen to know the late Orebaugh Christy because we both were wild about guns."

"Oh? Are you a collector?"

"No, I'm a crook."

Celery Keen's silver eyes seldom missed a trick. "That paper fan you have there. You carry it with you everywhere, Mr. Angelissimo?"

"Yeah, I carry it with me everywhere I go. It was a gift from my gypsy sweetheart, Gay Lombardo. She stopped going with me, though, because I was a ordinary crook without no future." Angelo wept a little. "I lost confidence in myself."

"Perhaps that's why you're a confidence man. 'The prickly thorn often bears soft roses,' said Ovid."

"What team did he manage?" Lefty Bilphrick inquired.

"I remember you from your halcyon days, Mr. Bilphrick. An all-time great pitcher, a phenomenal strikeout artist, till you injured your throwing arm while tossing a shortstop at the umpire. Tell me, Lefty: now that the golden days are gone, what does such a marvelous athlete do with his time?"

"I drink. I think everybody should have a hobby."

"Commendable. Now, then, the murder weapon." Celery squinted at the Colt single-action revolver beside the body. "Ah. Trigger's been filed off. Just as I thought. Well, Dad, I've solved the case."

"Oh, not again," moaned the inspector. "Well, go into your explanation and let's get on to the denouement."

"Angelo, you carry the gypsy fan a sweetheart gave you. The scarlet word could refer to you. Lefty, I think you struck out twenty-four men in one game, years ago."

"I had a lousy catcher," said Lefty. "He kept dropping the shortstop."

"And the word 'fan' is a sports term indicating a strikeout. You could be our guilty party. Now, Righty. You spend all your time watching baseball. That makes you a fan, so you, too, fit the bloody description."

"Go ride a subway," Righty suggested.

"Oh, you're innocent enough. Because Orebaugh Christy was trying to tell us that the murder weapon is a *fanner*. He couldn't finish the word before he died. Dad, two hands are needed to fire a fanner. In the days of the Old West, a gunman held the fanner against his right hip and used his left hand to knock the hammer back and fire the cartridge. Having only one arm, Righty must be innocent."

"Then that lets me out," said Lefty. "My throwin' arm is shot."

Celery Keen puffed out his slender chest. "By the process of elimination, that leaves one person."

"It's my environment," said Angelo bitterly. "I was an underprivileged gypsy. Momma was so poor she couldn't afford a crystal ball. I swiped a basketball for her from the school gym."

"Well, that's the way the ball bounces," murmured Celery.

Ten months passed, during which the reputation of Celery Keen, great amateur sleuth, spread across the world. He was called to London,

Paris, Hong Kong, Montreal, becoming despised by every law enforcement officer on Earth. Weary of his travels, Celery at last returned to New York.

"Son," said the aged inspector with a glower, "I been trying to reach you for nearly a year. Remember that pawnshop case about the gun collector?"

Celery nodded. "I was a veritable wizard in that case, Dad."

"Except," the inspector said wearily, "you forgot that, if a fanner could only be fired by two hands—"

"Yes?"

"It could be fired by *two one-handed men!* They finally confessed."

"They?" asked Celery faintly. "Who?"

"It seems Angelo held Christy in his chair. Righty held the Colt in his right hand and Lefty used his good left hand to knock back the hammer. Righty and Lefty confessed this morning—all three of 'em were guilty, son."

Celery Keen was lost in thought. Then his silver eyes took on a strange sparkle. "Dad? Does anyone else know about this?"

"Nope, son," said the old man. "Just me. I finally solved a case by myself."

Celery located the fanner in his desk drawer. "'Success is counted sweetest/By those who ne'er succeed,' according to Emily Dickinson."

Celery leveled the revolver. "Congratulations, Dad."

THE ENGLISH VILLAGE MYSTERY

Arthur Porges

Arthur Porges wrote only short stories, but—in his heyday, in the '50s and '60s—he wrote them prodigiously; it was not uncommon for his work to appear in three or four different magazines in a given month. A literary disciple of Anthony Boucher, Porges was a master of the impossible-crime and scientific-puzzle mystery. Sometimes, however, he dabbled in more humorous realms, authoring several Sherlock Holmes parodies featuring his own detective, Stately Homes. Porges also wrote two Ellery Queen parodies, each very tongue-in-cheek. "The English Village Mystery" was the first of them, followed by "The Indian Diamond Mystery."

Inspector Dewe East found himself in a most annoying predicament. With a promotion to assistant commissioner about to be awarded either to him or to Inspector South, East had the bad luck to be stuck with the most difficult case of his career. If he bungled it, the prize would fall to his rival.

East's superior, Commissioner North, a cold, blustery type, was obviously displeased.

"I'm not an unreasonable man," he growled, "but, after all, twelve murders in one village—and not a single clue to the identity of the criminal. It just won't do, East."

"I know," the inspector said glumly. "But they happened so fast. A dozen killings in two weeks. Somebody must be taking a course in Speed Murder," he added, hoping to release some of the tension, but the quip only made Commissioner North more furious.

"Don't make jokes!" he roared. "This is a serious matter. It's not as if the murders happened in London. Big population there, so nobody misses twelve people. But Tottering-on-the-Brink is the smallest community in all England. Fourteen permanent inhabitants—and twelve already killed. Only two left—you must have *some* idea who the murderer is, East!"

"The whole thing's so irrational," the inspector said. "No rhyme or reason to it—and not a smidgen of motive. But in a few more days, I hope—"

"By then, the village will be only a memory," North grunted. "And we'll be accused of messing up English history. I'll give you exactly forty-eight hours—not one minute more. After that, South gets the assignment."

He didn't say anything about the promotion, but East had no illusions. It was a matter of solve the case or lose out as new assistant commissioner.

"I'll get him," East said with cold determination. "You may count on it, sir."

"I just hope he doesn't get you," North said ungraciously. "So far, he's way ahead on points. Well, go to it, man."

In his desperation, East decided to do the unforgivable and consult a famous private detective. This was bad enough, since the Yard frowned on dealing with amateurs, but even worse was the fellow's non-English origin: he was an American, brash, airy, sometimes flippant, and given to hasty conclusions unsuited to the slow ways of British criminals. They objected to being captured before getting a good start on the job; always in a hurry, these blasted Yanks.

East knew that the American detective frequented a certain club when he visited London, and he found him there. It was not possible to miss him—he was so young, so cheerful, so self-assured. His name was Celery Green.

The American welcomed East with a warm smile and led him to a secluded corner.

"Now then, Inspector," he said. "What can I do for you?"

"I've got just a few hours to catch a very clever killer," East explained. "I've never asked for help in my life before, but this is a crisis."

"What are the circumstances?" Celery Green was no longer the nonchalant dilettante.

"Twelve murders. No motive. No point to them. Not a clue. That's the whole story in a nutshell."

"Who were the victims?" Celery said crisply.

"They all lived in Tottering-on-the-Brink. You've heard of it—the smallest village in England. Total population: fourteen people. No, fifteen now—a Mrs. Willow moved in three weeks ago. It isn't everybody can increase the population of a place by more than seven percent," he added.

"An outsider, eh?" Celery looked thoughtful. "Surely an obvious suspect. Why not pick her up and—"

"Not so fast," East objected. "Not so obvious a suspect as you might think. In most of the murders, the killer must have been known to the suspect, d'you see. They're a suspicious, insular lot there in Tottering. No one who hadn't lived in town for decades could get into the homes or stand alongside the victims. The last person—before Mrs. Willow—to come there was Miss Bristol, and they called her 'the stranger' for sixteen years, I'm told."

"The same sort of thing happens in New England," Celery admitted. "I could tell you about a town called Wrightsville—but carry on, Inspector."

"I can give you the names of the victims, as well as other information about them," East suggested.

"Good—let's have it." Celery was crisp again. "And details about the murder weapons, if you please."

East took out his notebook. "Let's see. The first to be murdered was Elsie Fyfe—stabbed through the heart from behind. Then came George Barton; somebody dropped a huge box of groceries—mainly tinned stuff, which is heavy—on him from a bluff over the ocean. He was lying on the sand; horrible mess. Besides being bashed, he was drowned in tinned soup.

"Major Pickett-Hall came next; he was banged on the head. Ram Dass, a Hindu, was killed in his garage—knocked out, and then finished off with car exhaust. Jane Hope was strangled, and so was Norman Quire. Harry Block had his skull smashed in with a big stone. Walter Lord was decapitated—'orrible!" In his agitation, the inspector lost an "h."

"That's eight." Celery was counting on his fingers. "Four more to go."

"Right—I have them all listed. The ninth was Amy Bristol—I believe I mentioned her. She was shot through the heart. And John Mahony: he was poisoned, and not quickly, either. Bad show, that. The came Mabel Slaughter; she was drowned in her own bathtub."

"More likely than being drowned in someone else's," Celery said drily. "That makes eleven. One more to go. Who was last?"

"Allen Gladstone Rigg-White, the mayor; fancy that. Blown to bits, poor chap."

Celery's silver eyes shone, and East held his breath. It was said that this energetic young American had amazed professionals with his brilliance. Was he the magician he was reputed to be? Would he pull a rabbit out of his hat? Inspector East almost wished he had some lettuce handy.

"Let me take your list," Celery was saying. "And the details about the weapons."

"It's all down in here," East said, laying the notebook on the table. "I certainly hope you can find some kind of pattern—it baffles me completely. And now there are only three left alive. One *must* be the killer. If we don't get him, Tottering-on-the-Brink will become a ghost town. An English village will have vanished from the face of the Earth." East sighed.

"No time for sentiment," Celery said briskly. "And the three survivors?"

"The newcomer, Mrs. Adele Willow, a Hector Guedalla, and a Miss Orange."

The great American detective rose. "Go home, Inspector, get a good night's sleep, and come back here tomorrow morning. I'll have the solution by then."

East gaped at him.

"How can you be so sure?"

"I'm conceited," Celery said frankly. "See you tomorrow, Inspector."

East thanked him in a choked voice and, with his eyes slightly glazed, left. He hoped this brash young man could keep his promise. It was East's only chance for the coveted promotion.

Early the next morning, Inspector East made a beeline for the club. Sure enough, Celery Green was already there, quivering with suppressed energy.

"Any luck?" the inspector demanded eagerly.

"It's not a matter of luck," the young detective said, trying to sound casual. "It's a matter of brains, imagination, and, above all, of logic."

East mumbled an apology.

"We'll go to Tottering-on-the-Brink at once," Celery said crunchily, "and capture our killer."

"But who—?" East began, only to be interrupted by a page.

"You're wanted on the telephone, Inspector," the page said.

With an exclamation of impatience, East strode off. When he returned, his eyes were hard.

"Guedalla's been killed," he reported. "Now we're down to just two—and both women, by gad!"

"Guedalla killed?" Celery exclaimed, his voice pithy with astonishment. "But that's impossible! How did it happen?"

"Run down by a car," East said savagely. "One of those huge American things," he added, giving Celery a reproachful look.

Celery shook his head slowly.

"If I weren't infallible," he said, "I'd almost think my solution was wrong. But if not Guedalla," he murmured, "then it must be—of course!" He grabbed East's arm. "We've got to hurry," he said. "Mrs. Willow is in great danger. She's due to be smothered any minute!"

"But—but—" the inspector objected, only to be hustled out to Celery's car, an ancient Duesenberg. Moments later, they were tearing through London on the way to Tottering-on-the-Brink.

When they arrived at the village, which was oddly quiet—thanks, no doubt, to the devastating drop in population—Celery had East direct him to Mrs. Willow's house. To their delight, the woman was unharmed. Nobody had been near her, she said; my, weren't things quiet today?

The two men withdrew, East giving her a suspicious stare.

"She's killed Miss Orange," Celery muttered. "But how was it done? It's just not possible! Is my theory all wrong?" His voice died away to a querulous mumble.

The inspector was bursting with curiosity, but he realized this was no time to ask questions. Instead, he led the way to Miss Orange's cottage. There, a distressing sight awaited them. The dowdy, plump body of the owner of the cottage was hanging by a rope at the back of the house.

"This makes no sense at all!" East exclaimed. "Wait. Mrs. Willow must have hanged the poor woman—that's it." He turned to Celery. "We must stop that killer before—"

He broke off, remembering with a shock that, if Mrs. Willow were guilty, eventually to be hanged, it was too late for Tottering-on-the-Brink: its population would be zero.

"Forget the Willow woman," Celery said calmly. "Look at the note that Miss Orange left." He handed it to East.

The inspector read it, his eyes popping.

"Suicide," he groaned. His face showed bewilderment. "I don't understand any of this, Celery."

"It's quite simple," the young American assured him. "Let's examine those names and weapons again. Elsie Fyfe—stabbed by a knife. George Barton—crushed by a carton. Ram Dass—suffocated with gas. Pickett-Hall—bashed by a round object, hard and heavy. I'd say a cricket ball! Don't you see? Fyfe—knife. Barton—carton. Dass—gas. Pickett-Hall—cricket ball."

East gulped. "But—but—" he gurgled.

"Coincidences? Is that what you're thinking? Then let me go on," Celery crackled. "Jane Hope—strangled with a rope. Norman Quire was also strangled—with a copper wire. And Harry Block's head was smashed, not with a stone, but with a rock. Walter Lord—decapitated with a sword."

"You mean—" East began thickly.

"Let me finish. Amy Bristol—shot with a pistol. John Mahony— poisoned with antimony…slow and nasty, as you said. And Mabel Slaughter was drowned in her bath. She died from"—he paused dramatically—"water."

The inspector had himself under control again, his trained mind working efficiently. "Look, Celery," he protested. "What about Rigg-White? That scuttles your theory—names and weapons rhyming. What murder weapon rhymes with Rigg-White?"

The younger man smiled. "Rigg-White was blown up," he reminded East. "You wrote down the means yourself in your notebook. Rigg-White—gelignite. Q.E.D."

"I must say," the inspector admitted weakly, "it does seem logical— in a peculiar sort of way. But who—?"

"A mad poet, of course. I saw that late last night," Celery said. "For a short time I thought it was Guedalla. But when he too was killed, I thought—but never mind. Miss Orange was our murderess."

"But why did she commit suicide? And what kept her from killing the Willow woman?"

"Ah," Celery said. "That's the crux of the matter. Think of this, East: all of the victims were either men or unmarried women—in short, people who use their own surnames. Now Miss Orange obviously hated all those whose names could be rhymed; hers couldn't, you know. No sonnets or love poems from the boys for Miss Orange. So she set about to kill the others, and always with a weapon that rhymed with the victim's name. Simple, isn't it?"

"But what about Mrs. Willow? She could have been smothered with a pillow—you did say she was in danger of being smothered."

"Or drowned in a billow," Celery added complacently. "But look at this copy of the local paper, printed before Miss Orange—ah—removed the editor. It mentions that Mrs. Willow's maiden name was Silver. Now, there's no rhyme for 'silver' in the English language. Miss Orange was so frustrated that, being obviously unbalanced anyway, she killed herself instead. She couldn't, in all conscience, murder Mrs. Willow under her husband's name. You see that, of course."

"It's all clear now," East said. "Maybe the commissioner will go easy in the circumstances. A very baffling case—the most baffling in the history of Scotland Yard." Then his face darkened. "Half a mo', Celery. What about Guedalla? What about him, hey?"

"The big American car that ran him down," Celery said, smiling triumphantly. "Without even checking—a pound to a ha'penny, Inspector—I'm betting it was an Impala!"

And Celery stalked off.

ELROY QUINN'S LAST CASE

Dennis M. Dubin

Dennis Dubin submitted the following story to EQMM *when he was a high-school senior, and its publication in the July 1967 issue made him one of the youngest authors ever to appear in the magazine. The story itself is an unusual mixture of parody and pastiche, defying easy categorization. Frederic Dannay's introduction concluded: "Be prepared—young Dennis will undoubtedly ride again!" Despite diligent application of our own sleuthing skills, though, we have unearthed no further information concerning the author or any subsequent published works. We are left to conclude that "Elroy Quinn's Last Case" was Dubin's sole contribution to detective fiction. It's a pity: it would have been fun to see what he might have come up with next!*

Sharp shadows were falling through the yellowed slats of the venetian blinds as Elroy Quinn groaned softly and adjusted himself and the book he was reading to take advantage of the failing light. No sooner was he more comfortable than he was startled by the ringing of the telephone. Moving slowly, he got up and groped for the receiver in the dimness.

My eyes are worse than ever, Elroy thought grimly.

Long ago, he had discarded his pince-nez for thicker, stronger lenses. Locating the telephone at last, he put it to his ear with a trembling hand. "Hello?" he said, in a low, gentle voice.

"Elroy?" came a firm deep basso in reply.

"Tom, Junior! I haven't heard from you for a year. Or more. What's the word in town?"

"The word is *crazy*. There's been a peculiar murder, the sort of thing you used to investigate with Dad. Interested?"

Elroy cackled with delight. "What is it, a dying message or a fantastic clue?"

"Could be either or both. Feel up to it? Say yes and I'll have a car around in half an hour."

"Yes!" shot back the enthusiastic if quavery reply.

"As you've probably read in the papers," said Inspector Thomas Velie, Junior, to Elroy as they traveled to the scene of the crime, "the king of Ubinorabia arrived here two days ago to begin talks on the huge oil deposit recently discovered in his country. The situation is explosive, to say the least. This is the first time since the Sixties that East and West will be sitting across a conference table and discussing something peacefully. Any incident, no matter how trivial, could lead to a breakup of the conference. And if that happens, the rift between the hemispheres will be widened beyond any possible negotiation."

Elroy whistled softly. "Things that bad? I've been a little out of touch, you know."

"Worse! Yet both sides want peace. It's just that they want other things, too. Like this oil. Well, anyway, the only sure way to break up the conference would be to get rid of the king. Then his son—"

"Son?"

"He's got one son, the heir of course to the throne. No one knows much about him; he's been at exclusive private schools in England since he was five. The point is that he's rumored to be violently opposed to the United States. If he were king, there'd be no conference. And there are men who would do almost anything to see him on the throne for that very reason."

Velie paused, then resumed in a low, hard voice. "Elroy," he said slowly, "I got a call from the Big Man himself. He said that this conference may be the last chance for world peace. He said that, if something happened to the king and his son were to ascend the throne, there'd be the devil to pay. Those were his exact words. Elroy, I can't let that happen."

"From what you've said, I assume the dead man is not the king. Then who is it?"

"It's one of the king's bodyguards, a man named Daja-nuna. He— wait, here we are."

They entered the sumptuous lobby of the city's newest hotel, where the king had taken an entire floor of rooms. Now it was bustling with police and reporters. Inspector Velie pushed his way into an elevator, herding Elroy in front of him. The elevator door slid shut, leaving a bewildered knot of reporters staring after them. In answer to an unspoken question, a grizzled long-faced veteran said suddenly, "That old guy— why, he looked like Elroy Quinn!"

"Aw, c'mon, Pop," said one of the younger journalists, "that would make him older than—than—"

His voice trailed off in embarrassment.

"There isn't much to tell," said Velie, as they gazed at the body sprawled on the luxurious bed. "According to this report that Doc Purty just sent up, death was instantaneous, resulting from a single bullet through the head."

"So there's no dying-message clue," Elroy muttered.

"No. But we've certainly got a fantastic one."

Both gazes shifted to the dead man's head, on which rested a gleaming, ornate plumed helmet such as had been used in the times of the gladiators and the arena.

"The way I see it," said Velie, "it was a case of mistaken identity. The king had just left to see the town. He took three of his bodyguards with him, and left this one behind to watch the rooms. Seeing that things were quiet, Daja-nuna must have lain down for a few moments. He fell asleep and was murdered by someone who thought that he was the king. He certainly does bear enough resemblance in size and build to be mistaken for him in the dark."

Velie turned to Elroy, only to find the old detective fingering a small statuette of two seemingly identical Thai cats and staring, unlistening, into space.

"What's that?" Velie demanded with ill-concealed annoyance.

"Curious," replied Elroy. "One of these cats has more than one tail."

Velie choked back an angry retort. He remembered how many times in the past Elroy had placed emphasis on the most trivial points, and how invariably they had turned out to be significant clues. "You think it's important?" he asked.

"If the king or one of his servants is around, you might ask them where this statuette came from."

Velie frowned, then handed the statuette to one of his men. After a whispered conference, the man left. He returned shortly and again conferred with Velie. Velie's eyebrows nearly shot off his head in surprise.

"Why, you old fox! Three servants and the king himself all swear they've never seen that statuette before."

Elroy sighed. "Then we have two clues, a gladiator's helmet and a pair of cats, one with a plethora of tails. Find the connection, and I think it will point directly at the murderer."

"It's beyond me," said Velie as they left. "I told you—it's your kind of case. Just like old times, Elroy."

They drove in a silence that was interrupted only when Elroy had a sudden long coughing spell. It reminded Velie of his passenger's age, and he decreased his speed.

"You'll be sure to phone me if something else turns up?" said Elroy as they parted.

"Of course. And if something occurs to *you*, you'll phone me personally at headquarters?"

"You can count on it. Thanks for calling me in, Tom—it *was* like old times."

"Yeah," said Velie. "'Night."

"'Night."

Two days later, Elroy himself answered the doorbell to find Velie standing there, his face flushed with excitement.

"There's been a new development. Thought I'd bring along the news—and the new clues with it." Reaching into a sack, he withdrew a large-sized sabot. Inside the wooden shoe was a small replica of a mummy case, oddly decorated and inscribed.

"No fingerprints, naturally," murmured Elroy.

"No. These were left near the king's bed, in the same place you found the statuette. We had a man watching the king's suite while he was out, but he was knocked on the head. Not very hard—just enough to daze him for a few minutes. But he didn't see the intruder." Velie paused. "Well, what do you think? Can you translate that red writing inside the mummy case?"

Elroy examined the miniature sarcophagus. "The inscription is in Greek."

"Greek! What does it say?"

"It's hard to read," said Elroy, squinting at the bright red lettering, "but, roughly translated, it means 'the beginning of crime.'"

"Too much for me," grumbled Velie. "I just don't get it."

"Not too puzzling—in fact, some of this business is quite obvious. Perhaps *too* obvious!" There was a trace of an old habit in Elroy's teasing drawl. "The murderer certainly intends to kill the king. But the death of Daja-nuna was not a case of mistaken identity. He was killed for another reason—most likely because he surprised the murderer in the act of trespassing in the king's suite."

"I don't follow you."

"The murderer *knew* that the king was away. That's why he came. He didn't expect anyone to be there."

"Then why did he come at all, if he intended to kill the king?"

"To plant his first clues—the helmet and the two cats. Just as he came last night to plant the shoe and the sarcophagus."

Velie thought for a moment. "Maybe he planted the clues just to taunt the police."

"I thought of that, but there are three objections. First, *no* murderer would carry such bulky objects on his person, knowing that his intended victim would be heavily guarded and therefore difficult to kill. Second, if the murderer wanted to plant clues after the murder of the king, why did he leave them after murdering the wrong man? He must have known that Daja-nuna was not the king as soon as he got close enough to put the helmet on his head. And, third, if the killer wanted to plant clues only after the king's death, why break into his rooms a second time, risking everything, to plant new clues?

"No," Elroy continued, "it seems quite obvious that the clues were meant to be planted *before* the assassination of the king. They are a challenge to the police to discover the murderer's identity *before* he kills the king. Or perhaps the murderer is just 'playing fair,' trusting the Fates to decide who will win, the killer or the police."

"Do you think, then, that he'll try to plant even more clues?"

"Very possibly. How soon does the king leave?"

"Not for another ten days, at least."

"Well, the killer certainly has plenty of time to plant more."

"Killing the king won't be easy now. Not only has he hired three more bodyguards, but I've detailed a dozen detectives to watch day and night. The biggest danger comes from the king himself. He insists on going out on the town—to the mangiest collection of nightclubs in the city. And he goes out every night"—Velie's voice lowered to a brief mutter, but Elroy distinctly heard the words—"the fat old lecher."

"Remember," Elroy interjected gently, "our man seems to know all about the king's movements."

"Well," said Velie, as he prepared to leave, "I'm doubling the police guard around the hotel. If he makes another attempt to plant his cryptic little clues, he'll be nabbed like *that*." He snapped his fingers.

"Meanwhile, Velie, we have to try to connect the clues we have now—to find out what meaning they have in common."

"I knew this was going to be a weird case, Elroy. That's why I called you in. 'Night."

"'Night," said Elroy softly, as he shut the door quickly to keep out the chill night air.

One blissful, peaceful, completely uneventful week passed. The cordon of men protecting the king began to relax. Relaxation, however, was not for Inspector Velie. He fretted and fumed and called Elroy daily. It seemed to Velie that the old master knew something—but Elroy would say nothing.

On the eighth day, it rained. It was a bitter, stinging rain that drove the city's citizens off the streets. By nightfall, the rain had changed into a thick, soupy London-type fog that swirled in the empty streets.

At nine that night, the king announced his intention of going to Club Midway, one of the shadier of the city's nightspots. The pleas and protests of his attendants and of the police escort were useless.

"The pompous old idiot!" snarled Velie, when one of his men telephoned the news. For a big man, he could move surprisingly fast; in less than ten minutes, he was in his car and speeding across the city in a furious race to intercept the king.

He was too late. He rounded the last corner on two wheels, just in time to hear the echoes of six quick rifle shots reverberating, then dying away. Even as he leaped from his car, hearing the cries of pursuit, he knew it was futile. The thickness of the fog made it easy for the murderer to escape.

But the king was not dead. Lying motionless in a hospital bed, he hovered between life and death. The doctors said that recovery was just as possible as death. It was an even bet.

The shots had been fired from the roof of a building across the way from the hotel. Here, Velie found his first understandable clue: an expensive rifle manufactured by a famous American firm. Tracing the owner was easy—too easy. Velie followed the trail to a shabby apartment in a squalid section of town. But nobody had ever seen the occupant—the landlady got her rent, and that was all she knew or cared about.

Inside the apartment, Velie found nothing except the box the gun had come in when it had been shipped to the address. Opening it, he found a note that read:

"For the *coup de grâce*—to end a king's life."

That was all. No fingerprints, no description of the occupant—nothing more to track down.

Velie had reached a dead end.

For the next ten days, as the world wondered and watched, Velie drove his staff mercilessly. Informers were paid huge sums, every tip was investigated, every wild theory was weighed and examined. The only interesting fact turned up in those ten days was that the king's son had not appeared, either to disrupt the conference or to claim the throne during his father's disability.

In the middle of the afternoon of the tenth day, the vision of the stooped, shrunken figure of Elroy Quinn flashed in Velie's bloodshot eyes. Suddenly it seemed to Velie that the only man in the world who could put all the clues together and name the killer, just by the power of his logical, deducto-analytic brain, was Elroy Quinn. "The old fox must know *something*," Velie mused aloud. He ate a quick lunch and drove out to see the great man himself.

He was met at the door by a stern and frowning doctor. From somewhere deep in the recesses of the house came a prolonged outburst of coughing. Then a hoarse voice called weakly, "Who's there, Doctor?"

"Tell him it's Tom Velie."

The doctor's countenance changed instantly. "Mr. Velie, you must be psychic! He's been asking for you. The poor man's in bad shape. At his advanced age, you know—"

Velie waited to hear no more. He shouldered past the doctor and into the sickroom. Elroy lay propped against pillows, a tall thin scarecrow of pajama and bone. His obvious relief at seeing Velie brought on another racking spell. But finally the old man, pale as death, his emaciated body quivering, pulled himself together—for a last effort.

"The mystery is solved," Elroy said hoarsely, his voice barely a whisper. "I wanted to tell you, but I was too ill. The king is not dead yet, is he?"

"No, the doctors say it could go either way. And you, you lively old fox—"

"This is the end of the line for me, I'm afraid." He cackled suddenly. "But I *am* an old fox, eh?" For a moment, his eyes flashed silver, as they had so often in the past.

Velie frowned and turned slightly away. It agonized him to see Elroy Quinn so obviously on his deathbed.

Elroy caught the movement and its meaning. "The murderer is a fox," he explained, with a crooked smile. Then he grimaced and shut his eyes in pain. When he opened them again, the dying man and the inspector stared at each other wordlessly for several seconds. Then Elroy said, in a startlingly strong voice, "I shot the king. There's a full report of my methods and motives in the drawer of my desk."

"You!" Velie gasped. "*You?*"

"Yes." The answer was as firm and steady as his gaze.

Velie was at a total loss. The world spun like a pinwheel, and then a whirlpool seemed to pull him down, threatening to drown him. He struggled for air. "Why? Just tell me—*why?*"

"Too long a story—haven't the strength—"

Then, summoning his last reserves, Elroy sat up slightly. When he spoke again, his voice was weak but surprisingly clear.

"I'll try to explain. As I've grown older, I've watched the world divide into two conflicting forces, with destruction inescapable for both sides. Then I learned of this conference, a giant step toward world peace, and I was determined that it must not fail. To ensure its success, I decided to investigate the force I knew was working toward the failure of the conference, and I unearthed a diabolical plot. If this conspiracy had succeeded in wrecking the conference, the world might be blowing itself apart at this very moment.

"Proof of the plot? I can give you nothing tangible, nothing to show the CIA or the FBI. I pieced it together from hundreds of fragments of information and hundreds of logical deductions based on those fragments. My problem was not to provide proof, or to expose the plot to the world. Had I tried to do either, the conference would certainly have been called off. No, my problem was to find a way to destroy the conspiracy, so that the conference could continue its work for world peace."

Velie could restrain himself no longer. "What plot?"

"Simply to kill the king and thus have his son ascend to the throne. But—the king himself was one of the plotters. The king was a dying man, and he knew it. He was completely under the influence of his son, the primary plotter, for whom he would do anything—"

"Wait a minute," interrupted Velie. "If the son had so much influence over the king, why didn't he just tell his father to abdicate?"

"The people of Ubinorabia would have revolted—it's all in my report."

These last words were smothered in a sustained attack of coughing. Finally Elroy resumed, his voice and manner noticeably weaker. "Taking all the factors of the problem into consideration, I came to the only possible solution—I killed the son."

"What?" sputtered Velie. "But you shot the king, not the son!"

"No. I did shoot the king—but I killed the son first. With one bullet through the head."

"Daja-nuna!" Velie smacked his forehead with the palm of his hand. "He wasn't a bodyguard—he was the son, accompanying his father in disguise. And when the son didn't show up later—how stupid of me not to think of it!"

"If Daja-nuna *had* been an innocent bodyguard who had caught me trespassing in the king's suite," said Elroy, "I could never have brought myself to kill him. It is not in me to kill the innocent." He paused for breath. "Once the son was dead, I thought the threat to world peace was over. But it wasn't. The king formed a violent hatred for this country, blaming it for his son's death. He made up his mind to wreck the conference himself, if only to honor his son's ambition. But he needed help— that's why he went to those shady nightclubs every night, to make contact with his son's accomplices. I had to shoot him before he could act on whatever advice the others gave him."

Elroy's voice faded, and he stared, glassy-eyed, at the ceiling. Silence lay heavy in the little room. Elroy broke it at last, mumbling, "Eyes no longer any good…I missed him…he's not dead." Then, with an almost superhuman effort, he raised himself and spoke clearly once again. "Face to face," the words tumbled out. "Don't you see, I had to come face to face with the problem and solve it the only way it *could* be solved. With both the king and his son dead, Ubinorabia will now be plunged into a huge power struggle. East and West will *have* to meet face to face over the conference table to prevent the ensuing civil war from escalating into a world conflict. Yes, it had to be done. I had to do it." His voice cracked, and he fell silent again.

This time, Velie broke the silence.

"But what about all those crazy clues: the helmet, the cats, the shoe, the sarcophagus. And the rifle with the strange message. That one came *after* the king was shot—"

"I had to leave one last clue—so you would come back here to see me—so I could explain—confess." Elroy's energy was draining fast. "I left the clues so they would point to me, only to me—"

"How in God's name did they point to *you*?"

Elroy managed a pathetic smile. "Names of my books—you know them, Velie. Gladiator helmet—*The Roman Hat Mystery.* Two Thai cats, one with more than one tail—*The Siamese Twin Mystery* and *Cat of Many Tails*. Sabot—*The Dutch Shoe Mystery.* Mummy case and inscription—*The Greek Coffin* and *The Scarlet Letters* and *The Origin of Evil.* Shot both with *The American Gun.* And all the others, throughout the case: *The Devil to Pay, Halfway House, And on the Eighth Day, Ten Days' Wonder, The Finishing Stroke*…and *The Murderer is a Fox*, you said it yourself, Velie. Yes, you were *Face to Face* with them—you know them, you've read them all—*The Player on the Other Side*—played fair with you—always have, always have.…"

Elroy's voice was suddenly filled with infinite weariness.

The door behind Velie opened, and the doctor entered. "Phone call for you, Mr. Velie."

Velie returned in a few minutes and stared at Elroy's parchment face until the sunken eyes flickered open.

"*The King is Dead,*" said Velie, continuing the inevitable pattern.

Elroy sighed—as if he understood that it had all been predestined. Then, reverting again to an old habit, he said: "Sleep after toil, port after stormy seas. Ease after war, death after life doth greatly please."

Elroy's last words were: "Edmund Spenser, *The Faerie Queene.*"

His eyes flashed silver—for only a moment. Then they closed, and his head bent toward the far window.

PART III

Potpourri

THE NORWEGIAN APPLE MYSTERY

James Holding

Between 1960 and 1972, James Holding—who ghosted three books in the Ellery Queen, Jr. series—wrote a total of ten short mystery stories, each of which takes place on a round-the-world cruise, recounting the adventures of the writing team of King Danforth and Martin Leroy, creators of the detective Leroy King. "The Norwegian Apple Mystery," published in the November 1960 EQMM, was the first in the series. All ten of the Danforth and Leroy stories have now been collected in one volume, The Zanzibar Shirt Mystery *(Crippen & Landru, 2018).*

Two hours after the stewardess found Angela Cameron lying dead in her bed in Cabin A-12, the news was all over the ship. That was pretty good going, even allowing for the fact that rumor is commonly conceded to fly faster on a ship at sea than anywhere else.

Most of the cruise passengers, of course, after forty-five days afloat, were eager for something besides shore excursions and shopping triumphs to gossip about; they seized this tidbit avidly, chewed it over, and passed it on to their neighbors with unusual celerity. Sunning themselves idly in the gaily striped deck chairs of the Norwegian cruise ship *Valhalla* as she plowed through the South China Sea toward Hong Kong, they chattered about Miss Cameron's death like a flock of hungry sparrows that suddenly discovers a slice of bread on the snow.

Despite the animation with which the passengers discussed the event, however, a general feeling of regret and even sadness spread with the news. For Angela Cameron had not only been vivacious, intelligent, pretty, and liberally endowed with sex appeal, she had actually been as well liked by the women passengers as by the men—which is saying a great deal for an attractive young woman traveling alone on a luxury cruise around the world.

The Danforths and the Leroys were sitting in the Promenade Bar, having a pre-luncheon gimlet, when they were first apprised of the fact that there had been a death on board. As the bar steward leaned forward to deposit a dish of salted nuts on their table, he said to King Danforth in a solemn undertone, "Too bad about Miss Cameron, sir."

Helen Leroy, who was blond, vital, and fast off the mark, spoke up before Danforth could say anything. "Miss Cameron?" she asked of the steward. "What about her, Eric?"

"I'm sorry, Madam," the Norwegian bar steward said in his stiff English, "I thought you might have heard. Miss Cameron is dead. Edith, her stewardess, found her this morning. She died while reading in bed."

"Oh, dear, what a shame," Carol Danforth said with instant sympathy. "She was such a lovely person. And how awful for Edith. What was it, Eric? Did Miss Cameron have a heart attack?"

"No, Madam," Eric said. "She choked to death on a bite of apple."

King Danforth and Martin Leroy exchanged glances. Death was no stranger to them. Indeed, they made a living from it. Under the pseudonym of Leroy King, the two men operated with fabulous success as a writing team specializing in stories of murder, mystery, and crime. Several dozen best-selling novels, scores of short stories, and numerous television and movie scripts about murder had made them world-famous. And here, on a cruise with their wives to get away from it all, the bar steward was saying—it might well have leapt directly from the page of one of their own mysteries—"No, Madam. She choked to death on a bite of apple."

Pressed by Helen and Carol, Eric gave them the details. It was obvious that the story had swept through the ship's crew like a brushfire in the Hollywood Hills. Miss Cameron usually had breakfast in her cabin. So Edith, her stewardess, unless warned away by a "Do Not Disturb" sign on the door of A-12, would normally enter Miss Cameron's cabin at ten o'clock, using her passkey, wake the lady, and take her breakfast order.

This morning, however, Miss Cameron had not awakened, nor did she need breakfast. Edith had found her clad in her nightgown, propped up against the pillows on her bed, a book fallen from one hand and a half-eaten apple from the other, her face dreadfully discolored and distorted, and her flesh beginning to turn cold. The reading lamp was still burning.

Although Miss Cameron was quite obviously past help, Edith had put through a hurried call for the ship's doctor. He was able only to confirm that poor Miss Cameron was indeed dead, and to point out the cause: a large fragment of the apple she had been eating was wedged tightly in her throat.

When the bar steward left them to their gimlets, Danforth wriggled his lanky frame in his chair, ran a hand over his crew cut, and said, a trifle sheepishly, "I am not callous and unfeeling about things like this. But I couldn't help thinking that *she choked to death on a bite of apple* would fit very well into one of our stories, Mart."

"I had the same thought," Leroy said, grinning. His dark eyes, short wide face, and compact body suggested Indian impassivity, but he denied it with every word and movement. "It's almost like being home again, working out a plot."

"Whoa, boys," Helen Leroy said. "This a vacation, remember? No plotting, no murder gimmicks, no looking for criminals to fit into stories—that was the agreement, right?"

"Right," Carol Danforth agreed emphatically. She was short and dark, like her husband's partner, with a brisk way of speaking. "So forget about it. Miss Cameron died a perfectly natural accidental death—to coin a contradiction in terms. Let her alone."

"But what a starting point for a mystery!" Her husband's eyes kindled.

"The first thing we'd have to postulate," Martin picked him up instantly, "is that the girl did *not* die a 'perfectly natural accidental death,' as Carol insists, but was murdered."

"Of course," Danforth said. "That's where the challenge lies. In figuring out how this perfectly natural accidental death could be made to appear that way by a murderer."

"And how he murdered her, and where, and why."

"Exactly."

"And who he was."

Their wives saw with resignation that the two incurable story plotters had the bit in their teeth and were not to be headed off. So rather than nag—and mellowed, moreover, by the gimlets they were drinking—they sighed and entered into the discussion.

"Before you apply your keen analytical brains to the solving of this murder that doesn't exist," Carol Danforth said, "do you realize that there are approximately seven hundred and fifty suspects aboard this ship? Four hundred crew members and three hundred and fifty passengers? Isn't that a few too many even for you two geniuses to sift successfully?"

"Not at all," her husband said. "Motive. Surely not *all* of those people would have a motive for killing an attractive girl like Miss Cameron."

"Not likely," Leroy agreed, "unless everybody on board found out Miss Cameron was a typhoid carrier, or fatally radioactive, or something like that."

Danforth shook his head. "Farfetched. Very few people would commit murder as a public service, even under such circumstances. No, it's got to be something more credible than that."

Helen Leroy said, "Well, I'm no writer, thank goodness, but if you want to be logical about it, *I'd* suggest that for one minute of respectful silence you turn your brilliant deductive powers on Miss Cameron's exceptionally fine figure."

King Danforth patted her hand and leaned back to sip at his gimlet thoughtfully. "Now we're getting somewhere, my sweet. A sex killing. That's more like it. This girl was very beautiful and, if you'll pardon a vulgarism, sensationally stacked. Suppose somebody made a pass at her, was ruthlessly repulsed, and killed her out of sexual frustration?"

"Hear, hear," Helen Leroy said. She was watching through the bar window the lazily lifting swells of blue sea that carried small antimacassars of lacy foam on their crests. "I'm getting bored with all this supposing. Doesn't that water look good enough to swim in?"

"Speaking of swimming," Danforth murmured, "the girl, Miss Cameron, was quite a fine swimmer herself. I have seen her churning back and forth in the ship's indoor swimming pool on occasion."

"In a bathing suit?" Leroy inquired.

"Of course."

"Then you're in a position to speak with authority on her figure, King. Was it enough to make a man commit murder?"

"It was," Danforth said appreciatively.

"This is the first I knew you'd been sneaking down to the pool to watch Angela Cameron do the Australian crawl," Carol Danforth said sharply. "Luring husbands to swimming pools! No wonder she got herself murdered!"

"If you will be guided by my long experience as a plotter," Martin Leroy said hastily, "let us for the moment drop the motive and settle a few questions about method. She choked on an apple, remember."

"Easy," Danforth replied. "She was strangled first. The bite of apple was merely shoved down her throat by her murderer and wedged there for the doctor to find—so he would think exactly what he *did* think."

"Ah, but the bar steward said nothing about marks on the lady's throat that might indicate a manual strangling."

"The murderer didn't choke her with his hands. He garroted her."

"Impossible. A garrote cord would leave a plainly visible mark."

"Who said anything about a cord? The murderer used something soft to choke her—like a bed sheet or a bath towel."

"A bed sheet," Helen Leroy laughed. "You men!"

"That would narrow down the suspects, though," Leroy grinned. "It ought to eliminate all the women aboard."

"Be serious," Danforth said with a frown. "This is a problem levity will not solve."

"All right. Where are we? We've got a resisting Miss Cameron strangled by a murderer, hypothetically male, using, say, a bath towel. Where do we go from there?"

"To lunch," Carol Danforth said grimly. "I'm starved."

"Don't anybody order an apple for dessert," Danforth said.

Their table was in the *Valhalla*'s forward dining room, familiarly called the Runic Room. As they seated themselves for luncheon, they could tell from the buzz of conversation enlivening the usually sedate saloon that Miss Cameron's death was being discussed all about them. But adhering to their long-established rule that no business be discussed during meals—long-established by the wives—the Danforths and the Leroys talked about yesterday's shore trip to Bangkok, where they had been privileged to see the breathtaking temples, towers and *cheddis* of that holy city.

The cruise ship had anchored at dawn off the mouth of the Menam River, unable to enter because of the extensive sandbar that effectively blocks the entrance to oceangoing ships. A huge flat-bottomed barge, handled by Chinese seamen, had chugged majestically out to the *Valhalla* from shore, taken aboard almost all the *Valhalla*'s passengers, ferried them triumphantly over the sandbar, and three hours later disembarked them at the wharves of Bangkok, twenty-five miles upriver. The full day of sightseeing in hundred-degree heat that ensued had been wearying, but worth it, they all agreed. It had been midnight when they climbed, exhausted, into their beds.

"That trip was rough enough to kill any but a hardened tourist," Leroy said. "I've never seen Helen as pooped as last night when we got back to the ship."

At this point, Danforth broke their rule. He had been thinking about Miss Cameron reading in bed. "Everybody who took that trip to Bangkok was completely beat last night," he said. "And that makes me think Miss Cameron wouldn't have been reading in bed after she got back on the ship. She'd have been sleeping, brother—worn out like the rest of us."

"So?"

"So she must have been reading in her bunk this *morning*. Woke up early, say, couldn't get back to sleep, picked up a book, turned on her reading light, felt the pangs of hunger stir, reached for an apple, and took a bite. How's that?"

"That's fine, Monsieur Dupin, but where does it get us?"

At that moment, Jackson Powell—Thos. Cook's Shore Excursion Manager on the ship—stopped by their table on his way out of the dining room. "It's too bad about Miss Cameron, isn't it?" he asked. "Especially after she missed seeing Bangkok. She was so looking forward to it."

"What do you mean, she missed it?" Danforth exclaimed. "Wasn't she ashore with the rest of us?"

Powell shook his head. "She had a reservation for the excursion, but she didn't go. I checked the list myself, and she wasn't there." He gazed morosely at the goat cheese Leroy was applying to a cracker. "She'll never see Bangkok now," he said profoundly and walked away.

Later, as they left the Runic Room, Leroy grinned self-consciously. "Go on up to our regular deck chairs, will you? I'll join you on the Sun Deck."

"Where are you going, Martin?" Helen Leroy demanded.

"Got a small errand to attend to in the aft dining room."

"That's where Miss Cameron's table was," his wife said. "You can't fool me. Why don't you forget it, darling?"

"Just a notion I want to ask about. See you in the sun, kids." And Leroy took off.

When he dropped into his chair on the Sun Deck five minutes later, Leroy was beaming. "I talked to her table steward. She didn't show up for any of her meals yesterday—or for dinner the night before!"

"Probably ate in her cabin," Carol Danforth said. "Can't we talk about *anything* else?"

But Danforth was muttering, "There's a way to find out." He left them, hurried down the starboard Sun Deck corridor to the elevator, and got off at A-deck. He went to his stateroom—A-20—let himself in, and rang for Edith, the stewardess.

She knocked on the door a few seconds later.

"Come in, Edith," he said. She was a lovely statuesque Norwegian girl with auburn hair and an incredible snow-and-roses complexion. Her eyes were a bit puffy and red, Danforth noticed. "Sorry about Miss Cameron," he said sympathetically. "It must have been hard for you, finding her like that."

"It was not good," Edith said, making the *good* sound like *goot*.

"Tell me, Edith. I hear Miss Cameron was not on the shore trip to Bangkok yesterday. And she didn't eat in the dining room either yesterday or the night before. Was she in her cabin all that time?"

The stewardess looked puzzled. "There is the 'Do Not Disturb' sign on her door all yesterday," she said, "and evening before. So I do not disturb her for dinner, breakfast, or luncheon. That is how I am told, when there is the sign 'Do Not Disturb.' Let her alone, yes?"

He raised his eyebrows. "So she stayed in her cabin all that time, even when she was supposed to be on the shore excursion to Bangkok?"

"Not all the time," Edith corrected. "At five o'clock in the afternoon, yesterday, I use my key and enter Miss Cameron's cabin. I am worried. I have not seen her since the afternoon before yesterday."

"And?"

"She is not in A-12. Nobody is there."

"Oh. And the bed, was it made up? Had it been slept in?"

"It is made up, although I have not made it up since morning before yesterday."

Danforth said, "She probably made it up herself yesterday. Slept so late she hated to bother you, maybe. Was her door locked when you went in yesterday?"

She nodded.

"And how about this morning when you—er—discovered her?"

"Not locked," the young stewardess said, obviously picturing in her memory how it had been. "Her door key is on the dressing table beside the fruit tray."

"And was the 'Do Not Disturb' sign gone from her door?"

"Yes."

"Did you touch her when you found her this morning?"

"Yes. Her arm when I shake her." Edith shuddered. "She is getting— she is getting—"

"Cold?"

Silently, she nodded.

"But still a little warm, too?"

"Still a little warm. But more colder. Colder than warm."

Danforth said, "Thanks, Edith. Mr. Leroy and I write stories about things like this, you know? We're always interested in how such things happen. And we liked Miss Cameron very much."

"She was nice," Edith said and left quickly.

Helen, Carol, and Martin were waiting for Danforth in their Sun Deck chairs when he returned, but not with any noticeable eagerness, because all three of them had dropped off into the well-fed, sun-induced post-luncheon nap that overcame most of the passengers regularly every afternoon.

"Hey!" King said loudly, sitting down in his deck chair.

They awoke with a simultaneous start.

Helen Leroy yawned. "You're back, King. Wish you'd stayed longer. I could have milked another half hour out of that nap."

"Listen," Danforth began eagerly.

"Oh, shut up, darling," Carol Danforth said. "We're all exhausted.

Go away somewhere else and plot your plans, or vice versa. Helen and I have had it."

"Not me!" said Leroy. "What's the good word from your recent investigation, King? You've been interviewing Edith, I assume."

"You assume right. Miss Cameron spent yesterday and the evening before in some mysterious limbo, Mart. She was not ashore in Bangkok. She was not in the dining room for any meals, as you yourself confirmed. And she was not in her cabin!"

"Not in her cabin?" his partner repeated, astonished.

"Edith says no. A 'Do Not Disturb' sign was up all day yesterday and the evening before. But Edith looked in at five yesterday. No Angela."

"What do you know," Leroy breathed. "Now there's a nice complication."

"It's nice complications that make the yarn," Danforth said sententiously. "So…where was she?"

"With the murderer," Leroy suggested. "Shacked up in *his* cabin while she repulsed his advances."

"Huh-uh. All the able-bodied men among the passengers were in Bangkok."

"The crew. It was obviously a member of the crew. *They* didn't go to Bangkok."

"True. They didn't."

They sat thinking in silence, watching the faint black stream of cinders from the *Valhalla*'s single stack go streaming away to port in the light breeze. Then Danforth said calmly, as though there had been no hiatus since his last remark, "The girl was murdered the day *before* yesterday. That would explain everything."

"The day before yesterday!" Leroy protested. "Impossible! The bar steward distinctly told us that Angela Cameron was just getting cold when Edith found her this morning. *Beginning* to get cold, I believe Eric said. They don't stay warm for thirty-six hours, Mastermind!"

"Yes, that *is* a problem. In Edith's own words, 'Miss Cameron had still a little warm, but more colder.'"

Silence once more.

Leroy suddenly said, "The average rate of body cooling is more or less one degree per hour, depending on the surrounding temperature and moisture."

Danforth looked at him respectfully. "You're quoting," he said. "But from what?"

"The *Encyclopedia Britannica*, I think. Or is it our own *The Swedish Match Mystery*? I don't remember. But I read it somewhere."

"So where," Danforth queried, "could a dead girl be stashed on this ship where the surrounding temperature and moisture might retard the cooling of her body?"

"The refrigerator," Helen Leroy said drowsily.

"Not the refrigerator, bright girl," her husband's partner shook his head. "That's where she is *now*. We want just the opposite effect."

Leroy had a faraway look in his eyes. "Friends," he announced, "I believe I've come up with the answer."

"Which is? And don't be so darn smug!" his wife exhorted him.

"Why, the natural, the obvious, the only possible place."

Danforth said, "Don't tell me. Let me guess. The steam room down on D-deck beside the swimming pool."

"Bingo! The steam room, of course. Where else?"

"Of course!"

Again silence descended upon the plotters.

This one lasted longer. But eventually Danforth broke it. "Say. The steam room is right off the swimming pool, next to the massage room. Miss Cameron was a regular swimmer in the pool each afternoon. In that very revealing suit. Somebody down there fell for her, but hard. Right?"

"You ought to know," his wife said.

"Somebody who saw her in that suit so frequently that he simply couldn't go on resisting his baser impulses. So, the day before yester-day—"

"Hold it, King, hold it." The interruption was Leroy's. "You keep trying to put the finger on somebody for this fictitious crime. I say we've got to work out how it *happened* first. Explain to me, if you please, the bit about the steam room. I've been in it. I've steamed myself like a soft shell clam with sinus trouble. I've lost six pounds in that room. But where could anybody hide a grown-up girl's body in that Spartan chamber?"

"Close your eyes, Mart," Danforth chortled. "Conjure up a picture of that steam room. It's got open framework wooden benches in it, like bleacher seats in a ballpark, for the customers to sit or recline on while steaming themselves thin. Correct?"

"Correct."

"Now think about the space *behind* those benches."

"Got it."

"Do you see?"

Leroy opened his eyes. "You're right. There's a space behind the benches about a foot and a half wide, backed by the wall of the steam room. And the back wall is solid. A body dropped in there would be hid-den."

"Exactly."

"Hidden from the customers, unless somebody happened to climb to the top row and look straight down the back."

"And the steam room wasn't used by more than a dozen people yesterday, remember. Most of us were ashore in Bangkok."

"Right!"

"So there's where the murderer kept Angela Cameron," Danforth said, "between the time he killed her and early this morning."

"When *did* he kill her, Swami?" Carol asked, in spite of herself.

"The probabilities seem fairly clear. What time does the indoor pool close?"

"Six o'clock."

"And Miss Cameron liked to do her swimming late in the afternoon, as I observed. Therefore, she probably went for her usual swim about five thirty, day before yesterday. She swam until the pool closed. By then, she was doubtless the only person left down there, aside from the staff. When she went into the ladies' dressing room to take off her wet suit and put on her robe, that's when it happened. The murderer, who had been waiting for just this opportunity, tried for his home run and got thrown out at first. So he killed her, to keep her from screaming the ship down or reporting him to the captain."

Leroy picked it up. "And then he put her in the steam room. The intense heat and moisture in there retarded—as you so delicately phrased it—the cooling of her body until the killer could get it back up to her cabin early this morning."

"Just a moment." Danforth raised a magisterial hand. "Why would he want to *delay* having her body found for a whole day?"

"Sheer terror of discovery, I should think," Carol said, now in it all the way.

"Perhaps he hoped to obscure the time of her death by allowing the mad confusion of the Bangkok shore excursion to intervene," Helen said.

"There could have been any number of reasons. The important thing is," Leroy said, "the killer stashes Angela behind the steam-room benches, then casually goes up to A-deck and drapes a 'Do Not Disturb' sign on her cabin door."

"He knows her cabin is A-12 from the tag on her door key."

"Yes. And he hangs out the sign to stall, to give him time to think, to plan."

"Check. But how does he get her body up to her cabin again, early this morning?"

"Maybe in a hamper of dirty towels from the swimming pool? The body covered up by laundry?"

"Perfect. He folds her body into a wheeled hamper, covers her with some soiled towels from the dressing rooms, and wheels her up to her cabin—pretending he's collecting laundry. And with no one stirring except crew members so early in the morning, he'd find it easy to wheel the cart right into her cabin at the proper moment. And out again, later."

"Not a very original method of body transport. But it could work."

"Of course it could work. Let's see, Edith said the door was locked yesterday afternoon when she went in and saw that Angela was missing. But it was not locked this morning when she discovered the body. What about that?" Danforth waited for suggestions.

Helen came through. "She had her room key with her when she went down to swim, naturally. So the murderer simply used her own key to get into A-12 when he took the body back."

"Very good. And why wasn't A-12 locked this morning when Edith discovered the body?"

Leroy said, "Because the killer had no way of locking the door after him when he left her cabin! They're not snap locks. And he had to leave her key *inside* the room because that's where it would naturally be when Miss Cameron was in her room. He couldn't take a chance that a missing key might arouse suspicion."

"Not bad," Danforth said. "That could be it."

Leroy sighed wistfully. "We could make an interesting story out of this, King, if we gave it the proper treatment. I particularly like the bath-towel touch. Victim strangled with bath towel, then concealed under same when wheeled to stateroom in laundry cart."

"And then," Danforth went on, ignoring him, "what happens? He's in her cabin now, with the body-laden cart. I say he dresses Miss Cameron in her nightie, puts her into bed, props her up, turns on the reading lamp, arranges a book near one hand, the apple near the other—and then scrams."

"Having first bitten a piece out of the apple and wedged it far down her throat." Leroy nodded. "I like it, King, I like it."

"Who's going to suspect murder? It was obviously an accident. Anyway, the killer comes out of A-12 with his cart and goes about his normal business, which is merely the taking of some soiled towels to the ship's laundry."

"The stairway down to the laundry is on A-deck, aft," Leroy said. "That fits."

"And poor Miss Cameron is found this morning at ten, dead in her bed, having choked to death on a bite of apple sometime during the night or early this morning. The victim of what my dear wife calls a perfectly natural accidental death." Danforth leaned back and lit a cigarette. "There we are. No holes in *that* fabric."

"But," said Helen Leroy.

"Are there buts?" King Danforth asked, "Do you mean there are loose ends?"

"One," she said succinctly. "Who's the man who couldn't resist his baser impulses when he saw Miss Cameron in a bathing suit?"

Danforth laughed. "You do have a point there," he said. "What do you think, Mart?"

"I am at an extreme disadvantage in this area of speculation," Leroy said. "I am not a swimmer." He slanted a look at Danforth. "I am not even drawn to swimming pools by sensational chassis, either singular or plural. In fact, I have never been down to D-deck for anything except a steam bath and massage. But if I were to pick out a member of the crew who could have fallen for Miss Cameron's charms at the swimming pool and killed her when he was denied them, I am in favor of that Neanderthal blond Viking type with the rabbit's teeth who's employed to pull you out of the pool if you start to drown. Isn't his name Nils?"

"The very fellow I was thinking of," Danforth agreed. "And he'd have ready access to the towels, too."

"And the laundry cart," Helen Leroy said. "But I know Nils quite well. He's sweet."

Perhaps your chassis is not sensational enough to arouse the beast in him, her husband considered saying, but he thought better of it.

"Well, children," Danforth said, "if fact were as strange as Leroy King's fiction, which it unfortunately ain't, that's the way poor Angela Cameron would have got hers."

"Face it," Leroy sighed. "Miss Cameron just had the bad luck to choke to death on her apple. And to be quite fair to Nils, the lad at the swimming pool, I'd say that, if he went to an orthodontist and got those outboard teeth of his brought into line, he'd be better-looking, more appealing, and more gentle than either gentleman in this present company."

"And that," Carol Danforth said heartily, "is fact, not fiction!"

At dinner, they were in high spirits and ordered a bottle of champagne. "To celebrate," Leroy said, "our solution of the Norwegian Apple Mystery."

They had stingers on the rocks in the ballroom after dinner, while playing Bingo games that were always won by other passengers. Then they danced until midnight to the excellent music of the all-Scandinavian jazz band.

And when they finally descended to their cabins on A-deck to turn in, they were pleasantly aware of the fact that, despite its tragic ending for one of their fellow passengers, the day had been stimulating.

To get to their staterooms from the elevator, they had to pass the door of Cabin A-12, recently occupied by the late Miss Angela Cameron. As they approached it, the door to A-12 opened and Edith, their stewardess, stepped out into the corridor, carrying a fruit tray. She bobbed her auburn head at them and started to pass. Danforth put out his hand and restrained her.

"Hi, Edith," he said. "Something else happening in A-12?"

"No, Mr. Danforth," she said. "I am cleaning up Miss Cameron's stateroom, packing her things. To take off the ship with her when we arrive in Hong Kong. It is now all finished. Her parents radio to have her cremated in Hong Kong, and send ashes home on airplane."

"Poor thing," Helen Leroy said, suddenly feeling very guilty. But then she looked at the dish of fruit that Edith was taking from A-12 to dispose of in her service pantry.

Leroy was looking at it, too. He reached out and took an apple from the tray. "Is this the apple Miss Cameron was eating when she choked?"

Edith nodded.

"Look at that," Leroy whispered, holding out the apple.

Its flesh had turned brown where someone had taken a single large bite out of it.

The tooth marks showed clearly along the top edges of the bite. They could not possibly have been made by the small even teeth of Angela Cameron. Unmistakably, they had been carved into the fruit by two very large, protruding front teeth.

THE MAN WHO READ ELLERY QUEEN

William Brittain

After "The Man Who Read John Dickson Carr" and "The Man Who Read Ellery Queen" appeared back to back in the December 1965 EQMM, *junior-high-school English teacher William Brittain contributed nine additional "Man Who Read" stories to the magazine, along with thirty-two tales featuring high-school science teacher Leonard Strang. In the early 1980s, Brittain turned his attention from crime stories to novels for young readers; his* The Wish Giver *was a Newberry Honor Award recipient in 1983. Our children's gain was our loss—but there's good news for mystery readers: all eleven of the "Man Who Read" stories and five of the Mr. Strangs have been collected as* The Man Who Read Mr. Strang: The Short Fiction of William Brittain *(Crippen & Landru, 2018).*

To make the transition to institutional living easier, each resident of the Goodwell Senior Citizens Home was allowed to retain one item of personal property. Some of the old men kept their stamp collections, others preferred to treasure voluminous photograph albums. One senior citizen, Gregory Wyczech, had a 1907 ten-dollar gold piece that was almost as precious to him as life itself. Aside from the single personal item, all the necessities and luxuries—food, clothing, bedding, and recreational material—were furnished by the home.

The only thing that Arthur Mindy brought with him when he entered the Goodwell Home was a complete collection of books by Ellery Queen.

Shortly after his admittance, arranged by a daughter who had grown weary of ministering to the constant needs of an eighty-year-old man, Arthur Mindy sat in his small room, discussing his choice with Roy Carstairs, the first-floor attendant.

"I read my first Ellery Queen mystery at the age of forty-five," said Arthur, finishing his meager lunch. "It was at the beginning of the Depression, and I had plenty of time for reading. For a long time, I dreamed of solving a mystery just the way Ellery does."

"What's so different about the way he solves mysteries?" Carstairs asked.

"The pure logic of his solutions is beautiful," Arthur answered. "He uses only the smallest wisps of evidence, and from these he is able to arrive at the only possible solution. Take *The Roman Hat Mystery*, Ellery's first novel. I read it thirty-five years ago. It was solved when Ellery made deductions from an opera hat found near the body of the murdered man. In other books, the pivotal clues have been things like a shoelace, a bottle of iodine, a collar, a packet of matches—all so insignificant! And sometimes the vital clues are things that *should* be there but aren't, what Ellery calls 'invisible clues.'

"It's always been my ambition," Arthur went on dreamily, "to solve a mystery using only the one or two seemingly vague clues that Ellery Queen finds sufficient." He looked at the light brown walls of his tiny room and sighed. "But now I guess I'll never get the chance."

"Yeah, but Mr. Mindy," Carstairs said, "you got to remember that—"

Whatever it was Arthur had to remember may never be known. At that moment, a shout—the thin cracked voice of an old man—issued from the hallway outside the door.

Carstairs sprang from his chair and through the half-open door, followed at a more leisurely pace by Mindy. They were brought up short by the scene in front of them.

In the middle of the thickly carpeted hall, Gregory Wyczech, dressed only in the light green pajamas and robe which were almost a uniform at the home, was engaged in a boxing match with another similarly dressed resident. Although the sparring form of both men would have done mild credit to a Jack Dempsey or a Joe Louis, each man was standing well out of reach of the other.

While Carstairs stepped between the two combatants, Arthur Mindy looked at Wyczech's opponent. Eugene Dennison had been admitted to the home some time before Arthur. After a short but unsuccessful attempt on the part of the other men to become friendly, Dennison had been classified as a "cold fish." He never had any visitors, and his haughty manner repelled even the most amiable of advances. He refused to take part in any of the home's recreational activities. Television bored him. In the crowded world of the Goodwell Home, he walked aloof and alone.

Dennison stood stiffly just outside Gregory Wyczech's door as Wyczech circled him, chattering like an angry monkey. "He stole my eagle," Wyczech repeated, over and over.

"Your what?" Carstairs' eyebrows shot up.

"My eagle. My ten-dollar gold coin. He stole it!"

"Mr. Carstairs." Dennison spoke for the first time. His imperious tone brought silence to the hallway, which by this time was beginning to fill with old men. "Mr. Carstairs, I have not stolen his eagle or whatever it is. I was on my way to the dispensary to renew my supply of pills. I took the elevator down, since at my age the prospect of three flights of stairs is appalling. Congratulating myself for not having picked up a sliver from the wooden floor of that infernal machine, I came out of the elevator door—which, unfortunately for me, is next to Mr. Wyczech's door. Then this idiot came around the corner, entered his room and burst out again, striking out at me. Naturally, I fought back."

"You stole it," Wyczech said again.

"I didn't."

"You did!"

"I did *not*."

"Wait a minute," said Carstairs. "How do you know he stole it, Mr. Wyczech?"

"Here's what happened," said Wyczech, catching his breath. "I'd just gone down the hall and around the corner to wash my hands. My gold coin was in its envelope on the table, and I wanted to wash before handling it. When I got back, just a minute later, the gold piece was gone, and this—this thief in the night was walking away from the door of my room. So I took a swing at him."

"You must have hit him fairly hard. I see you cut his cheek quite badly." Arthur pointed to a rather long, deep wound on Dennison's cheek, from which fresh blood was now oozing.

"To lapse into the vernacular," said Dennison, "he never laid a glove on me. That's where I cut myself shaving this morning."

"Could anybody else have taken the coin?" asked Carstairs.

"Nobody would have had time," said Wyczech. "I wasn't gone that long. And no one else was around." Dennison looked at the many pairs of accusing eyes turned in his direction. Then he opened the front of his robe and spread it dramatically. "If I submit to a search, will that satisfy everybody?"

Dennison shrugged off the robe and flung it at Wyczech. He removed the tops of his pajamas, loosened the bottoms, let them fall to the floor, and shuffled out of them. He stood on the green carpet, naked as a jaybird, without losing a particle of his massive dignity.

The clothing was quickly searched, even the seams and buttonholes. Nothing. No gold coin.

"He must have swallowed it," sputtered Wyczech.

"Mr. Carstairs, I leave it to you," said Dennison, in the manner of a parent speaking to a dull-witted child. "You know the condition of what's left of my stomach. Considering that my diet for the past several years has consisted only of oatmeal and milk, could I have swallowed a piece of salami, much less a gold coin?"

"That's true, Mr. Wyczech," said Carstairs reluctantly.

Wyczech examined Dennison's hair and the inside of his mouth without results. Then he shrugged. "I still say he stole it. He was the only one who could have."

"Mr. Dennison," said Carstairs, "you go back to your room. I'll take care of Mr. Wyczech."

With a shrug, Dennison reclaimed his clothing and, not bothering to put it on, shuffled to the carpeted stairway across from Wyczech's room.

"Just a moment, please!" The men in the hallway looked to see who had spoken, and then Arthur Mindy stepped forward and faced Carstairs and Dennison.

"If you gentlemen would indulge me, I think perhaps I might be of some assistance. This case is reminiscent of 'The Black Ledger,' a story in *Q.B.I.—Queen's Bureau of Investigation*. In that story, Ellery kept a long list of known criminals on his person the entire time he was being minutely searched by some desperate individuals who were determined to find the list. Ellery was stripped to the buff, just like Mr. Dennison here."

"Where did Ellery hide it?" asked Carstairs.

"That would be telling. I'll lend you the book sometime."

The attendant shook his head sadly. He was sure something had snapped in Arthur's mind.

"Now," Arthur continued, "if Mr. Dennison *did* take the coin, what did he do with it? Where did he hide it? Unless we can find that out, he's innocent by default. Let's see if the problem will yield to logic."

"Like Ellery Queen?" asked Carstairs, attempting to humor Arthur.

"Precisely. Now I ask you to consider two pieces of evidence, Mr. Carstairs. The first is that long, deep cut on Mr. Dennison's cheek."

"So he cut himself shaving, Mr. Mindy," said Carstairs. "What about it?"

"And the second is that Mr. Dennison is now preparing to climb the stairs to his room," Arthur concluded.

"So what?" moaned Wyczech. "Come on, great detective. Where's my coin?"

Arthur smiled. "You know," he said, "in Ellery Queen's earlier novels and in many of his short stories, there's a point at which the reader is challenged to solve the mystery using only the facts given in the story. I'm sorely tempted to use that device right now."

"Mindy!" screamed Wyczech. "You can't torture me like this! Where's my gold eagle?"

"Very well," said Arthur, "let's first consider the cut on Dennison's cheek. He says he cut himself shaving this morning. That would have been at least two hours ago, since lunch was just served. But you all noticed the cut is bleeding again. *Fresh* blood. Why?"

"Because Mr. Wyczech hit him?" Carstairs suggested.

"By Dennison's own admission, Wyczech never laid a glove on him. But tell me, Mr. Carstairs, what do you do when you cut yourself shaving?"

"Use a styptic pencil."

"But suppose the cut is long and deep?"

"I'd stick a piece of adhesive plaster over it."

"Exactly. Adhesive plaster. And if Dennison had just torn a piece of adhesive tape from his face, it would have reopened a long deep cut. Right?"

"Right," said Carstairs.

"So now we have Dennison provided with a piece of adhesive plaster. Where is that adhesive tape? Evidence Number Two: what did he just do when he was told to leave? He went to the stairway, in spite of the fact that there is an automatic elevator waiting right here for him. What is so attractive about the stairway?"

"So he wanted some exercise," said Wyczech. "Get to the point."

"The point," said Arthur, "is that the stairs are carpeted, while the floor of the elevator is bare wood. When Dennison left the elevator and noticed the door to Wyczech's room open, he walked in—probably just out of curiosity—and saw the coin. He couldn't resist taking it, but as he went back into the hall, he heard Wyczech returning. So he had to conceal the coin in a place where it could not be found even if he were searched, but where it would be available to him as soon as he was allowed to leave."

"I don't get it," moaned Wyczech. "Why didn't he go back to his room by the elevator?"

"He would have clicked."

"*Clicked?*"

"Clicked. Logically, the only place the coin could be is the one place on his person that we failed to search."

Arthur savored the silence of the men in the hall. At the age of eighty, he had finally been given his golden moment.

"You'll find it taped to the bottom of his foot."

Dennison was quickly forced to sit on the bottom stair, and on the ball of his right foot was found the gold coin, held there by a thin strip of adhesive plaster—just as Arthur Mindy had deduced. Dennison's face was now a mask of hatred. Then the mask came apart.

"I didn't mean to do it!" he cried out. "I just wanted something all to myself—something that belonged to me and not to everybody else, too. You men—you have relatives to come and see you. They bring you gifts and tell you about their families. You don't know what it's like to be really alone. I've got nobody—nothing." His thin body was racked by sobbing.

Gregory Wyczech sat down on the bottom step and put his arm around Dennison's shoulders. "I tell you what," he soothed. "You and me, we're gonna be partners. I'm giving you a half interest in my gold coin, see. Every other week you get to keep it all to yourself."

The two old men stood up and crossed the hall, while Carstairs gazed at Arthur Mindy in awe.

"Thank you, Mr. Queen," he heard Arthur Mindy murmur.

E.Q. GRIFFEN EARNS HIS NAME

Josh Pachter

Author's Note: I was sixteen years old when I wrote "E.Q. Griffen Earns His Name," seventeen by the time it appeared in the "Department of First Stories" in the December 1968 EQMM. In his introduction, Fred Dannay wrote: "Another 'first' by a teenager (God bless 'em!)...it is always a happy event to welcome young blood to the circulatory system of the mystery story." A second E.Q. Griffen story was in the May 1970 issue of the magazine—and I'm bringing E.Q. back again, half a century older, in a fiftieth-anniversary story titled "50," which will be in the November/December 2018 issue.

For the third time in as many minutes, Ellery Queen removed his horn-rimmed glasses (they just don't *make* good pince-nez any more) and carefully polished the lenses.

"Shades of Circe!" he muttered. "How can I be so abysmally dense?"

Ellery's vexation stemmed from his total inability to find the solution to a mystery that even John Hamish Watson would have been able to see through without the benefit of a second glance. But: "It's there," E.Q. groaned, "if only I knew what it was!"

"My goodness, Ellery," a feminine voice intruded, "don't tell me our little problem has got you talking to yourself?"

With a moan of embarrassment and despair, the great detective fled the room.

That Alison Field, he thought, as he paced the sidewalk in front of the Fields' home. *Why can't she realize that being a detective isn't as easy as it seems in books. It's hard work! I just* wish *I could show her!*

Ellery Queen's last name was Griffen, and he was sixteen years old.

About an hour before his hasty departure from the Fields' kitchen, Ellery had received a frantic telephone call from Mrs. Leora Field. "Ellery," she had said, "is anybody else home? Well, then, could *you* come over, please? Right away!"

When Ellery had arrived, the woman had led him into her kitchen and pointed a trembling finger at an open window. "They're gone! Do something, Ellery, they're gone!"

"What's gone?" the boy asked sensibly.

"My pies!" she shrieked. "My beautiful pies!"

Finally, the story came out. Leora Field had spent that day baking three large apple pies for a church bazaar to be held the next afternoon. Later, she had taken Alison, her only child, to a dental appointment, leaving the pies on the windowsill to cool. When they returned, the pies were missing.

Ellery's investigation had uncovered only one clue: an Italian postage stamp, which he found lying face down beneath the window. The stamp was golden brown and dark brown, and had been issued in 1964— Ellery had looked it up in his *Scott Catalogue.* The design of the stamp illustrated Italian sports.

Ellery reflected, and decided there were only four people known to him who could possibly be connected with foreign postage stamps: Charles Green, who owned the local stamp shop; Greg Zorn, a boy of Ellery's age who worked at Green's store every day after school; and two stamp collectors, Al Williams and Steve Holden. Steve's mother was in charge of the church bazaar.

Even though the Italian stamp seemed to be the only clue, Ellery simply could not figure out how to eliminate any of his suspects. A few phone calls established that not one of the four had an alibi for the crime period. And now Alison Field was needling him.

Suddenly a cry split the quiet late-afternoon air: "Ellery! *Ellery!"*

It was the detective's mother and, relieved, he trotted off toward home and dinner.

Something will hit me sooner or later, he thought.

The greatest compliment a Griffen child could receive was to be told that he had "earned his name."

Inspector Ross Griffen, of the Tyson County Police Force, had grown up on a rich diet of detective fiction and, in respectful memory of Sherlock Holmes, Hercule Poirot, Arsène Lupin, Bulldog Drummond and the other heroes of his youth, he had named each of his eleven children after one of them. And the inspector had introduced his sons and daughter to the joys of detection at early ages, teaching them to use their minds and wits to their fullest advantage.

A Griffen "earned his name" when he was able to solve a criminal problem in the manner of his namesake. Although these problems were usually made up round robin at the dinner table or read out of a book, the children had on several occasions used their detective powers to help solve cases their father had brought home with him.

Jane Marple Griffen, Peter Wimsey Griffen, Albert Campion Griffen, and John Jericho Griffen had pointed out clues that had led to the solution of two burglaries and one case of arson. Parker Pyne Griffen, Gideon Fell Griffen, and Augustus Van Dusen Griffen had earned their names on make-believe crimes, while Sherlock Holmes, Perry Mason, and Nero Wolfe, being younger than ten years of age, had understandably not yet shown much creativity.

Inspector Griffen's biggest disappointment was Ellery. Not that the boy didn't try; he was always advancing ingenious theories, but he always seemed to be wrong.

So when, that Thursday evening, his father sat down at the table with a singularly puzzled and abstracted look on his face, Ellery kept quiet about his own problem and asked, "What's up, Dad?"

"Not now, El," the inspector answered. "I'll tell you about it after dinner."

But after dinner Griffen went into his study (a rare treat for a policeman with eleven children), and sat down with the phone. Hoping to get some information about their father's case, the Griffen children turned on the radio to an all-news station and listened. After the usual roundup of national and international news, the announcer delivered a local report:

"At an unknown time last night, Collier's Jewelers on South Firthson Avenue, under twenty-four-hour high-security guard, was broken into and robbed of a twenty-two-thousand-dollar diamond necklace. Police investigation, led by Inspector Ross Griffen, has thus far failed to discover the identity of the thief or thieves or how they managed to enter the building. The necklace was found missing this morning from a seemingly untouched display case by Geoffrey Collier, the store's owner and manager, during a routine search of the building. The police were immediately notified. Timothy Tierney, night guard, neither saw nor heard anything out of the ordinary last night. An intricate burglar-alarm system failed to go off. For further information on last night's robbery of Collier's Jewelers, stay tuned to…."

At the mention of the name Collier, Parker had sat up very straight and listened intently to the broadcast. At its conclusion, he exclaimed, "Boy! Anyone clever enough to get into Collier's is really going to be tough to catch."

"What do you mean, Park?" Jane asked.

"You know my friend Dickie Albert? Well, his brother Paul works at that jewelry store, and Paul was telling Dick and me about it. That place is as safe as Fort Knox."

"If this is Dad's case," Ellery put in, "we'd better know the layout. How about describing it to us?"

"From what Paul Albert told me, old man Collier has that whole place set up with just one purpose in mind: not letting any merchandise out of the store until it's been paid for. And up to now he's done a good job of it, too. So far, there have been three burglary attempts, and each time the crooks were caught before they even got into the store.

"Here's the way it works. Every night, before closing up, Collier locks all the windows from the inside. There are bars over each window on the outside. He double locks the back door, and then, with Tierney standing guard outside, Collier searches the entire building. After the search, he double locks the front door, gives the only duplicates of those two keys to Tierney, and leaves for home.

"When he comes back the next morning, Tierney unlocks the front door, returns the keys, and then the two of them search the store together. There's a series of alarms covering both doors, all the windows, and all the showcases. Like I said, safe as Fort Knox."

"Obviously not," Albert commented drily.

Augustus looked up from a magazine, yawned, and said, "It shouldn't require a Thinking Machine to inform you that, with all these precautions, it had to be an inside job."

Shaking his head, Parker replied, "I doubt it. According to Paul, Collier even put his porter through a strict security check. Believe me, anyone who can get a job at Collier's is one hundred percent honest. That guy Collier doesn't take any chances."

The study door opened, and Inspector Griffen walked out. He crossed the living room to his easy chair and dropped into it. Eyes closed, he slowly massaged his forehead. Finally he spoke: "All right, kids. If you're still interested, I'll tell you about the case."

"We kn-know most of the facts, D-d-dad," John Jericho stammered. Unlike his tall red-haired namesake, John was short, dark, and occasionally spoke with a stutter. "How about if we just ask q-q-questions about the points we're not clear on?"

"Fine with me, son," the inspector replied. "What would you like to know?"

"F-first of all, was the n-normal routine followed last night?"

"Yes, it was, everything as usual: windows and doors locked, et cetera."

"And the necklace was definitely in the case when Collier left?" Jane asked.

The inspector nodded, then elaborated. "It's by far the most valuable piece in the store, and Collier checks it just before he leaves. He's sure it was there last night."

Gideon, lost in thought until this time, looked up and said, "I rather think you've been ignoring the obvious. What about this man Tierney? People have gone rotten for far less than twenty-two thousand dollars. Money's the motive, the keys are the means, and Tierney had opportunity all last night."

"Collier stands by Tierney and every one of his other employees, but we're having them all checked out, anyway. I've got Captain Harris, my best man, on it, and I should be hearing from him any minute."

"I could explain this 'miracle' two other ways," continued Gideon, neither a doctor nor fat, but hoping to become the former and trying to stall off the latter. "Tierney could be innocent, but he could have left his post for a while—to get a beer, say—or even have dozed off for just long enough."

"I'll have all that information soon," the inspector said.

Albert spoke up: "Of course the burglar alarms were on all last night? No signs of tampering, nothing out of order?"

"Nothing," his father said. "There's a bell-and-light hookup at headquarters. If the alarm is tripped, or tampered with, the bell goes off, and, if there's any internal malfunction, the light starts flashing."

"What about those window bars?" Augustus asked.

"If I understand the point of your question, son, then the answer is no. Not even a circus midget could have passed between those bars. In fact, I think it would be safe to say that whoever got into Collier's Jewelers had a harder time of it than Professor Van Dusen had getting out of Cell 13."

A silence followed, shattered after some seconds by the ringing of the phone. Nero Wolfe Griffen rose, according to custom, and crossed to the kitchen. He picked up the receiver and, thanks to its long cord, was able to carry it back to his father.

"Hello, Griffen speaking…yeah, Harris…all of them…? All night, huh…? Okay, thanks a lot." Inspector Griffen handed the phone back to his son, who walked once more to the kitchen.

Wolfe cradled the phone.

"Well, kids, that seems to let out Tierney," the inspector said. "Harris is convinced the night guard is completely innocent, and that he didn't leave his post all last night."

Inspector Griffen's eyes swept the room tiredly, then came to rest on Ellery. "What about you, El?" he asked. "You haven't said a word so far. Have you got any questions?"

"Just one, Dad," Ellery responded. "Whose fingerprints were found on the rifled display case?"

The inspector looked startled and replied, "It's funny you should ask that. We dusted every inch of that case, and it looks, according to what we found, like it just wasn't touched. Every print on it belonged there; there were no strange ones. Not a single area had been wiped off. And gloves seem to be out. Although wearing gloves will eliminate finger-prints, the gloves themselves leave marks or smudges on most materials. Not traceable to any particular pair, of course, but identifiable as having been made by gloves. That help you any, Ellery?"

"It might."

Inspector Griffen stood up. "Kids," he said, "I'm due back at head-quarters at eight, and it's seven-thirty. Unless there are any suggestions, I'll leave now."

There were suggestions.

Jane said, "This reminds me of an incident that occurred back in high school, when Violet Bronson, a beautiful girl with deep blue—"

And Parker said, "The crime was quite obviously committed by some poor misguided—"

And Gideon said, "With all the doors and windows locked—"

And Augustus S.F.X. Van Dusen said, "Logically—"

And then, wonder of wonders, Ellery said, "I know the answer."

Inspector Griffen sat down heavily, breathed deeply, and listened to the silence. Finally he managed to ask, "What?"

"I said," Ellery repeated, "I know the answer. And I do. Not only do I know who robbed Collier's, but I know how and why."

"You're sure?" the inspector asked incredulously.

Ellery pulled off his glasses and thought for a moment. Then he nod-ded and said, "Yes, I'm sure."

"Then tell us, son."

"Of course. There are," he began, "two ways this crime could have been committed without leaving a single fingerprint, mark, or clue. The first is that the lack of clues indicates the lack of a crime—that is, the necklace was not stolen at all but merely mislaid."

"But we—" his father interrupted.

"Don't interrupt," Wolfe grumbled.

Ellery continued: "But we can eliminate this possibility, because a thorough police search failed to turn up the gems. Besides, they were definitely seen by Mr. Collier when he made his rounds last night.

"You especially, Sherlock, should know that 'when you have elimi-nated the impossible, whatever remains, however improbable, must be the truth.' So eliminating our first possibility indicates that the second one must be the truth. But before we discuss that, let's consider the ways in which the thief could have entered the store to commit the robbery.

"The front of Collier's," Ellery went on, "is guarded by Timothy Tierney, who has been found to be one hundred percent trustworthy. He remained at his post all night, making entry through the front impossible. There are other stores on both sides of the jewelry store, but with no connecting doors or partitions. The back windows were locked and barred, and found to have been undisturbed. The same goes for the back door, so rear entry can also be ruled out. I've been in the store, and I know that there are no other ways in—no fire escape, no skylight, no chimney. And we can't forget the burglar alarms—ready to go off at any intrusion.

"These facts all boil down to this: *there is no way that anyone could have entered Collier's after closing and stolen that necklace!*

"But since we have established that it *was* stolen, then the theft must have occurred *before* closing.

"Could the thief have taken the necklace and left before the building was locked up? No, since Collier saw it before closing up for the night.

"Could he have hidden in the building until after closing, stolen the jewels, and then left? Or waited until morning, managing to escape during the confusion caused by the discovery of the theft? No again: he would have been found during Collier's nightly search. And don't forget, no strange fingerprints were found on the display case."

"I've got it!" Jane cried. "Vickie Harding did the same thing up at the University. You know Vickie, Ellery, she's that cute girl with the long blond—"

"Get to the point, Jane!" snapped Peter, the oldest.

The Griffens' only girl blushed. "Oh, yes, sorry. I do ramble so. Anyway, one day last semester, Vickie forgot to bring her lunch to school. Rather than ask me for a loan so she could buy something in the cafeteria, she sneaked one of my sandwiches out of my lunch bag, leaving some crumpled-up paper in its place so that I wouldn't notice anything missing until later. Of course, I easily deduced that Vickie had taken the sandwich and confronted her. She broke down and confessed. I forgave her, and we've been the best of friends ever since."

"And just how does that help?" Parker sneered.

Jane looked at her younger brother furiously and continued, "Obviously the same thing happened here. The thief took the necklace before the store closed, leaving a paste replica in its place. Then, when Collier made his search, he thought the genuine necklace was still there!"

Parker clapped his hands with glee and pounced. "And just what happened to this replica," he demanded. "Did it get up and walk away? Or did the successful diamond thief decide to come back later and steal the fake, too?"

Jane's mouth fell open.

"May I continue?" Ellery asked politely. "This brings us back to the second possibility—that the theft was committed before, not after, Collier's Jewelers was closed for the night.

"The biggest question still is: How was the necklace stolen without leaving either fingerprints or marks or smudges on the display case?

"But isn't it possible that we've been looking at this point from the wrong angle, that the thief's prints *are* on the case, and that we just didn't recognize them as belonging to the crook? In other words, that this *was* an inside job, after all?

"Assuming this to be true, the theft must have been committed *after* Mr. Collier looked into the case, but *before* the thief left the building."

Breaking his silence, Inspector Griffen said, "But, Ellery, Collier always conducts his search after all store personnel have already left."

"Exactly!" Ellery exclaimed triumphantly. "So it should be as clear as daylight that the thief must have been—"

"C-C-Collier!" John Jericho yelled.

"It's not too uncommon an occurrence," Inspector Griffen explained at breakfast the next morning. The jewelry-store owner had confessed, and the stolen necklace was now residing in a police safe.

"Collier had been backing a risky stock too heavily, and his firm was bankrupt. The brokers were pressing him to pay the large balance of his account, and he needed cash in a hurry. So Collier stole his own jewels, expecting to collect their full value from his insurance company, plus another five to ten thousand dollars by selling the diamonds through a fence."

"How did he manage it, Dad?" Albert asked.

"I told you that Collier and Tierney search the store together every morning, but Collier conducts the evening search by himself, with Tierney on guard outside. So it was easy for him to unlock the display case, slip the necklace into his pocket, and then relock the case. He probably figured that, even though Tierney had passed a rigorous security check, the guard would be blamed, since he had the perfect opportunity to commit the crime. But I suppose you deduced all this, Ellery. What I'd like to know is what put you on to it so quickly?"

Ellery beamed. "You know that Ellery Queen, after whom I'm named, often solves his cases through interpretation of seemingly insignificant clues: a piece of sugar in a dead man's hand, a cut-out piece of paper from the Sunday comics, a cryptic dying message.

"Well, Ellery once solved a case because there was no top hat where there should have been one, and another case when he noticed the statuette of a bridegroom missing from a newlywed's apartment. These two cases came to my mind when I realized that *this* case was also characterized by a lack of clues, by a clue that was missing.

"Finally, I realized that this *lack* of clues was a clue in itself, indicating that the theft must have been perpetrated by someone whose fingerprints on the display case would not be suspicious. This obviously pointed to an insider, and to the logical conclusion that it was Collier himself who stole the necklace."

"Ellery," Inspector Griffen said proudly, "you've earned your name."

Noon that day found Ellery Queen Griffen pounding on the front door of Leora Field's home. After a short while, Mrs. Field opened the door and ushered Ellery into the kitchen, where Mrs. Sandy Holden was sipping from a mug of steaming coffee.

"Ellery," she began, and coughed apologetically, "I think that little matter—"

The detective interrupted, "Yes, yes, that's why I'm here! I've got the case all solved! The answer hit me last night, after I managed to— ahem—clear up another slight matter. You see, that postage stamp was a blind! It was planted at the scene of the crime to throw suspicion on three innocent boys, your son included, Mrs. Holden."

"But, Ellery," Leora Field said.

"Just a minute, please. After deducing that this was all a frame-up, I began to wonder who could have possibly had access to that stamp—"

"But, Ellery," she said again.

"In a moment. I went through all the people I know, matching up motive and opportunity, but I got nowhere."

"Ellery!" Mrs. Field pleaded.

Paying no attention, the young criminologist continued: "Then I found someone. Someone who works every day in Benton's Grocery, which is *right next door to Green's Stamp Shop!* Peter Gould, who merely had to walk next door to purchase that stamp."

The victimized housewife looked at her friend, shrugged, and let Ellery go on.

"So it was Peter Gould who stole your pies, Peter Gould who planted that stamp, Peter Gould who—just the other day—told me that your daughter had refused to go to the movies with him! So, out of revenge, he tried to ruin your contribution to the church bazaar. The case," E.Q. concluded, "is solved!"

"Ellery," Mrs. Field said patiently, "there never was a case. This whole thing was just a big mistake."

"Excuse me?" Ellery said calmly.

"There never *was* a case, Ellery. Sandy—Mrs. Holden—came by to pick up those pies yesterday afternoon, but, as I told you, I was out with Alison. She didn't know that, though, so she went around back, thinking that I was here in the kitchen and perhaps couldn't hear the front door-bell. She saw the pies on the windowsill, and, when she realized I wasn't home, she took them. Peter Gould had nothing to do with it."

"But—but—" Ellery stammered. "My reasoning! There was nothing wrong with it! I—wait a second! What about that stamp?"

"I think I can explain that," Sandy Holden said. "I didn't want to take the pies without letting Leora know, so I left a note. You know that my son Steve collects postage stamps. Well, I picked that one up for him at Green's store, along with some others that Steve ordered, and they were all in a glassine envelope in my purse. When I was looking for a pencil and paper to leave the note—well, somehow the stamp must have fallen out."

"But the note!" Ellery insisted. "What about the note?"

"Oh," she continued, "I forgot. I wrote the note and put it on the kitchen table, this one right here. The breeze through the open window must have blown it off. When I came over for coffee this morning, I learned that Leora thought the pies had been stolen, and I explained the whole thing. We found the note over there in the corner."

"But," Ellery said, "but—"

"Sorry, Ellery, but I'm afraid you were all wrong."

"But," Ellery said, "but—"

"Oh, Ellery," Alison giggled from the doorway.

THE LAST CHECK

Patricia McGerr

When Pat McGerr's "The Last Check" appeared in the March 1972 issue of EQMM, *Fred Dannay's very brief introduction promised "further comments" at the end of the story. Far be it from us to second-guess Ellery Queen! We'll let you get right to the story, and save our—and Dannay's—comments until after you've read it....*

Stephen Coleman was alone in his study. A checkbook lay open in front of him, a stack of bills near his left hand. He looked at the top bill, checked the column of figures, and frowned his disapproval. *Waste*, he told himself, *sheer waste. Doesn't anybody but me know the value of money?*

Stephen Coleman was a rich man but a careful one. A joint checking account had encouraged the extravagance of his first wife, and he had not made the same mistake with his second. Instead, it was his custom to examine the monthly accounts and personally pay every bill. Tonight, he had no choice but to pay the exorbitant grocery bill. Tomorrow, he would make sure that both his wife and their cook understood that such profligacy must cease.

His pen was poised over the check when a metallic click drew his attention to the study door. It opened, and a familiar figure entered. "Still up?" he said in mild surprise. "I thought everyone was—"

Then he saw the weapon in the gloved hand, and his eyes widened in shock. "You're not—you can't—"

But a glance at the other's face told him protest was useless. He barely had time to scribble his name at the bottom of the blank check before the gun blazed and the pen dropped from his hand.

The killer hurried to the victim's side to place the gun in his hand and curve his finger around the trigger and then, after a quick appraisal of the objects on the desk, ran from the room. The shot roused the other occupants of the house, and they came with haste to the study. The murderer also returned to mingle with the others and join in their expressions of horror and disbelief at the apparent suicide. One of them phoned a doctor, who in turn summoned the police.

Coleman was pronounced dead on arrival. While the lab squad took pictures and collected physical evidence, Captain Rogan roamed the study.

"Look at this." He called his aide's attention to an alcove lined with books. "The man was a real fan."

"Mysteries, huh?" Sergeant Pringle looked over his shoulder. "If the killer read them, he'd have known better than to try to pass off a death as suicide when the gun was too far away to leave a powder burn."

"Unfortunately, however, he—or she—knew enough about fingerprints not to leave any on the gun, except the corpse's. These aren't just mysteries, though," Rogan added. "Have you noticed? They're all by the same author: Ellery Queen. Why, there must be more than fifty! You read any of them?"

"Sure I have." The sergeant scanned some of the titles. "He's the one whose victims often leave dying messages that finger the murderer. Too bad Coleman didn't take a leaf from those books and write us a clue."

"I think he did," the captain said. "Okay, Ernie." He nodded to the photographer. "If you've got all the angles, they can take the body away."

Rogan moved back to the desk and stared at the blank check that Coleman had used his last few seconds of life to sign. "He was trying to tell us something. The question is—what?"

A short time later, with the body removed and the technical men gone, Rogan sat in the dead man's chair and studied the two men and two women who were ranged in a semicircle on the other side of the desk.

Three of them lived in the house: Blanche Coleman, the new-made widow; her stepson Desmond Coleman; and the cook, Eva Rojack. The fourth, a guest for the weekend, was Ralph Frampton, treasurer of Coleman Enterprises, Inc.

Each told substantially the same story. They were all in their rooms, all in bed at the time of the murder. Frampton said he was studying a financial report he intended to discuss with his employer the next day. The others claimed they were asleep until the sound of the shot wakened them. They put on robes and slippers and converged on the study. It was a time of excitement and confusion, and no one was clear on the order in which they had arrived there.

In any case, that was not a significant point, since the study was on the second floor at the end of a corridor onto which all the bedrooms opened except that of the cook. Her room connected with the kitchen and was almost directly below the study. Every one of them could, as they said, have heard the shot and come to investigate. Any one of them might have fired the shot and ducked back into his or her own room—or, in the cook's case, down the stairs—to emerge again with the others.

"All of you," Rogan summed up, "had equal opportunity. The weapon belonged to the deceased and was regularly kept in an unlocked drawer of the desk. Presumably, all of you knew it was there and could have slipped in during the day and taken it. So we—"

"I did not!" the cook interrupted. She was a dark angular woman in her middle forties, whose English was precise though slightly accented. She had answered the captain's questions with distrustful brevity, but mention of the gun made her, for the first time, voluble. "I know nothing of a gun. I have nothing to do with guns. I do not wish to be in a house with one."

"Really?" Rogan gave her his full attention. "You sound as if you've had some bad experience with firearms."

"In my own country"—she shivered, cut off the sentence. "But that was long ago. I do not want to remember it."

"What *is* your country, Mrs. Rojack?"

"I am of Bohemia. But no more, not since I was a child. Now I am United States citizen. And I do not want to live where there are guns."

"I see. Does anyone else deny knowledge that the gun was here?"

"I knew Steve had a gun, of course," Frampton volunteered. "He talked about getting one last year, when there were some robberies in the area. But I had no idea where he kept it."

"How about you, Mrs. Coleman? You knew there was a gun in your husband's desk?"

"Certainly I knew." A plump, pretty blonde, she leaned forward, and her mauve chiffon wrapper opened to reveal a matching nightgown whose décolletage furnished ample evidence of her attractions. "He was very nervous about the robberies and even made me learn to shoot. But that was months ago. I'd forgotten all about it."

"And you?" The captain turned to the bearded young man beside her. "Did you—?"

"Sure I did." Desmond didn't wait for him to complete the question. "I knew he had it. I knew where he kept it. I knew how to use it. But I didn't shoot the old man, even though I had good cause."

"What was your cause?"

"The usual," Desmond replied carelessly. "He didn't dig my life-style. But if you're sniffing for motives, there are plenty lying around."

His glance flicked to Frampton. "Like maybe the account books didn't quite balance."

"That's not funny, Desmond," the treasurer snapped.

"So who's joking? You weren't invited for a weekend of fun and games. All afternoon, the two of you were holed up in here, going over figures. And the way the old man was shouting at you made it clear he didn't like the way you were adding them up."

"The last quarter showed a loss," Frampton conceded. "But that wasn't my fault. And certainly there was no question of dishonesty."

"If you say so," Desmond shrugged. "Anyway, it'll all come out in the audit." He switched his malice to his stepmother. "How about you, Blanchie? You so hot for your Latin lover you decided to anticipate the divorce with a bullet?"

"Why, you sneaky little insect! How do you—?" She turned on him furiously, then broke off to resume a more moderate tone. "I don't know what you're talking about."

"Be frank with the fuzz," Desmond advised kindly. "They'll find out, anyway. All the neighbors know about you and Angelo. I think even Dad was catching on, and then you'd have been out on your tail without a dime. Now you can have both love *and* money. Isn't that neat?"

"You're insufferable," she said angrily. "Since you find it so amusing to spread suspicion, why not tell the detectives about the quarrel you had with your father at dinner?"

"I've already admitted we didn't get on."

"Didn't get on," she echoed scornfully. "That hardly describes the ugly scene at the table. Don't you agree, Mr. Frampton?"

"He put up with a lot from you, Des," the older man corroborated. "But you finally pushed him too far. I think he meant it when he told you he was through supporting an ingrate."

"What was it he said?" The widow showed satisfaction in remembering. "'You've had your last check from me. From now on, you earn your bread or you don't eat.'"

"Motives for everyone." Desmond was undaunted. "Except Little Eva." He turned to the cook. "How about it? Are you part of some dark Bohemian plot to avenge your honor?"

"You always like to joke," she told him solemnly. "I think when your papa is dead is wrong time for joking."

"Speaking of time"—the captain checked his watch—"I don't think we'll learn any more tonight. You can all go back to bed. I'll talk with you again in the morning."

He stood in the doorway and watched as Mrs. Coleman, Desmond, and Frampton walked down the hall to their rooms and the cook vanished down the back stairs. Then he returned to the desk.

"Not much forwarder, eh?" the sergeant commented. "Think there's anything in what the son said about Frampton fixing the books and the wife having a boyfriend?"

"We'll find out," Rogan promised. "Meanwhile, we have this." He fingered the signed blank check. "I'm sure he's told us who shot him, if we only knew how to read it."

"It doesn't make sense," Pringle argued. "If he had time to write a name, why didn't he put down the killer's? Oh, I know how it is in the books on the wall." He gestured toward the Ellery Queen corner. "The dying message is always a puzzle that only the wiseguy private dick can figure out. But Coleman wasn't writing riddles. He wanted his killer caught. So why make it hard for us?"

"For the same reason the dying message in the books has to be obscure: so the murderer won't destroy it. Do you think whoever shot Coleman would have left behind a paper with his or her name on it for us to find?"

"No, I guess not." The sergeant frowned. "If the boy were called Stephen Coleman, Junior, the name on the check would mean something. But his name is Desmond. And the last name can point to either the son or the wife, so that's no help, unless—say, what about the fight at dinner? Coleman could count on somebody telling us about that, maybe repeating what he said to young Desmond about the 'last check.' This *is* a last check, all right."

"Could be." Rogan rubbed his chin thoughtfully. "At least we're moving in the right direction. It's not *what* he wrote but what he wrote it *on* that's significant. A check. What does that make you think of?"

"My wife," Pringle answered promptly. "She's the runaway check writer at our house."

"Maybe here, too. That is, Coleman wrote the checks, but we'll probably find out most of the bills he was paying were hers."

"That's reaching," the sergeant demurred. "He also paid bills for the boy. And the top one there is from a fancy grocer, which could point to the cook. But she's the only one nobody's dredged up a motive for."

"Which doesn't prove she hasn't got one," Rogan pointed out. "How are you at geography, Ned?"

"I know where the precinct lines intersect," he answered. "What are you getting at?"

"There's no such country as Bohemia anymore," Rogan explained. "It's now part of Czechoslovakia."

"You mean the lady's a Czech?" He looked at the slip of paper in the captain's hand. "Well, what do you know? He really *was* leaving us a message. But why would the cook—?"

"Not so fast," Rogan cautioned. "There's somebody else among the suspects to whom a check has a special application. What's a big part of a treasurer's job?"

"Writing checks," the sergeant answered glumly. "Hell, Captain, Coleman may have thought he was handing us a clue, but what's it worth when it points to everybody in the house?"

"It can't be that broad," Rogan countered. "He was saying something very specific. If the check itself, the piece of paper, was the vital clue, he didn't have to take the time to sign it. Any kind of mark—an X, a circle—would have called our attention to it as his last message. But he rushed to sign his whole name on it before he died."

"Maybe not," the sergeant suggested. "Maybe it isn't a dying message at all. Coleman was sitting here paying bills. He might have signed the check before the killer came in."

The captain shook his head. "Coleman had a firm, neat signature. This one was written in such a hurry it's barely legible. Besides, nobody puts his name on a check before he fills in the rest of it."

"My wife does," Pringle said. "It's a bad habit, and I keep warning her some day somebody will get hold of one of her signed blank checks and write in any amount he likes. But you're right. A man like Coleman would never be so unbusinesslike."

"That's it!" Rogan exclaimed. "You've hit it, Sergeant. *A signed blank check!* That's the dying message."

"Yeah, I know." Pringle was puzzled by his superior's enthusiasm.

"I think you'd better knock on Mrs. Coleman's door and tell her I'd like to see her. She's probably not sleeping yet."

His guess was confirmed by the speed with which the sergeant returned with the widow.

"I don't understand," she protested. "Of course I want to help in every way I can to find out who killed my husband. But what do you need to ask me that's so important it can't wait till morning?"

"I have something to *tell* you," he corrected her, "and it's *very* important. I'm about to charge you with your husband's murder, and I must inform you of your right to have a lawyer—"

"I don't need a lawyer!" she exploded, "and you can't charge me. You have no proof, no evidence, nothing but the word of that spiteful boy."

"Was he lying about—what was the name?—Angelo?"

"So I have a friend," she admitted. "That doesn't mean I killed my husband."

"We have your husband's word for that," the captain told her. "He didn't have much time before he died, but he had enough time to identify you as his murderer."

"You're bluffing," she said. "He didn't write anything about me."

"He wrote this." Rogan held out the check. Reluctantly, with eyes narrowing and lips pressed tightly together, she moved closer to the desk to examine the piece of paper. As she looked at it, the worry left her face.

"Yes," she said triumphantly. "That's *all* he wrote. His own name. Nothing at all about me. Do you think I'm so stupid I'd have left—oh!" She cut herself short. "You're trying to trick me. But I'm not going to answer any more questions."

"I don't *have* any more questions," Rogan told her. "I just want you to get dressed and come with us to headquarters."

"But that's crazy! All you have is his signature. How can you call that a message about *me*?"

"Your name is Blanche, Mrs. Coleman," Rogan answered. "That's why your husband signed this check. He wanted to give us a piece of paper that was blank, except for a signature—in other words, a *carte blanche*."

Here, as promised, is Fred Dannay's afterword to the story:

Editor's Note: Is the story you have just finished a parody or a pastiche of Ellery Queen? Or is it a new form, a new variation of "parody-pastiche"? We asked author Patricia McGerr to give her views, and here is what she wrote to us: "Since talking to you, I've thought a bit more about the category to which my story, 'The Last Check,' belongs. It's not a parody or a pastiche, since the Famous Detective isn't present either in caricature or in carbon. Nor is the intent, as in the stories by Robert L. Fish and Jon L. Breen, comic. But its ancestry is clear. For while there are many Ellery Queen stories with no dying message, the thought of a dying message automatically brings Ellery Queen to mind. So what I really attempted was a straightforward account of two EQ readers (the victim and the detective). It seemed logical that a man steeped in the EQ canon would, if about to be killed, leave a cryptic clue to the identity of his murderer; and that, of course, required an investigator of similar literary taste, to recognize and interpret the dying message."

THE DEATH OF THE MALLORY QUEEN

Lawrence Block

Up to now, we've presented you with stories riffing on Ellery Queen the character and Ellery Queen the author. But Ellery Queen was also an editor, and in the story that follows it's that piece of the EQ puzzle that comes to the fore. As you'll see, "The Death of the Mallory *Queen" is more closely connected to Nero Wolfe than it is to Ellery Queen, but we hope you'll agree that the Mallory/Ellery element makes it worthy of inclusion in this collection. Lawrence Block provides the following introduction:*

Author's Note: I first wrote about Chip Harrison in 1970, in a coming-of-age novel called No Score *that could have been* Lecher in the Rye. *A second book,* Chip Harrison Scores Again, *followed a couple of years later, and, when I got the urge to write more about the lad, I had the idea of putting him to work for a private detective, a Nero Wolfe wannabe named Leo Haig. This worked, and Chip starred in two more novels,* Make Out With Murder *and* The Topless Tulip Caper. *They were intended as an homage to Rex Stout, although I understand he was not amused. "The Death of the* Mallory *Queen" was the first Chip Harrison short story, published in 1984. It was full of inside gags, with luminaries like Ellery Queen and Joan Kahn and Carol Bremer and the good Otto Penzler given altered names and sex-change operations, but I couldn't find a magazine to give it a home and tucked it into a collection,* Like a Lamb to Slaughter. *As for my own connection to Ellery Queen, I placed several stories with the magazine, starting with "A Bad Night for Burglars" in 1977. (Fred Dannay, who never met a title he didn't long to change, called it "Gentleman's Agreement," a title used to good effect some years previously by Laura Hobson.) It was Fred who published my first story about an idiosyncratic defense attorney named Martin Ehrengraf, and who suggested I write more about the fellow; that there's now a book of a dozen Ehrengraf stories* (Defender of the Innocent) *is in part his doing.*

"I am going to be murdered," Mavis Mallory said, "and I want you to do something about it."

Haig did something, all right. He spun around in his swivel chair and stared into the fish tank. There's a whole roomful of tanks on the top floor, and other aquariums, which he wishes I would call aquaria, scattered throughout the house. (Well, not the whole house. The whole house is a carriage house on West Twentieth Street, and on the top two floors live Leo Haig and Wong Fat and more tropical fish than you could shake a jar of tubifex worms at, but the lower two floors are still occupied by Madam Juana and her girls. How do you say *filles de joie* in Spanish, anyway? Never mind. If all of this sounds a little like a cut-rate, low-rent version of Nero Wolfe's establishment on West Thirty-Fifth Street, the similarity is not accidental. Haig, you see, was a lifelong reader of detective fiction, and a penny-ante breeder of tropical fish until a legacy made him financially independent. And he was a special fan of the Wolfe canon, and he thinks that Wolfe really exists, and that if he, Leo Haig, does a good enough job with the cases that come his way, sooner or later he might get invited to dine at the master's table.)

"Mr. Haig—"

"*Huff*," Haig said.

Except that he didn't exactly *say* huff. He *went* huff. He's been reading books lately by Sondra Ray and Leonard Orr and Phil Laut, books on rebirthing and physical immortality, and the gist of it seems to be that if you do enough deep circular breathing and clear out your limiting deathist thoughts, you can live forever. I don't know how he's doing with his deathist thoughts, but he's been breathing up a storm lately, as if air were going to be rationed any moment and he wants to get the jump on it.

He huffed again and studied the rasboras, which were the fish that were to-and-froing it in the ten-gallon tank behind his desk. Their little gills never stopped working, so I figured they'd live forever, too, unless their deathist thoughts were lurking to do them in. Haig gave another huff and turned around to look at our client.

She was worth looking at. Tall, willowy, richly curved, with a mane of incredible red hair. Last August, I went up to Vermont toward the end of the month, and all the trees were green except here and there you'd see one in the midst of all that green that had been touched by an early frost and turned an absolutely flaming scarlet, and that was the color of Mavis Mallory's hair. Haig's been quoting a lot of lines lately about the rich abundance of the universe we live in, especially when I suggest he's spending too much on fish and equipment, and looking at our client I had to agree with him. We live in an abundant world, all right.

"Murdered," he said.

She nodded.

"By whom?"

"I don't know."

"For what reason?"

"I don't know."

"And you want me to prevent it."

"No."

His eyes widened. "I beg your pardon?"

"How could you prevent it?" She wrinkled her nose at him. "I understand you're a genius, but what defense could you provide against a determined killer? You're not exactly the physical type."

Haig, who has been described as looking like a basketball with an Afro, huffed in reply. "My own efforts are largely in the cerebral sphere," he admitted. "But my associate, Mr. Harrison, is physically resourceful, and"—he made a tent of his fingertips—"still, your point is well taken. Neither Mr. Harrison nor I are bodyguards. If you wish a bodyguard, there are larger agencies which—"

But she was shaking her head. "A waste of time," she said. "The whole Secret Service can't protect a president from a lone deranged assassin. If I'm destined to be murdered, I'm willing to accede to my destiny."

"*Huff,*" Haig huffed.

"What I want you to do," she said, "and Mr. Harrison, of course, except that he's so young I feel odd calling him by his last name." She smiled winningly at me. "Unless you object to the familiarity?"

"Call me Chip," I said.

"I'm delighted. And you must call me Mavis."

"*Huff.*"

"Who wants to murder you?" I asked.

"Oh, dear," she said, "it sometimes seems to me that everyone does. It's been four years since I took over as publisher of *Mallory's Mystery Magazine* upon my father's death, and you'd be amazed how many enemies you can make in a business like this."

Haig asked if she could name some of them.

"Well, there's Abner Jenks. He'd been editor for years and thought he'd have a freer hand with my father out of the picture. When I reshuffled the corporate structure and created Mavis Publications, Inc., I found out he'd been taking kickbacks from authors and agents in return for buying their stories. I got rid of him and took over the editorial duties myself."

"And what became of Jenks?"

"I pay him fifty cents a manuscript to read slush-pile submissions.

He picks up some freelance work for other magazines as well, and he has plenty of time to work on his own historical novel about the Venerable Bede. Actually," she said, "he ought to be grateful to me."

"Indeed," Haig said.

"And there's Darrell Crenna. He's the owner of Mysterious Ink, the mystery bookshop on upper Madison Avenue. He wanted Dorothea Trill, the Englishwoman who writes those marvelous gardening mysteries, to do a signing at his store. In fact, he'd advertised the appearance, and I had to remind him that Miss Trill's contract with Mavis Publications forbids her from making any appearances in the States without our authorization."

"Which you refused to give."

"I felt it would cheapen the value of Dorothea's personal appearances to have her make too many of them. After all, Crenna talked an author out of giving a story to *Mallory's* on the same grounds, so you could say he was merely hoist with his own petard. Or strangled by his own clematis vine, like the woman in Dorothea's latest." Her face clouded. "I hope I haven't spoiled the ending for you?"

"I've already read it," Haig said.

"I'm glad of that. Or I should have to add you to the list of persons with a motive for murdering me, shouldn't I? Let me see now. Lotte Benzler belongs on the list. You must know her shop. The Murder Store?"

Haig knew it well, and said so. "And I trust you've supplied Ms. Benzler with an equally strong motive? Kept an author from her door? Refused her permission to reprint a story from *Mallory's* in one of the anthologies she edits?"

"Actually," our client said, "I fear I did something rather more dramatic than that. You know Bart Halloran?"

"The creator of Rocky Sledge, who's so hard-boiled he makes Mike Hammer seemed poached? I've read him, of course, but I don't know him."

"Poor Lotte came to know him very well," Mavis Mallory purred, "and then I met dear Bart, and then it was I who came to know him very well." She sighed. "I don't think Lotte has ever forgiven me. All's fair in love and publishing, but some people don't seem to realize it."

"So there are three people with a motive for murdering you."

"Oh, I'm sure there are more than three. Let's not forget Bart, shall we? He was able to shrug it off when I dropped him, but he took it harder when his latest got a bad review in *Mallory's*. But I thought *Kiss My Gat* was a bad book, and why should I say otherwise?" She sighed again. "Poor Bart," she said. "I understand his sales are slipping. Still, he's still a name, isn't he? And he'll be there Friday night."

"Indeed?" Haig raised his eyebrows. He's been practicing in front of the mirror, trying to raise just one eyebrow, but so far he hasn't got the knack of it. "And just where will Mr. Halloran be Friday night?"

"Where they'll all be," Mavis Mallory said. "At Town Hall, for the panel discussion and reception to celebrate the twenty-fifth anniversary of *Mallory's Mystery Magazine*. Do you know, I believe everyone with a motive to murder me will be gathered together in one room?" She shivered happily. "What more could a mystery fan ask for?"

"Don't attend," Haig said.

"Don't be ridiculous," she told him. "I'm Mavis Mallory of Mavis Publications. I am *Mallory's*—in fact, I've been called the *Mallory* Queen. I'll be chairing the panel discussion and hosting the celebration. How could I possibly fail to be present?"

"Then get bodyguards."

"They'd put such a damper on the festivities. And I already told you they'd be powerless against a determined killer."

"Miss Mallory—"

"And please don't tell me to wear a bulletproof vest. They haven't yet designed one that flatters the full-figured woman."

I swallowed, reminded again that we live in an abundant universe.

"You'll be killed," Haig said flatly.

"Yes," said our client, "I rather suspect I shall. I'm paying you a five thousand dollar retainer now, in cash, because you might have a problem cashing a check if I were killed before it cleared. And I've added a codicil to my will calling for payment to you of an additional twenty thousand dollars upon your solving the circumstances of my death. And I do trust you and Chip will attend the reception Friday night? Even if I'm not killed, it should be an interesting evening."

"I have read of a tribe of Africans," Haig said dreamily, "who know for certain that gunshot wounds are fatal. When one of their number is wounded by gunfire, he falls immediately to the ground and lies still, waiting for death. He does this even if he's only been nicked in the finger, and, by the following morning, death will have inevitably claimed him."

"That's interesting," I said. "Has it got anything to do with the *Mallory* Queen?"

"It has everything to do with her. The woman"—he huffed again, and I don't think it had much to do with circular breathing—"the damnable woman is convinced she will be murdered. It would profoundly disappoint her to be proved wrong. She *wants* to be murdered, Chip, and her thoughts are creative, even as yours and mine. In all likelihood, she will die on Friday night. She would have it no other way."

"If she stayed home," I said. "If she hired bodyguards—"

"She will do neither. But it would not matter if she did. The woman is entirely under the influence of her own death urge. Her death urge is stronger than her life urge. How could she live in such circumstances?"

"If that's how you feel, why did you take her money?"

"Because all abundance is a gift from the universe," he said loftily. "Further, she engaged us not to protect her but to avenge her, to solve her murder. I am perfectly willing to undertake to do that." *Huff.* "You'll attend the reception Friday night, of course."

"To watch our client get the ax?"

"Or the dart from the blowpipe, or the poisoned cocktail, or the bullet, or the bite from the coral snake, or what you will. Perhaps you'll see something that will enable us to solve her murder on the spot and earn the balance of our fee."

"Won't you be there? I thought you'd planned to go."

"I had," he said. "But that was before Miss Mallory transformed the occasion from pleasure to business. Nero Wolfe never leaves his house on business, and I think the practice a sound one. You will attend in my stead, Chip. You will be my eyes and my legs. *Huff.*"

I was still saying things like *Yes, but* when he swept out of the room and left for an appointment with his rebirther. Once a week, he goes all the way up to Washington Heights, where a woman named Lori Schneiderman gets sixty dollars for letting him stretch out on her floor and watching him breathe. It seems to me that for that kind of money he could do his huffing in a bed at the Plaza Hotel, but what do I know?

He'd left a page full of scribbling on his desk, and I cleared it off to keep any further clients from spotting it. *I, Leo, am safe and immortal right now,* he'd written five times. *You, Leo, are safe and immortal right now,* he'd written another five times. *Leo is safe and immortal right now,* he'd written a final five times. This was how he was working through his unconscious death urge and strengthening his life urge. I tell you, a person has to go through a lot of crap if he wants to live forever.

Friday night found me at Town Hall, predictably enough. I wore my suit for the occasion and got there early enough to snag a seat down front, where I could keep a private eye on things. There were plenty of things to keep an eye on. The audience swarmed with readers and writers of mystery and detective fiction, and if you want an idea of who was in the house, just write out a list of your twenty-five favorite authors and be sure that seventeen or eighteen of them were there. I saw some familiar faces, a woman who'd had a long run as the imperiled heroine of a

Broadway suspense melodrama, a man who'd played a police officer for three years on network television, and others whom I recognized from films or television but couldn't place out of context.

On stage, our client Mavis Mallory occupied the moderator's chair. She was wearing a strapless and backless floor-length black dress, and in combination with her creamy skin and fiery hair, its effect was dramatic. If I could have changed one thing, it would have been the color of the dress. I suppose Haig would have said it was the color of her unconscious death urge.

Her panelists were arranged in a semicircle around her. I recognized some but not others, but before I could extend my knowledge through subtle investigative technique, the entire panel was introduced. The members included Darrell Crenna of Mysterious Ink and Lotte Benzler of the Murder Store. The two sat on either side of our client, and I just hoped she'd be safe from the daggers they were looking at each other.

Rocky Sledge's creator, dressed in his standard outfit of chinos and a tee shirt, with the sleeve rolled to contain a pack of unfiltered Camels, was introduced as Bartholomew Halloran. "Make that Bart," he snapped. *If you know what's good for you*, he might have added.

Halloran was sitting at Mavis Mallory's left. A tall and very slender woman with elaborately coiffed hair and a lorgnette sat between him and Darrell Crenna. She turned out to be Dorothea Trill, the Englishwoman who wrote gardening mysteries. I always figured the chief gardening mystery was what to do with all the zucchini. Miss Trill seemed a little looped, but maybe it was the lorgnette.

On our client's other side, next to Lotte Benzler, sat a man named Austin Porterfield. He was a Distinguished Professor of English Literature at New York University, and he'd recently published a rather learned obituary of the mystery story in the *New York Review of Books*. According to him, mystery fiction had drawn its strength over the years from the broad base of its popular appeal. Now other genres had more readers, and thus mystery writers were missing the mark. If they wanted to be artistically important, he advised them, then get busy producing Harlequin romances and books about nurses and stewardesses.

On Mr. Porterfield's other side was Janice Cowan, perhaps the most prominent book editor in the mystery field. For years, she had moved from one important publishing house to another, and at each of them she had her own private imprint. "A Jan Cowan Novel of Suspense" was a good guarantee of literary excellence, whoever happened to be Miss Cowan's employer that year.

After the last of the panelists had been introduced, a thin, weedy man in a dark suit passed quickly among the group with a beverage tray, then scurried off the stage. Mavis Mallory took a sip of her drink, something colorless in a stemmed glass, and leaned toward the microphone.

"What Happens Next?" she intoned. "That's the title of our little discussion tonight, and it's a suitable title for a discussion on this occasion. A credo of *Mallory's Mystery Magazine* has always been that our sort of fiction is only effective insofar as the reader cares deeply what happens next, what takes place on the page he or she has yet to read. Tonight, though, we are here to discuss what happens next in mystery and suspense fiction. What trends have reached their peaks, and what trends are swelling just beyond the horizon."

She cleared her throat, took another sip of her drink. "Has the tough private eye passed his prime? Is the lineal descendant of Sam Spade and Philip Marlowe just a tedious outmoded macho sap?" She paused to smile pleasantly at Bart Halloran, who glowered back at her. "Conversely, has the American reader lost interest forever in the mannered English mystery? Are we ready to bid adieu to the body in the library, or"—she paused for an amiable nod at the slightly cockeyed Miss Trill— "the corpse in the formal gardens?"

"Is the mystery, if you'll pardon the expression, dead as a literary genre? One of our number"—and a cheerless smile for Professor Porterfield—"would have us all turn to writing *Love's Saccharine Savagery* and *Penny Wyse, Stockyard Nurse*. Is the mystery bookshop, a store specializing in our brand of fiction, an idea whose time has come—and gone? And what do book publishers have to say on this subject? One of our number has worked for so many of them, she should be unusually qualified to comment."

Mavis certainly had the full attention of her fellow panelists. Now, to make sure she held the attention of the audience as well, she leaned forward, a particularly arresting move given the nature of the strapless, backless black number she was more or less wearing. Her hands tightened on the microphone.

"Please help me give our panel members full attention," she said, "as we turn the page to find out"—she paused dramatically—"What Happens Next!"

What happened next was that the lights went out. All of them, all at once, with a great crackling noise of electrical failure. Somebody screamed, and then so did somebody else, and then screaming became kind of popular. A shot rang out. There were more screams, and then another shot, and then everybody was shouting at once, and then some lights came on.

Guess who was dead.

* * * *

That was Friday night. Tuesday afternoon, Haig was sitting back in his chair on his side of our huge old partners' desk. He didn't have his feet up—I'd broken him of that habit—but I could see he wanted to. Instead, he contented himself with taking a pipe apart and putting it back together again. He had tried smoking pipes, thinking it a good mannerism for a detective, but it never took, so now he fiddles with them. It looks pretty dumb, but it's better than putting his feet up on the desk.

"I don't suppose you're wondering why I summoned you all here," he said.

They weren't wondering. They all knew, all of the panelists from the other night, plus two old friends of ours, a cop named Gregorio who wears clothes that could never be purchased on a policeman's salary, and another cop named Seidenwall, who wears clothes that could. They knew they'd been gathered together to watch Leo Haig pull a rabbit out of a hat, and it was going to be a neat trick because it looked as though he didn't even have the hat.

"We're here to clear up the mysterious circumstances of the death of Mavis Mallory. All of you assembled here, except for the two gentlemen of the law, had a motive for her murder. All of you had the opportunity. All of you thus exist under a cloud of suspicion. As a result, you should all be happy to learn that you have nothing to fear from my investigation. Mavis Mallory committed suicide."

"Suicide!" Gregorio exploded. "I've heard you make some ridiculous statements in your time, but that one grabs the gateau. You have the nerve to sit there like a toad on a lily pad and tell me the redheaded dame killed herself?"

"Nerve?" Haig mused. "Is nerve ever required to tell the truth?"

"Truth? You wouldn't recognize the truth if it dove into one of your fish tanks and swam around eating up all the brine shrimp. The Mallory woman got hit by everything short of tactical nuclear weapons. There were two bullets in her from different guns. She had a wavy-bladed knife stuck in her back and a short dagger in her chest, or maybe it was the other way around. The back of her skull was dented by a blow from a blunt instrument. There was enough rat poison in her system to put the Pied Piper out of business, and there were traces of curare, a South American arrow poison, in her martini glass. Did I leave something out?"

"Her heart had stopped beating," Haig said.

"Is that a fact? If you ask me, it had its reasons. And you sit there and call it suicide. That's some suicide."

Haig sat there and breathed, in and out, in and out, in the relaxed, connected breathing rhythm that Lori Schneiderman had taught him. Meanwhile they all watched him, and I in turn watched them. We had them arranged just the way they'd been on the panel, with Detective Vincent Gregorio sitting in the middle where Mavis Mallory had been. Reading left to right, I was looking at Bart Halloran, Dorothea Trill, Darrell Crenna, Gregorio, Lotte Benzler, Austin Porterfield and Janice Cowan. Detective Wallace Seidenwall sat behind the others, sort of off to the side and next to the wall. If this were novel length, I'd say what each of them was wearing and who scowled and who looked interested, but Haig says there's not enough plot here for a novel and that you have to be more concise in short stories, so just figure they were all feeling about the way you'd feel if you were sitting around watching a fat little detective practice rhythmic breathing.

"Some suicide," Haig said. "Indeed. Some years ago a reporter went to a remote county in Texas to investigate the death of a man who'd been trying to expose irregularities in election procedures. The coroner had recorded the death as suicide, and the reporter checked the autopsy and discovered that the deceased had been shot six times in the back with a high-powered rifle. He confronted the coroner with this fact and demanded to know how the man had dared call the death suicide. 'Yep,' drawled the coroner. 'Worst case of suicide I ever saw in my life.'"

Gregorio just stared at him.

"So it is with Miss Mallory," Haig continued. "Hers is the worst case of suicide in my experience. Miss Mallory was helplessly under the influence of her own unconscious death urge. She came to me, knowing that she was being drawn toward death, and yet she had not the slightest impulse to gain protection. She wished only that I contract to investigate her demise and see to its resolution. She deliberately assembled seven persons who had reason to rejoice in her death, and enacted a little drama in front of an audience. She—"

"Six persons," Gregorio said, gesturing to the three on either side of him. "Unless you're counting her, or unless all of a sudden I get to be a suspect."

Haig rang a little bell on his desktop, and that was Wong Fat's cue to usher in a skinny guy in a dark suit. "Mr. Abner Jenks," Haig announced. "Former editor of *Mallory's Mystery Magazine*, demoted to slush reader and part-time assistant."

"He passed the drinks," Dorothea Trill remembered. "So that's how she got the rat poison."

"I certainly didn't poison her," Jenks whined. "Nor did I shoot her or stab her or hit her over the head or—"

Haig held up a hand. There was a pipe stem in it, but it still silenced everybody. "You all had motives," he said. "None of you intended to act on them. None of you planned to make an attempt on Miss Mallory's life. Yet thought is creative and Mavis Mallory's thoughts were power-ful. Some people attract money to them, or love, or fame. Miss Mallory attracted violent death."

"You're making a big deal out of nothing," Gregorio said. "You're saying she wanted to die, and that's fine, but it's still a crime to give her a hand with it, and that's what every single one of them did. What's that movie, something about the Orient Express, and they all stab the guy? That's what we got here, and I think what I gotta do is book 'em all on a conspiracy charge."

"That would be the act of a witling," Haig said. "First of all, there was no conspiracy. Perhaps more important, there was no murder."

"Just a suicide."

"Precisely," said Haig. *Huff.* "In a real sense, all death is suicide. As long as a man's life urge is stronger than his death urge, he is im-mortal and invulnerable. Once the balance shifts, he has an unbreakable appointment in Samarra. But Miss Mallory's death is suicide in a much stricter sense of the word. No one else tried to kill her, and no one else succeeded. She unquestionably created her own death."

"And shot herself?" Gregorio demanded. "And stuck knives in her-self, and bopped herself over the head? And—"

"No," Haig said. *Huff.* "I could tell you that she drew the bullets and knives to herself by the force of her thoughts, but I would be wasting my"—*huff!*—"breath. The point is metaphysical, and in the present con-text immaterial. The bullets were not aimed at her, nor did they kill her. Neither did the stabbings, the blow to the head, the poison."

"Then what did?"

"The stopping of her heart."

"Well, that's what kills everyone," Gregorio said, as if explaining something to a child. "That's how you know someone's dead. The heart stops."

Haig sighed heavily, and I don't know if it was circular breathing or resignation. Then he started telling them how it happened.

"Miss Mallory's death urge created a powerful impulse toward vio-lence," he said. "All seven of you, the six panelists and Mr. Jenks, had motives for killing the woman. But you are not murderous people, and you had no intention of committing acts of violence. Quite without con-scious intent, you found yourselves bringing weapons to the Town Hall event. Perhaps you thought to display them to an audience of mystery fans. Perhaps you felt a need for a self-defense capability. It hardly mat-ters what went through your minds.

"All of you, as I said, had reason to hate Miss Mallory. In addition, each of you had reason to hate one or more of your fellow panel members. Miss Benzler and Mr. Crenna are rival booksellers; their cordial loathing for one another is legendary. Mr. Halloran was romantically involved with the panel's female members, while Mr. Porterfield and Mr. Jenks were briefly, uh, closeted together in friendship. Miss Trill had been very harshly dealt with in some writings of Mr. Porterfield. Miss Cowan had bought books by Mr. Halloran and Miss Trill, then left the books stranded when she moved on to another employer. I could go on, but what's the point? Each and every one of you may be said to have had a sound desire to murder each and every one of your fellows, but in the ordinary course of things nothing would have come of any of these desires. We all commit dozens of mental murders a day, yet few of us dream of acting on any of them."

"I'm sure there's a point to this," Austin Porterfield said.

"Indeed there is, sir, and I am fast approaching it. Miss Mallory leaned forward, grasping her microphone, pausing for full dramatic value, and the lights went out. And it was then that knives and guns and blunt instruments and poison came into play."

The office lights dimmed as Wong Fat operated a wall switch. There was a sharp intake of breath, although the room didn't get all that dark, and there was a balancing *huff* from Haig. "The room went dark," he said. "That was Miss Mallory's doing. She chose the moment, not just unconsciously, but with knowing purpose. She wanted to make a dramatic point, and she succeeded beyond her wildest dreams.

"As soon as those lights went out, everyone's murderous impulses, already stirred up by Mavis Mallory's death urge, were immeasurably augmented. Mr. Crenna drew a Malayan kris and moved to stab it into the heart of his competitor, Miss Benzler. At the same time, Miss Benzler drew a poniard of her own and circled around to direct it at Mr. Crenna's back. Neither could see. Neither was well oriented. And Mavis Mallory's unconscious death urge drew both blades to her own body, even as it drew the bullet Mr. Porterfield meant for Mr. Jenks, the deadly blow Mr. Halloran meant for Cowan, the bullet Miss Cowan intended for Miss Trill, and the curare Miss Trill had meant to place in Mr. Halloran's glass.

"Curare, incidentally, works only if introduced into the bloodstream; it would have been quite ineffective if ingested. The rat poison Miss Mallory did ingest was warfarin, which would ultimately have caused her death by internal bleeding; it was in the glass when Abner Jenks served it to her."

"Then Jenks tried to kill her," Gregorio said.

Haig shook his head. "Jenks did not put the poison in the glass," he said. "Miss Lotte Benzler had placed the poison in the glass before Miss Mallory picked it up."

"Then Miss Benzler—"

"Was not trying to kill Miss Mallory, either," Haig said, "because she placed the poison in the glass she intended to take for herself. She had previously ingested a massive dose of Vitamin K, a coagulant that is the standard antidote for warfarin, and intended to survive a phony murder attempt on stage, both to publicize the Murder Store and to discredit her competitor, Mr. Crenna. At the time, of course, she'd had no conscious intention of sticking a poniard into the same Mr. Crenna, the very poniard that wound up in Miss Mallory."

"You're saying they all tried to kill each other," Gregorio said. "And they all killed her instead."

"But they didn't succeed."

"They didn't? How do you figure that? She's dead as a bent doornail."

"She was already dead."

"How?"

"Dead of electrocution," Haig told him. "Mavis Mallory put out all the lights in Town Hall by short-circuiting the microphone. She got more than she bargained for, although in a sense it was precisely what she'd bargained for. In the course of shorting out the building's electrical system, she herself was subjected to an electrical charge that induced immediate and permanent cardiac arrest. The warfarin had not yet had time to begin inducing fatal internal bleeding. The knives and bullets pierced the skin of a woman who was already dead. The bludgeon crushed a dead woman's skull. Miss Mallory killed herself."

Wong Fat brought the lights up. Gregorio blinked at the brightness. "That's a pretty uncertain way to do yourself in," he said. "It's not like she had her foot in a pail of water. You don't necessarily get a shock shorting out a line that way, and the shock's not necessarily a fatal one."

"The woman did not consciously plan her own death," Haig told him. "An official verdict of suicide would be of dubious validity. Accidental death, I suppose, is what the certificate would properly read." He huffed mightily. "Accidental death! As that Texas sheriff would say, it's quite the worst case of accidental death I've ever witnessed."

And that's what it went down as, accidental death. No charges were ever pressed against any of the seven, although it drove Gregorio crazy that they all walked out of there untouched. But what could you get them for? Mutilating a corpse? It would be hard to prove who did what, and it would be even harder to prove that they'd been trying to kill each other. As far as Haig was concerned, they were all acting under the influence of Mavis Mallory's death urge, and were only faintly responsible for their actions.

"The woman was ready to die, Chip," he said, "and die she did. She wanted me to solve her death and I've solved it, I trust to the satisfaction of the lawyers for her estate. And you've got a good case to write up. It won't make a novel, and there's not nearly enough sex in it to satisfy the book-buying public, but I shouldn't wonder that it will make a good short story. Perhaps for *Mallory's Mystery Magazine*, or a publication of equal stature."

He stood up. "I'm going uptown," he announced, "to get rebirthed. I suggest you come along. I think Wolfe must have been a devotee of rebirthing, and Archie as well."

I asked him how he figured that.

"Rebirthing reverses the aging process," he explained. "How else do you suppose the great detectives manage to endure for generations without getting a day older? Archie Goodwin was a brash young man in *Fer-de-Lance* in 1934. He was still the same youthful wisenheimer forty years later. I told you once, Chip, that your association with me would make it possible for you to remain eighteen years old forever. Now it seems that I can lead you not only to the immortality of ink and paper but to genuine physical immortality. If you and I work to purge ourselves of the effects of birth trauma, and if we use our breath to cleanse our cells, and if we stamp out deathist thoughts once and forever—"

"Huh," I said. But wouldn't you know it? It came out *huff*.

THE RANSOM OF EQMM #1

Arthur Vidro

Author's Note: Growing up, I never bought a poster. Got through high school and college without defacing my walls. But then, as an adult, I saw, in the October 1989 issue of Ellery Queen's Mystery Magazine, *an ad for a limited-edition poster. I clipped the coupon, mailed a check, and bought it—a huge blow-up of the cover of the Fall 1941* EQMM. *Three years later, I bought a bunch of old issues of the magazine, including Fall 1941, and immediately noticed a discrepancy between my poster and the actual issue. In 2011, the hoopla surrounding* EQMM's *seventieth anniversary spurred me to create a story around that discrepancy. Though I focused on the magazine, not Ellery, I paid homage to the Queen books by including two of their police characters. To have included Ellery, I felt, would have been an act of sacrilege.*

The pride of my life is my full run of *Ellery Queen's Mystery Magazine*. In, of course, excellent condition. No browning or brittle pages. No rips. No coupons clipped. No doodling on the covers. No mailing labels. With reluctance, I allow on the contents page small check marks recommending specific stories; have to allow the previous owners some leeway. Otherwise, these magazines are in delicious condition.

The debut issue, dated Fall 1941, has seven stories, one each by Dashiell Hammett, Margery Allingham, T.S. Stribling, Anthony Abbot, Cornell Woolrich, Frederick Hazlitt Brennan, and Ellery Queen. Other authors published in the first year of *EQMM* include Agatha Christie, Melville Davisson Post, Frederick Irving Anderson, John Dickson Carr, R. Austin Freeman, Ben Hecht, Edgar Wallace, Lawrence G. Blochman, Stuart Palmer, and Jacques Futrelle. Quite a roster.

Unlike many collectors, I have read all the stories in my collection.

When the local newspaper got wind of my run of all seventy years' worth of *EQMM*, they sent a cub reporter with notebook and camera. I even unlocked the glass case so he could shoot some snapshots without battling glare.

At least he asked permission before touching. "Mind if I move them around and look through a few?" he asked.

"Go right ahead, young man, but be careful."

"I'm very careful with books, and these magazines are like small books." He started setting up his photo shoot.

The end result landed on page 3 of the weekly *Shinn Corners Courier*:

70-Year-Old Local Man Showcases 70-Year-Old Magazine Collection

by Mark Wayne Howard

Some people collect coins or stamps or dolls or trains. One local resident has a full collection of more than 800 issues of *Ellery Queen's Mystery Magazine*, the leading fiction magazine of its genre. You won't find it on sale in Shinn Corners anymore, but that's because most of its business is by subscription. Homer Slocum adds ten issues each year to his growing collection by motoring to Boston to buy each copy as it hits the newsstands there. He claims he can't subscribe, because "having a mailing label affixed ruins an issue's collectability."

The magazine was founded in 1941 by the famous mystery writer Ellery Queen and publisher Lawrence E. Spivak.

Slocum's collection is preserved behind glass in barrister bookcases. The accompanying photos show how the height and width of the digest-sized magazine fluctuated throughout the decades. The earliest issues all face the viewer front-on because, explains Slocum, it wasn't until 1949 that the magazine was bound with a square spine on which the issue's date and year could be printed.

"I'm sure there are some other collectors out there who, like me, have a full run of *EQMM*, but the number isn't large," says Slocum.

Even the current *EQMM* publisher, Dell Magazines, does not possess a full run of the title.

But why collect this particular magazine?

Slocum says he's always been partial to short stories, especially mysteries, and he feels an affinity with *EQMM* because both he and it were brought into this world on the same day, September 25, 1941.

That first issue has appreciated greatly and a typical one would fetch several hundred dollars in the open market. Slocum believes his copy, being in excellent condition, could command several times that amount.

(If any other *Courier* readers have extensive collections, we'd love to highlight them.)

The article did not divulge my address, but I'm listed in the county phone book, so anyone with half a brain could have figured out where my collection was housed. And our town has plenty of folks with half a brain.

Next day, much to my dismay, the gawkers started arriving. People I barely knew or knew not at all would ring the doorbell for a look at The Collection. Young and old, male and female, even a whole den of Cub Scouts, traipsed through my home.

After a few days, I'd had enough. Placed my "Keep Out" and "Gone Fishing" signs on my porch swing and stopped letting people in. Had to get my collection back in order.

But I couldn't.

For the Fall 1941 issue of *EQMM* was gone.

I ransacked my house looking for it, but it wasn't there. Called my insurance company and learned collectibles are not covered under my homeowner's policy. Moseyed over to the police station to file a missing magazine report.

A large, beefy sergeant named Thomas Velie was on duty and handled the paperwork.

"Dee-skrip-shun?" he asked.

"Five and a half inches wide. A smidgen over seven and a half inches tall. About three-eighths of an inch thick."

He sighed. "You expect us to take mesh-ure-ments of every magazine we come across? Give me something better to go on."

"A hundred and twenty-eight white pages in off-brown wrappers."

"Rappers?"

"Soft paper covers. The front is dominated by a George Salter illustration of a man whose eyeglasses reflect the hunt for a killer." About this time the sergeant put down his pencil. "And the back is dominated by a letter Q in quotation marks."

"So you want us to look for a magazine with a Q on the back cover?"

"Not an ordinary Q. This one has two tails through it."

The sergeant chuckled and called over a police officer who was sipping a cup of coffee in the corner. "Mr. Slocum, this here is Officer Arthur Johnson. Mr. Slocum wants us to mind our Ps and Qs—or at least he wants us to be on the lookout, Johnson, for a Q with two tails through it. Ain't that right, Mr. Slocum?"

"Why, yes," I stammered.

"Now tell us, Maestro," the sergeant continued, "why does this particular Q on the back cover have two tails when one tail is good enough for all them other Qs?"

"One tail represents Manfred Lee and the other tail represents Frederic Dannay. You see, together they wrote as Ellery Queen."

The sergeant nodded with feigned comprehension. "Well, sure, Mr. Slocum, sir. That explains everything." He crumpled up the paper on which he'd been writing. "Johnson and I will look at every Q in town until we find us the one with the two tails, and when we find it we'll let you know right away. And in the meantime, you be careful, Mr. Slocum, not to climb any trees."

I didn't understand. "Not to climb trees?"

"Wouldn't want the squirrels to mistake you for a nut!" Velie roared at his joke, Johnson chuckled, and I slinked away.

I'd have to find *EQMM* #1 on my own.

Each night over supper I open the day's mail and, once a week, pore over the local newspaper.

The following edition of the *Courier* included, in the Police Log, a report of the missing magazine. It concluded with: "Distinctive features: on rear wrapper is the letter Q with an unusual variation."

Two evenings later, still mourning the loss of my *EQMM* #1, I dined at home on chicken soup with rice and a slab of rye bread. My incoming correspondence included the usual items plus one envelope that bore a local postmark but no return address. Inside was a slip of plain white paper on which was typed:

> Here is picture proving we have your magazine and have not hurt it. To get it back, leave $500 cash in brown paper bag under elm tree outside police station. Tonight. Midnight. Or else it's curtains for your magazine. Each night you do not pay, we will draw an extra tail through the back-page double-tailed Q. Heck, we'll even draw extra Qs. With permanent marker.

This was the enclosed picture:

I ran off a copy of the ransom note en route to the police station. Velie and Johnson were on duty alone and didn't seem to notice me.

"Did you lend him the money?" asked Velie.

"No," said Johnson. "Not this time. Told him if he gets into debt without the family's help, then he should get out of it without our help. Don't think he'll ever learn his les—"

"Good evening," I spoke up. Their faces sank. Unfortunately, they remembered me.

I presented the ransom note to the smirking Velie. "I don't expect you to find my magazine, Sergeant; that's my worry. But I plan to leave a bag filled with money outside your police station tonight. Can you post someone to nab the greedy bugger?"

The sergeant rubbed his jaw and pocketed the note. "Now that we have some ev-ee-dence, we can spare a man for one night. Johnson here will be glad to take the midnight watch."

The small, balding officer flinched. "I will? But, Velie, you're much bigger than me. What if the thief is huge and—"

"You'll be armed; the thief probably won't be. Thanks for volunteering." Johnson went to the coffeepot. Velie beamed at me. "Mr. Slocum, if the thief shows up, we'll catch him."

"Oh, the thief won't show up," I said. "I just want you to apprehend whoever sent this note."

"Isn't that the thief?"

"No. But thanks for your help. I'll be back a few minutes before midnight with the drop-off bag. Should I come in here first or just leave it at the tree?"

"Leave it at the tree. He might be watching the place. And just to be safe, when you put down the bag, make some noise."

"What noise? And why?"

"Any loud noise. Cough, sneeze, walk with a cane or long umbrella. This way we'll know it's you and be alert." He lowered his voice to a rumbling whisper and winked. "It's to wake Johnson up. He don't know it yet, but last week we switched the station-house brew to decaf."

I hustled home to work on my larger problem, finding the missing magazine.

The dim light of my porch bulb showed I had company. There on my porch swing, nibbling a doughnut over a paper sack and sipping a takeout coffee, was cub reporter Mark Wayne Howard. Beside him lay a shoebox. He hailed me with a sheepish grin.

"Been waiting for you. Thought you'd want this back." He neatly set down the coffee and handed me the box. I lifted the lid.

Inside, resting on a small fleecy lining and a bed of color photographs, was my *EQMM* #1.

After placing the magazine back in its rightful place of prominence, we sat down to admire the collection anew.

"Why did you take my magazine?" I asked.

"Sorry. Wasn't thinking. I saw the authors' names and started flipping pages and reading…couldn't put it down…so I took it with me to read all the stories in full. But then I got sick for several days. Couldn't sit up in bed, let alone read. Got my strength back today."

"Wish you'd have just asked me first. I don't mind your reading it if you're careful."

"Gee, sir, I didn't realize I was causing such a problem until I read the police report. But here it is, and none the worse for wear. Okay if I tell my editor the crime is solved?"

"Not yet, young man. The magazine's disappearance is solved. But we still have a criminal to catch." I showed him my copy of the ransom note.

"Whew. That's something. May I tag along and earn a scoop?"

"You sure you don't know anything about this ransom note?"

He blanched. "No, I swear! I didn't even know about the double-tailed Q—you never mentioned it in our interview."

"Never mentioned it? No, I didn't…not to you nor the gawkers—of course! That's the key clue!"

"Key clue, sir?"

"Never mind that. Did you shoot a picture of my *EQMM* #1?"

"Sure did. But it didn't run in the *Courier*. Editor published only a few, mostly closeups of the more bloody and sexy covers. All the photos we didn't use are in the shoebox. Thought you might like them enough that you wouldn't get me into trouble for, er, borrowing your magazine."

"Ah," I said. "A peace offering? Very well, I accept. Get that photo from the box and follow me. We've work to do."

The young journalist trailed me as I retrieved from my games room a large stack of Monopoly currency and then searched with increasing annoyance for a brown paper sack. But there was none in the house. I berated myself for always bringing my own cloth bags to the shops. My companion finally gave me his bag. I tossed the false currency onto the doughnut crumbs and coffee droplets, sealed the bag with a few rubber bands, grabbed a walking stick from my closet, and off we went to nab a crook.

I drove us to the police station, parked a full block away, turned off my lights. As we waited the few minutes to midnight, I gave the young journalist some instructions. Then I headed to the elm tree. I poked harshly at the ground with my walking stick, but the darned thing had a rubber tip on it, like a silencer. So when I reached the tree trunk I resorted to a few wheezes that blossomed into a coughing fit.

I dropped the bag at the trunk base, walked away as sharply as my seventy-year-old legs allowed, then ducked for cover behind a thicket of bushes.

Silence for nearly a minute. Then my car engine kicked in, and I heard the auto pull away. Good boy, that journalist. Doing exactly as I told him. Immediately after came the sound of cautious but rapid footsteps. They got nearer and I craned to look.

A lanky man-shaped figure in a ski mask hastened through the dim night straight to the elm. He scooped up the paper bag and began sprinting my way.

Then everything happened at once.

I jumped up, aimed my flashlight at the felon, and snapped it on. "Stop, crook! You're surrounded!" I brandished the walking stick like a club.

My car engine revved louder as it skidded toward us, and the car headlights snapped on, blinding the petrified thug.

Officer Johnson, in plain clothes, leapt from a nearby thicket, gun in hand. "Police! Freeze! Don't make me shoot! You are under arrest!" I hadn't counted on the police's help, but was grateful for it.

The crook raised his hands, still holding the paper bag.

Young Mr. Howard ran from the car, its headlights still on us, and removed the fellow's mask.

"Chester!" exclaimed Johnson.

The unmasked man shielded his face from the light and whimpered. "Uncle Arthur, please let me go. I didn't hurt anyone, and I won't do it again. But I was gambling too much again, and had to pay off my bookie and—"

"Shut up!" said Johnson. "You are under arrest for trying to ransom issue #1 of *Ellery Queen's Mystery Magazine*. You have the right to remain silent. I strongly encourage you to exercise that right, else I'll get your parents here pronto and they'll give you a good whipping. Into the station house, everyone!"

Johnson, Howard, and I sat in the station house, drinking precinct coffee, until Sergeant Velie arrived to take charge. In another room, Chester was locked up in the constabulary's one holding cell.

"Good work, Johnson. You too, Mr. Slocum," Velie said after being updated. "Quite a shocker, Johnson, your nephew being the culprit."

"Didn't shock me," I said. "I knew the person who sent the ransom note had to be one of you two officers, or else someone who knew you fairly well."

Johnson turned red and Velie scratched his head.

"How did you dope that out, Maestro?"

"Simple. The note mentioned the Q with the two tails. But the police report in the newspaper didn't mention the two tails. And when Mr. Howard here wrote the feature article about my collection, he didn't mention the tails either—because he didn't know about them. The only time I mentioned them was here—to you, Sergeant, and you, Officer Johnson. So one or both of you were guilty, or else one of you had mentioned it to the ransomer…."

Johnson turned a deeper shade of scarlet. "Yeah, I shouldn't have done it, but I told my missus the whole story about the missing *EQMM*; thought she'd get a laugh about that Q business."

"Joanne's trustworthy," said Velie. "I could see your telling her. But your deadbeat nephew? Come on!"

"Well, he was mooching a meal off us, so he heard it, too. Big mistake. My mistake."

"For discussing police business in front of Chester, I suspend you for a week without pay." Johnson shrugged and stood up as if to leave. "Stick around. Suspension starts next week. Can't get Hesse or Piggott to cover for you until then." Johnson placidly sat back down. "And when you do return, you have a full month of daily coffeepot-cleaning duty."

"Ouch!" Johnson winced. "I don't care what happens to Chester. And I could use a few days off. But a month of cleaning that coffeepot? That hurts worst of all."

Velie removed the rubber bands from the paper bag. "Let's count and pocket—I mean, file away the ev-ee-dence." He dumped out the contents. "*Monopoly* money?" he snorted.

"Afraid so, Sergeant," smiled journalist Howard.

"Well, let's count it anyway and file it away." Velie methodically tabulated the pseudo-cash while eating the few doughnut remnants large enough to be worth his while. He unlocked a desk drawer and tossed the bag in, then removed the ransom envelope from the drawer.

"One thing I don't understand, Maestro." Velie studied the paper. "When you brought us this ransom note, you said you already knew the sender wasn't the thief. How did you know?"

"Yeah, how?" asked Howard. "The *Courier*'s readers will want to know."

"Easy, Sergeant. One glance at the photo that came with the note told me right away that the sender did not have my magazine." Velie laid down the photo from the ransom envelope and scrutinized it.

"Mr. Howard," I said, "please give us the photo you took of my magazine." He placed on the table, beside the ransomer's *EQMM* picture, this snapshot:

"You see the difference, of course," I stated.

The sergeant pondered, Howard looked blank, and Johnson squinted with intensity.

Finally the small balding officer spoke. "You mean that your magazine has just a little bit of wear and tear, but the picture that was mailed to you looks like a flawless example?"

"Well, that's true enough, but the evidence to me was much more glaring. You still don't see it?"

They all shook their heads.

"Check the price."

"Oho!" said Velie. "Your copy sold for twenty-five cents but Chester sent you a picture showing a twenty-cent issue?"

"Bingo," I smiled. "That's how I knew right away that the ransomer was a fraud."

"But how could the magazine have two different prices?" asked Howard.

"It pretty much had only one price, for twenty-five cents. Near as I can figure it, the publishers had planned on a twenty-cent price but shortly before there was much or even any distribution, raised it to twenty-five. But the publisher kept the twenty-cent version in its files. Whenever it chose to re-create the image of the first issue, the non-existent twenty-cent version was used."

"How," asked Johnson, "did my nephew get hold of the twenty-cent image?"

"Probably off the Internet. It's a paradise for false information. Fools like your nephew tend to believe everything they read on it. But the image must be there somewhere. Back in 1976, *EQMM*'s publisher, which was Davis Publications then, offered readers a poster-size version of the cover of *EQMM* #1, in a limited numbered set of three hundred and fifty, all of them signed by Fred Dannay. That poster showed the misleading or erroneous twenty-cent price. It was a sort of thirty-fifth anniversary celebration."

"Gee," said Howard. "Bet it sold like hot cakes."

"Not really, son. As late as 1989, Davis was still trying to sell the last few of the three hundred and fifty posters. Now let's cut ahead to 2005. To celebrate the hundredth birthdays of Manny Lee and Fred Dannay, *EQMM*'s publisher—by this time Dell Magazines—sponsored a symposium and exhibition at Columbia University. To advertise the event, it made up postcards bearing the image of a flawless twenty-cent *EQMM* #1 from its files—or perhaps they enhanced the poster image. So either from that postcard or from the poster, Chester got an image, pretended it was a photograph he had taken, and sent it to me."

"Don't any twenty-cent issues of *EQMM* #1 exist?" asked Howard.

"Well," I hedged, "I have heard of one, in the possession of the Queen estate. But even that one, with a twenty-cent cover price, says in small print inside, 'Published quarterly by The American Mercury, Inc., at twenty-five cents a copy.' So I don't think, despite the posters and postcards, that twenty-cent copies were ever sold to the public. Then, of course, there was an Armed Forces edition without any price—"

Howard put down his notebook and pencil. "My head is spinning," he said. "I need to go home and sleep. Can you give me a ride and then tomorrow I'll write up the story?"

"If that's all right with the sergeant here," I beamed.

"Sure, Maestro, sure, get yourselves home and take your screwball *EQMM* knowledge with you. We'll handle the rest of the case from this end."

I drove Howard back to his car at my house. As he inserted his key he asked me one more favor, to which I agreed.

"Mr. Slocum," he asked, "there are so many great stories to read. Could I stop by tomorrow and borrow *EQMM* #2?"

THE TEN-CENT MURDER

Joseph Goodrich

*Author's Note: With the exception of a slight case of murder,
almost everything in this story is true: Dashiell Hammett taught
a class in mystery writing at the Jefferson Institute in Manhattan, his friend and colleague Fred Dannay was an occasional
guest lecturer, freedom of speech and thought was under siege
from homegrown fascists like Senator Joseph McCarthy and his
Red Scare. What must it have been like to be in that classroom,
with two masters of their craft sharing their secrets with a group
of tyros? The historical record, alas, doesn't tell us much, so
"The Ten-Cent Murder" is a roundabout bit of speculation on
what might have (could have?) happened. After all, there are
worse ways to learn about mystery writing than by watching two
of the profession's finest track down a killer!*

Fred Dannay, in a dark-gray overcoat and fedora, heavy briefcase
swinging at his side, walked quickly along West Tenth Street. An editorial meeting at *Ellery Queen's Mystery Magazine* had gone on longer
than anticipated, and he was running late. It was eight minutes after six
on an early autumn evening in 1951. The sky was lambent. The trees still
had their leaves, obscuring the brick and stone of the buildings that lined
the block, but the air was chillier than a week ago. He was glad he'd
worn the overcoat. If only he'd brought his scarf….

He pressed the buzzer of the garden apartment at number 28 and
waited.

Dashiell Hammett, tall and painfully thin, with a shock of white hair
and a dark mustache, opened the door. He was wearing a crisp white shirt
with French cuffs and onyx cufflinks and sharply creased brown slacks.
He greeted Fred, who was shorter by at least a foot, hung up his hat and
overcoat, and led him from the small foyer into the living room.

"Sorry I'm late."

"No need to apologize. Drink?"

"Do we have time?"

"They'll wait for us."

"A small one, then."

Dash fixed drinks.

Fred sat on a chair near the fireplace. The grate was filled with cigarette butts and crumpled up legal-pad pages. He took a scotch-and-water from Dash. "Thank you." He unbuttoned his jacket and exhaled with a sigh. "It's good to be here."

"How's your day in the city been?" Dash poured a scotch, no water, for himself.

Fred sipped his drink. "The train in was late this morning. I missed a meeting with Stanley. Things are crazy at the magazine. I've been trying all day to catch up."

"Have you succeeded?"

Fred lifted his bulging briefcase and let it drop back to the floor with a thud. "Not until I've read these."

Hammett whistled. "Jesus."

"I just hope there's a decent story in the lot. Two would better."

"Don't push your luck."

Fred laughed. "We get a lot of dreck, it's true." He took off his glasses and rubbed his eyes.

"You all right?"

"Headache." He massaged his temples. "I've had it all day."

"Sure you want to come to class tonight? You wouldn't rather head back to Larchmont and get some rest?"

"I promised I'd be there," Fred said doggedly, "and I'll be there."

"I appreciate it. I know the students are looking forward to meeting you."

Fred put his glasses on. "Any writers in the class?"

"Too soon to tell. They should have a character assignment ready for tonight. That'll help sort out the sheep from the lambs."

"How many students, this time around?"

"Three."

Fred was surprised. "Only three?"

"Students have been scared away from the school."

"My God, these are perilous times."

"They're getting worse." Dash sat in the chair across from Fred and lit a cigarette. He gestured to a yellow legal pad and several typewritten pages on the coffee table. "I've spent my day working on that."

Light danced in Fred's eyes. "A new story?"

"A begging letter. It's for the school. They asked me to take a look at it." He smiled. "I'm nothing but a glorified proofreader these days."

"May I?"

"Be my guest."

Fred leaned forward and collected the typewritten pages. He adjusted his glasses, then started reading:

> The Jefferson School of Social Science was founded in 1944, and occupies a nine-story building in downtown Manhattan. It is an adult evening school that teaches Marxism, the philosophy and social science of the working class. It analyzes the nature of capitalist and socialist society and studies the general laws of social change, with special emphasis on the United States.

Hammett watched him, smoke unfurling from his cigarette.

> Today the United States Department of Justice is trying to shut down the Jefferson School—the first time in history our Government has moved to close a school on the basis of what it teaches. Such thought-control measures are not new in this period of the "Cold War." Many Americans have fallen victim to the growing menace of McCarthyism.

Fred looked up from the page. "They can't actually shut it down, can they?"

Before Dash could answer, the telephone rang. He tossed his cigarette into the fireplace, crossed the room and picked up the receiver.

"ORegon 3-3797," he said. A voice buzzed on the other end.

Fred watched Dash listening to his caller, then went back to the typewritten page:

> They include teachers and students, trade union leaders, writers and publishers, artists and entertainers, leaders of the Negro people, and foreign-born persons who have lived here for decades. Thousands have been "investigated" by Congressional committees, hounded by the F.B.I., pilloried in the press, fired from their jobs, deported, barred from travel abroad, or sent to prison—on the basis of what they think and advocate, or what they are suspected of thinking.

Fred took another sip of his scotch-and-water.

> The drive to intimidate the non-conformists of our time has become so severe that what Supreme Court Justice William O. Douglas calls "The Black Silence of Fear" has begun to settle over the people of our country. Much of this drive against

"I'll be there as soon as I can," Dash said.

Fred looked up. He could tell from Dash's expression that something was wrong. He set the page aside.

Dash dropped the receiver into its cradle. He took a long swig of scotch and lit another cigarette.

"What's happened?"

Dash exhaled smoke. "Can they shut the place down? Isn't that what you asked, just before the phone rang?"

"That's right."

"Their chances just got a hell of a lot better." Dash downed the rest of his scotch. "That was Peggy Parsons, one of the board members. There's been a murder."

"At the school?"

"Yes." Dash flicked his cigarette into the fireplace and got to his feet. "They want me to talk to the police." He left the room.

Fred stood up and walked to the bedroom door. Dash stood at the mir-ror, tying his tie with quick, efficient movements. "Who's been killed?"

"One of the staff members."

"Do they have any idea who did it?"

Dash slipped into a tan-and-black-checked sports coat. "They think it was one of my students." He crossed into the foyer and put on his hat and overcoat. "There won't be any class tonight. You can get an early train home."

"Are you kidding me?" Fred, briefcase in hand, bustled into the foy-er. He grabbed his overcoat. "I'm coming with you. I wouldn't miss this for the world."

"I'll be glad to have you there. And from what Peggy told me, it sounds like this murder is right up your alley."

"How do you mean?"

Dash would say nothing more. Fred slapped his hat on and followed him out of the apartment.

The black-and-yellow Plymouth De Luxe taxicab let them out in front of the Jefferson School of Social Science, a nondescript building at Sixteenth and Sixth. They showed their identification to a policeman, massive in his brass-buttoned tunic and cap, and got into the self-ser-vice elevator. Dash pushed the button for the seventh floor. The elevator ground its way upward.

"We're lucky," he said, breaking the silence he'd maintained since leaving West Tenth Street.

"We are?"

Dash gave Fred a grim smile. "Usually the elevator's out of order."

While they waited for Detective McAlpine, Dash and Fred talked with Margaret Parsons in an empty classroom. Mrs. Parsons was a striking dark-haired woman in her early forties who favored dungarees and pearls. She came from old money and had new ideas about how to spend it. She funded organizations dedicated to social justice, the improvement of race relations, American-Soviet Friendship, and a dozen other causes. She taught an evening class in Dialectical Materialism and, like Dash, was on the school's board.

At twenty minutes to six, Mrs. Parsons had found the body of Morris Rabinowitz, the school's registrar, lying dead on the floor of his office, a letter opener protruding from his neck. Rabinowitz's desk had been forced open and searched. Only one thing was missing: a list of the students currently enrolled in the school. Mrs. Parsons had notified the police and then called Dash.

"You see how horrible this is," Mrs. Parsons said. "Not only is Mr. Rabinowitz dead, but the student list is gone."

"What's so important about the list?' Fred asked.

Dash lit a cigarette. "The school guards that list carefully. If it fell into the wrong hands, it could be used to blacklist or blackmail the students on it."

"We may do away with keeping any lists at all." Mrs. Parsons drew her mink tighter about her. "If this doesn't close us down for good."

Dash aimed a plume of smoke toward the ceiling. "They think it was one of my students?"

"Yes. They were all seen around Mr. Rabinowitz's office within twenty minutes of the time I found him."

"Between five-twenty and five-forty or so?"

"That's right."

"No one else was around?"

"No. It looks like whoever killed poor Mr. Rabinowitz is one of your students."

"Who saw them?" Fred said.

"Bridie, the cleaning woman."

"Where are they now?" Hammett said.

Mrs. Parsons gestured toward one of the faded green walls. "In one of the classrooms. Waiting to be questioned."

"Who are they?" Fred said. "What are their names?"

Dash held up a finger for each student. "Penny Meyer. Brendan Nicholl. Salvatore Quarta."

"Wait a second. Penny, Nicholl, Quarta. Their names are all coins, or damn near. You've got to be kidding me."

"I wish I was."

"And that's not all." Mrs. Parsons twisted her strand of her pearls. "Mr. Rabinowitz was found with a dime clutched in his hand."

"A dying clue?" Fred shook his head in disbelief. "This is like something out of one of the Queen stories."

"Now you see why I'm glad you're here," Dash said.

"Ellery would know what to do. I'm afraid I don't."

"If only Ellery Queen *were* here," Mrs. Parsons said. "He could solve the murder and save the school."

Fred looked thoughtful. "Would it really?"

Mrs. Parson sighed deeply "At this point, Mr. Dannay, *anything* would help."

Fred paced. Hammett watched him, amused. He could see the wheels turning in Fred's mind.

Fred stopped abruptly. "I wonder," he said, "if Detective McAlpine would let us talk with the students?"

It turned out that McAlpine—a long gray figure in a blue serge suit and a snap-brim fedora—would, but only after he'd questioned them. After a long wait, Fred, Dash and Mrs. Parsons were taken to the glum trio of students.

Penny Meyer was in her late twenties, with ash-blond hair and a deep tan left over from the summer. She was dressed in a bright red tam o' shanter, a black turtleneck sweater, a red-and-black plaid skirt and black flats.

Brendan Nicholl was in his late twenties. He wore a camel hair sport coat, blue shirt and tie, chino trousers and brown loafers. A crew haircut and horn-rimmed glasses heightened his resemblance to *Call Me Madam*'s Russell Nype.

Salvatore Quarta was the odd man out. He was well into his fifties, heavy-set, with a dark complexion and a workingman's hands. His suit was off the rack and his shoes were badly in need of a polish. He was sweating. He looked up from a manuscript held together with a large silver paperclip, then quickly looked down again.

Penny stood up. "Mr. Hammett, isn't it terrible what happened? We couldn't be more upset about it all."

Nicholl and Quarta followed Penny's lead and stood. Dash introduced Fred. Penny said it was an honor to meet him and how nice it was of him to come to Mr. Hammett's mystery-writing class. Nicholl expressed the hope that Mr. Dannay would return when things had settled down. Quarta told Fred how much he'd enjoyed *The Origin of Evil* and asked, "Are you working on another mystery?"

"I'm working on one now," Fred said, smiling.

He chatted for another couple of minutes with the students, asking them about their work and their lives, while Dash and Mrs. Parsons watched. Then he crossed to Dash and said in an undertone: "I think I'm on to something."

Dash whispered back. "What?"

They talked together quietly for a time.

"I noticed that, too," Dash said.

"Do you want to handle it?"

Dash shook his head. "No. My detective days are over."

"Then I'll ask McAlpine to check on it."

Fred stepped into the hall. A uniformed officer took him to McAlpine. Fred made his request.

McAlpine removed his hat and scratched his head. "The Hall of Records is closed for the day."

"Can you get someone to open it up?"

"I *could*, but I'd need a damned good reason."

"I think I can give you one."

Fred told McAlpine what he'd told Dash. McAlpine listened intently, then hurried off down the hall.

Fred rejoined Dash and Mrs. Parsons. "McAlpine's calling now. He thinks it'll take about an hour to get an answer."

"What is it you're waiting to find out about?" Mrs. Parsons said.

"A wedding ring," Fred said.

"A wedding ring? Why?"

"Unless I'm greatly mistaken, one is missing."

"Who's missing one?"

"One of the students."

Mrs. Parsons looked puzzled. "But none of them is married. I heard you asking them about that. So how can a wedding ring be missing?"

Fred refused to say another word.

Frustrated, Mrs. Parsons turned to Dash. "Do you know what he's talking about?"

"Yes, but I'm not telling either."

"You're *impossible*." She sat down at one of the desks and folded her arms. "So what am I supposed to *do* for an hour?"

Dash brought out his pack of cigarettes. "Smoke if you got 'em."

Conversation had run out ten minutes before McAlpine and a uniformed officer entered. McAlpine hurried over to Fred and said something to him under his breath. Fred nodded, and McAlpine took a seat.

Fred stood up. Every eye turned to him. He adjusted his glasses and cleared his throat. "Ladies and gentlemen, Detective McAlpine has very kindly given me the floor. It's been a long evening for us all, so I'll try to wrap things up here as quickly as possible."

But he took his time before he spoke.

"Morris Rabinowitz was murdered tonight by someone who wanted the list of students currently attending the Jefferson School. I don't know why the killer wanted it, but Mr. Hammett and Mrs. Parsons assure me there are some very good—or should I say some very bad—reasons for stealing such a list. There's a *lot* I don't know. I never knew Mr. Rabinowitz, for instance, though I'm sorry he's dead. John Donne was right: 'Any man's death diminishes me, because I am involved in mankind.' Mr. Rabinowitz's death diminishes everyone in this room—even his killer."

McAlpine muttered something under his breath, but Fred paid no attention.

"I certainly don't know where the list is. It may be hidden somewhere on the premises, it may be tucked into a shoe or a briefcase, though I presume you've all been searched—or will be. I only know two things. The first is that there are three suspects, all students in Mr. Hammett's mystery-writing class. The second is that I was lied to this evening."

Fred slowly approached Penny Meyer and fixed his gaze on her. The young woman looked up at him with a blank, pleasant expression. "By whom, Mr. Dannay?"

"By you, Miss Meyer. For starters."

The young woman frowned. "I don't know what you mean. I haven't told any lies."

"Earlier this evening you said you're not married."

"I didn't lie. I'm not."

"You got a lovely tan this summer, Miss Meyer," Fred said.

"Thank you. I spent a lot of time at the beach."

"I can see you did. And that's why I couldn't help noticing the white band of skin on the fourth finger of your left hand. That strip of untanned skin is exactly where a wedding ring should be. But you said you weren't married. My only conclusion is that you lied to me. Unless you have another explanation?"

The young woman was silent, lips pursed, and she studied the toe of her left shoe, as if by concentrating hard enough she could make the room and everyone in it disappear.

"Do you have another explanation?" Fred was gentle but remorseless. "If you do, I'd like to hear it."

"So would I," growled McAlpine.

"Well, Miss Meyer? *Do* you have an alternate explanation?"

The dark head nodded. "Yes, I have." The young woman's voice wasn't much louder than a whisper. "But I wish I didn't have to tell you."

"Why is that?"

"Because it's"—Penny faltered, licked her lips, tried again—"it's too painful." She looked up at Fred, her dark eyes liquid with sorrow. "You were right, Mr. Dannay. I did lie to you. I *was* married. It was foolish to try to hide it from you. I'm sorry. But it's just so hard to talk about"—a tear ran down her cheek—"about Jimmy."

"Jimmy?"

"Jimmy McKelway," Penny said with a sigh. "He was a soldier. We were married just before he was sent to Korea. He died in the Battle of Taejon. It was only the other day I decided to stop wearing his ring." She lifted up her left hand, fingers outspread, then let it drop back onto her lap. "He was a hero, my Jimmy, and I loved him—but I have to live my own life." Her voice throbbed. "You understand that, don't you, Mr. Dannay? It's not bad of me, is it? It can't be. I loved him, but I have to be free."

Fred studied the young woman as she shakily dug a handkerchief out of her purse and wiped at her eyes. "That's a very touching story, Miss Meyer. It'd be even more touching if it were true."

Brendan Nicholl sprang to his feet. "How dare you speak to her like that? Hasn't she been through enough without—"

Detective McAlpine cut him off. "You'll get a chance to talk. Don't worry. For the moment, why don't you just sit down and shut up." The young man sat, staring daggers at McAlpine who, unfazed, gestured to Fred. "Go on, Mr. Dannay."

Fred's tone was mild. "As I was saying, Miss Meyer—your husband isn't dead, and he was never a soldier in Korea. According to the Hall of Records, your husband is very much alive. In fact, he's sitting right next to you. His name is Brendan Nicholl."

"That's ludicrous," the young man said. "I didn't even *know* Miss Meyer until I met her in Mr. Hammett's class. We're not married—we never have been—and as far as I know, we never will be. I wish you'd get that through your heads."

Fred turned to Hammett. "Good, isn't he?"

Hammett exhaled smoke. "He's good. He's very good. I like the note of righteous indignation he worked in. It's very effective. I almost believe him."

Mrs. Parsons stirred at Hammett's side. "Why don't you?"

"The records," Hammett said. "Right, Fred?"

"Exactly." Fred looked at the young man, who sat glowering at his desk. "The records show that you and Miss Meyer are married. Why you both chose to conceal it—why Miss Meyer isn't wearing her ring—I don't know. But I *do* know this. Judging by the paperback books and newspapers on his desk, Mr. Rabinowitz loved games and crossword puzzles and word play. Unable to speak due to a wound in the throat, he still managed to leave a clue to his killer's identity. As he was dying, he dug into his jacket pocket and picked out a coin, which was found in his clenched fist."

Fred stuffed his hands into his jacket pockets and made a slow circle of the room. "A coin. Doesn't that strike you as strange? I mean, we have a *room* full of coins here, don't we? *Penny* Meyer, Brendan *Nicholl* and—stretching things a little—Salvatore *Quarta*. But the coin we found in Mr. Rabinowitz's hand was a *dime*. How could a dime tell us who killed him? I asked Detective McAlpine what kind of change Mr. Rabinowitz had in his pockets. He told me: two dimes and a half-dollar. Nothing else. So Mr. Rabinowitz chose the dime on purpose. But what was that purpose? Who did Mr. Rabinowitz identify as his killer?" He peered at Hammett. "Dash?"

Hammett might have raised an eyebrow a fraction of an inch, and he might not have, but he said nothing.

"Mrs. Parsons?"

Mrs. Parsons shrugged. "I haven't the slightest, Mr. Dannay."

"Neither did I," Fred said, "until I found out that Penny and Brendan are married. Then it all fell into place." He crossed to the two young people. "Mr. Rabinowitz identified you as clearly as if he'd spoken your names. Do you know how he did it?"

Penny looked sideways at Brendan.

"Do you?"

Brendan opened his mouth to speak.

Before he could say a word, Fred slapped a coin onto Penny's desk. Everyone in the room—even McAlpine and the uniformed officer—jumped at the *thwack* of flesh and metal meeting wood.

"Rabinowitz identified his killers with a dime," Fred said, pointing at the coin. "And, after all, what is a dime but *two Nicholls*?"

It didn't take McAlpine long to get the details. Brendan Nicholl and Penny Meyer had been searching Rabinowitz's desk when the registrar returned unexpectedly. They'd tried to talk him out of calling the police, but Rabinowitz wouldn't give in. Brendan grabbed him when he tried to leave. They struggled. Penny stabbed him in the neck with the letter opener from the desk. They thought he was dead, but he wasn't—

not quite. They'd hidden the list in a desk in an empty classroom and planned to sell it to one of the rabid anti-Communist organizations that had sprung up over the last few years.

As the school registrar, Rabinowitz knew that Meyers and Nicholl were married. Penny often went by her maiden name. She and Nicholl were experts at the badger game and frequently posed as brother and sister. But that was over now. It was *all* over now.

A week later, Salvatore Quarta had dinner with Fred and Dash at the garden apartment on West Tenth. As two-thirds of the students had been arrested and the class had been canceled, Dash felt he owed Quarta something. After a steak dinner, drink in hand, Quarta read his short story aloud. Fred and Dash offered their critique. It wasn't bad, not bad at all. Some things to fix, some things to think about…but not bad.

As he was buttoning his overcoat, Quarta said, "Say, Mr. Dannay, I was wondering." He pulled a flat cap out of an overcoat pocket and put it on. "If I was to write up what happened last week at the school as a kind of story—as a piece of fiction, like—I was wondering if maybe you'd think about putting it in *EQMM*? If it was any good, of course."

"Stranger things have happened," Fred said.

They made their goodbyes and, talking nineteen to the dozen, walked off into the chilly autumn darkness. Dash locked the door behind them and sank onto the sofa. He lit a cigarette and smoked it in the ringing silence of the apartment.

He poured himself another drink and went into a small study off the bedroom. A typewriter with a blank sheet of paper rested on a small table. He sat in front of it and contemplated the keys with that old familiar ache. Maybe tonight. Maybe tonight….

ACKNOWLEDGMENTS

Many people provided invaluable assistance in the preparation of this book. We thank them, one and all, especially:

Larry Block, **Jon Breen**, **Joe Goodrich**, **Mike Nevins**, and **Arthur Vidro** for providing copies of their stories and permission to include them in this volume.

Janet Hutchings, **Jackie Sherbow**, and **Deanna McLafferty** at *EQMM* and **Kurt Sercu** in Belgium for tracking down some of the hard-to-find material.

Rémi Schultz in France for providing a copy of Thomas Narcejac's "*Le mystère des ballons rouge*," **Rebecca K. Jones** for translating it into English, and **Editions Denoël** in Paris for obtaining the reprint rights from Narcejac's estate.

Patricia Hoch for granting permission to include her husband Ed's story. **Virginia Brittain** for granting permission to include her husband Bill's story, and Bill's daughter **Susan Brittain Gawley** for her kind assistance. **Richard Simms** and **Joel Hoffman** for helping to arrange permission to include the story by **Arthur Porges**. **John Betancourt** and **Carla Coupe** at Wildside Press and **Vaughne Lee Hansen** at the Virginia Kidd Agency for granting permission to include the story by James Holding. **Carol Demont** at Penny Publications for granting permission to include the stories by **Dennis M. Dubin**, **Patricia McGerr**, **Norma Schier**, and **J.N. Williamson**, which originally appeared in *Ellery Queen's Mystery Magazine*. And **Kim Jorgensen**, reference librarian at the Bennett Martin Public Library in Lincoln, Nebraska, for information about Patricia McGerr.

John Betancourt and **Carla Coupe** of Wildside Press for their commitment to seeing *The Misadventures of Ellery Queen* appear in print.

Richard and **Douglas Dannay**, **Rand Lee** and **Patricia Lee Caldwell**, and the **Frederic Dannay Literary Property Trust** and **Manfred B. Lee Family Literary Property Trust**, faithful guardians of the literary legacy of Fred Dannay and Manny Lee, for their enthusiastic support, and for giving us permission to use the Ellery Queen name and character.

And, most of all, thanks to **Frederic Dannay** and **Manfred B. Lee**,

whose creation of Ellery Queen in 1929 inspired the authors of the stories contained in this volume.

ABOUT THE CONTRIBUTORS

DALE C. ANDREWS (1949–) is a lifelong Ellery Queen fan and the author of three Ellery Queen pastiches, all of which were originally published in *Ellery Queen's Mystery Magazine*. He has been a regular contributor on *SleuthSayers*, the mystery short story writers' blog, and a guest contributor on *Something Is Going to Happen*, the *EQMM* mystery blog. He previously was the Deputy Assistant General Counsel for Litigation at the U.S. Department of Transportation and an adjunct professor at the University of Denver.

LAWRENCE BLOCK (1938–) has been writing and publishing books and short stories, most of them in the field of crime fiction, for sixty years. As is perhaps inevitable in such a long career, he's won a handful of awards along the way, and has occasionally shouldered his way onto a bestseller list. Now and then something of his gets dramatized via film or TV. What pleases him most, however, is the fact that virtually his entire backlist, including no end of pseudonymous erotica originally printed on non-acid-free paper, is now—through the miracle of e-books and print-on-demand paperbacks—back in print, delighting a whole new generation of readers and bringing him wealth beyond the dreams of avarice.

JON L. BREEN (1943–) is the author of eight novels (two of which were shortlisted for Dagger Awards), over a hundred short stories, and two Edgar-Award-winning reference books, *What About Murder: A Guide to Books About Mystery and Detective Fiction* and *Novel Verdicts: A Guide to Courtroom Fiction*. His first story, a parody of Ed McBain's 87th Precinct books, appeared in *EQMM* in 1967, and he wrote *EQMM's* "Jury Box" book-review column for about thirty years. His critical work also appears in *Mystery Scene* and *The Weekly Standard*.

RICHARD DANNAY (1939–), one of Frederic Dannay's sons, is a New York City lawyer and litigator specializing in copyright and publishing law. His copyright cases have involved matters such as John Steinbeck's works, the novel and movie *Jurassic Park*, Dorothy Parker's poems, and Grateful Dead concert posters. He has published articles on copyright law's controversial "fair use" doctrine, and is a past president of the Copyright Society of the USA. He's also a book collector and member of the Grolier Club.

Little is known about **DENNIS M. DUBIN**. According to editor Fred Dannay's introduction to "Elroy Quinn's Last Case," which appeared in the "Department of First Stories" in the July 1967 issue of *EQMM*, Dubin was a senior at New Hyde Park Memorial High School when he wrote the story. Though Dannay promised that "young Dennis will undoubtedly ride again," he does not seem to have ever published any further fiction, and all efforts to track him down have thus far proven unsuccessful.

JOSEPH GOODRICH (1963–) is a playwright and author. His *Panic* won the 2008 Edgar Award for Best Play, his adaptation of EQ's *Calamity Town* received the 2016 Calgary Theater Critics' Award for Best New Script, and he has also adapted Rex Stout's *The Red Box* and *Might As Well Be Dead* for the stage. He is the editor of *Blood Relations: The Selected Letters of Ellery Queen, 1947-1950*, and his fiction has appeared in *EQMM, AHMM*, and two MWA anthologies. A former Calderwood Fellow at the McDowell Colony, he lives in NYC.

EDWARD D. HOCH (1930-2008) was the author of almost a thousand published short stories under his own name and many pseudonyms; from May 1973 until after his death in 2008, *EQMM* published at least one new Hoch story in every single issue. Under the supervision of Manfred B. Lee, he ghosted *The Blue Movie Murders*, a paperback original published as by Ellery Queen (though not containing the EQ character), and, after Lee's death, he wrote "The Reindeer Clue," a short story published as by Ellery Queen and featuring the EQ character, which first appeared in *The National Enquirer* in 1975.

JAMES HOLDING (1907-1997) wrote both mystery stories and juveniles, including ten "Leroy King" pastiches for *EQMM*, three titles in the Ellery Queen, Jr. series, twenty "Library Cop" stories, and a series featuring Brazilian photographer/hitman Manuel Andradas. In addition to fiction, Holding also wrote travel articles and was an accomplished poet.

REBECCA K. JONES (1986–) is a practicing attorney in Arizona, specializing in criminal law. Her first short story, "History on the Bedroom Wall," was published in *EQMM* in 2009.

RAND LEE (1951–) is the son of Manfred B. Lee, co-author of the Ellery Queen mysteries. An alumnus of St. John's College, he is a freelance writer and psychic consultant based in Santa Fe, New Mexico. His science-fiction and fantasy short stories have appeared in *Asimov's Science Fiction Magazine*, *The Magazine of Fantasy & Science Fiction*, *Amazing Stories*, and in several anthologies. His most recent work, a science fiction murder mystery, *Centaur Station*, is forthcoming.

PATRICIA McGERR (1917-1985) won the French *Grand Prix de Literature Policiere* for her 1951 novel, *Follow, As the Night*, and an *EQMM*/MWA prize for her 1968 short story, "Match Point in Berlin." The author of sixteen novels, she also wrote a series of short stories featuring secret agent Selena Mead. Several films have been based on her work, most recently *The Legend of Johnny Lingo* (2003).

THOMAS NARCEJAC (1908-1998) was the pseudonym of Pierre Ayroud, who wrote collaboratively with Pierre Boileau as Boileau-Narcejac. Their best-known work was *D'entre les morts* (1954), which was filmed by Alfred Hitchcock as *Vertigo* in 1958. A collection of Narcejac's pastiches of famous fictional detectives was published in France as *Usurpation d'identité*.

FRANCIS M. NEVINS (1943–) had a day job, until his retirement, as a professor at St. Louis University School of Law. Away from the lectern, he has written more than forty short stories (which have appeared in *EQMM*, *Alfred Hitchcock's Mystery Magazine*, and other national magazines) and six mystery novels. He has also edited more than fifteen mystery anthologies and collections and is the author of several nonfiction books on the genre, two of which have won him Edgar awards from Mystery Writers of America. One of his latest contributions to the field is *Ellery Queen: The Art of Detection* (Perfect Crime Books, 2013).

JOSH PACHTER (1951–) is a writer, editor and translator. Almost a hundred of his short crime stories have appeared in *EQMM, AHMM, New Black Mask, Espionage,* and many other periodicals, anthologies, and year's-best collections. *The Tree of Life* (Wildside Press, 2015) collected all ten of his Mahboob Chaudri stories. He collaborated with Belgian author Bavo Dhooge on *Styx* (Simon & Schuster, 2015). He co-edited *Amsterdam Noir* (Akashic Books, 2018) with Dutch writer René Appel and edited *The Man Who Read Mr. Strang: The Short Fiction of William Brittain* (Crippen & Landru, 2018).

ARTHUR PORGES (1915-2006) was best known for his science-fiction and fantasy stories, but he also wrote a significant body of crime fiction and was a regular contributor to both *EQMM* and *AHMM*. In addition to his two EQ pastiches, he also wrote a series of Sherlockian pastiches featuring "Stately Homes."

NORMA SCHIER (1930-1995) contributed ten unusual pastiches to *EQMM* between 1965 and 1970. In each case, her byline was an anagram of the name of a noted crime writer, and all of the proper names in the stories were also anagrams. In 1979, the Mysterious Press collected all ten of these stories—plus five more—as *The Anagram Detectives*.

KURT SERCU (1963–) is the founder and proprietor of *Ellery Queen—A Website on Deduction*, the most extensive EQ resource on the Internet (http://queen.spaceports.com). He lives in Belgium, where he is the head nurse at the AZ Alma hospital in Eeklo.

ARTHUR VIDRO (1962–) wrote the introduction to T.S. Stribling's *Dr. Poggioli: Criminologist* (2004) and was the proofreader on Ellery Queen's *The Adventure of the Murdered Moths and Other Radio Mysteries* (2005); both books were published by Crippen & Landru. He works as a freelance editor and proofreader (mysteries a specialty) and self-publishes the thrice-yearly journal *(Give Me That) Old-Time Detection*, which explores detective fiction of the past. His mystery-fiction articles have also appeared in the British publication *CADS*.

J.N. WILLIAMSON (1932-2005) was the author of more than 40 novels and 150 short stories, primarily in the horror and science-fiction genres. He received a lifetime achievement award from the Horror Writers of America in 2003.

CPSIA information can be obtained
at www.ICGtesting.com
Printed in the USA
BVHW030506030919
557385BV00004B/34/P